BRONZED
betrayals

**The Bodies of Art Mystery Series
by Ritter Ames**

Praise for the Bodies of Art Mystery Series

"Ames, with her great writing and brilliant story, has created a masterpiece of her own in *Marked Masters*. She leaves her readers doing their own research between the pages. Like Laurel, Ritter keeps the story with its rightful owner—the reader."

– Crimespree Magazine

"Boasting a great cast of characters, good conversations and the global background, this was a very enjoyable read and I look forward to the third book in this exciting series."

– Dru's Book Musing

"An intricately woven tale with plenty of action and suspense. The story is crafted in such a way to keep readers guessing...characters are well-written with smart and witty dialogue. An enjoyable read."

– A Cozy Book Nook

"Funny, fast paced and just a smidge of romance. What more could you ask for? Bring on the next one!"

– T. Sue Versteeg,
Author of *My Ex-Boyfriend's Wedding*

"A high-octane, fast-paced thrill ride of a mystery adventure that will definitely leave you anxious for the next installment."

– Girl with Book Lungs

"Incredible attention to detail. The author creates a world that you truly can get lost in. The book is also a fast-paced, fun read. I'm looking forward to reading book two."

– A Girl and Her ebook

"The book takes you on car chases, shooting, great locations around the world all in the hopes of finding a missing friend and lost artifact. I read the book three times enjoying each time."

– Book Him Danno

"This fast-paced mystery had me reading far past my usual time for bed. I simply couldn't put it down because I was so drawn into the story. It's simply wonderful!"

"Takes off as fast as a speeding locomotive...The twists in this story will keep you reading until the amazing end...Have a great deal of fun while delving into the art trade filled with betrayal, old secrets, greed, and some extremely strange gifts."

"To save the day, Laurel takes you with her every step of the way on subways, planes, fast cars, and motorcycles all while being in danger. This book is truly a keeper, jump in and go for a ride!"

"This fast-paced, action-filled whodunit was enjoyable and hard to put down...it was fun to watch the pieces come together in this well-written drama. I'm looking forward to the next book in this series."

"This third book in the Bodies of Art Mystery series is as engaging and entertaining a worldwide romp as the first two books, and I highly recommend the entire series. Ritter Ames has penned a marvelous story with Laurel Beacham continuing to show her cleverness and intuition portraying a strong character...I was thrilled!"

"Once again I have to hold on to my hat while we zip around Europe and land in lovely Florence where author Ritter Ames lures me in with her delightful vignette of Italian life seen through the eyes of an art expert."

BRONZED
betrayals

A BODIES OF ART MYSTERY

RITTER
AMES

HENERY PRESS

Copyright

BRONZED BETRAYALS
A Bodies of Art Mystery
Part of the Henery Press Mystery Collection

First Edition | June 2018

Henery Press, LLC
www.henerypress.com

Trade Paperback ISBN-13: 978-1-63511-354-9
Digital epub ISBN-13: 978-1-63511-355-6
Kindle ISBN-13: 978-1-63511-356-3
Hardcover ISBN-13: 978-1-63511-357-0

Printed in the United States of America

To all the family and friends who consistently believe in me.
And, of course, the team at Henery Press
—both past editorial staff and current—as well as the wonderful
marketing people and support staff.

ACKNOWLEDGMENTS

So many people need a spotlight shone on them for helping me and so many authors in our careers. From bloggers like Dru Ann Love, Jenna Czaplewski and Christine Gentes, to super fans like Jeanie Jackson, Gale Sroelov, Eleanor Cawood Jones (who is also an awesome author in her own right, by the way), and all the members of my street team. Seriously, that is only a small sample.

I could probably fill an entire book with just names of all the wonderful readers who keep us authors going with kind words, early reviews, and the comradery that comes from loving our fictional characters. I applaud each of you.

They say, "Find a job you love and you'll never work a day in your life." I won't say writing is exactly like that, as some days I almost believe that a job slogging uphill in the mud might be easier. Days when the words won't come, or when reading revisions points out every redundancy that crept into the work, or when the characters get backed into a corner and there doesn't appear to be any good way out—those are all challenges, sure. However, when it all comes together, when the final words flow, there isn't a better career opportunity in the world, and it's every wonderful reader out there who makes the difference.

Thank you all.

ONE

The club relied on trendy darkness mixed with strobing colored lights to create an atmosphere I'd tried to avoid since the year after college. Unfortunately, the woman throwing the party for her new husband's sixtieth birthday was only twenty-three, and if she wanted a loud, drunken Monday night extravaganza with beautiful people decades younger than hubby, he and his checkbook were happy to buy into this wifestyle. Even if he risked a heart attack. I'd put my money on six months.

Oh well, she'll look smashing in a black mini and veil, I thought.

We were using the party invite as a cover. I needed an alibi for later, and this kind of over the top celebration provided such an option. As head of the London office of the Beacham Foundation, I stayed on the party lists for nearly every rich person who dallied in any form of art collection, preservation, philanthropy or as just a hanger-on to the scene. Which meant I tended to save my RSVPing for times when there were fundraisers, or I needed to meet someone in particular who was slated to attend. Neither of those cases fit this Bacchus brouhaha, but the party set a perfect alibi mechanism for leaving people with an impression that I was there later when I...wasn't. Something essential within the next hour's timeframe.

The Russian and his wife left the dance floor and had been holding court at a corner table for most of the evening, his red face showing the effects of too much alcohol and exertion. His flirty trophy wife also seemed to hop in his lap the second his blood pressure appeared to be lowering a smidgeon. I wondered how much she stood to inherit and how hard she'd work to make it happen sooner rather than later.

Six months might be optimistic, I concluded.

My right temple throbbed. The impending migraine could easily have had its roots in the techno-house party beat pounding redundantly from the perimeter speakers. Or possibly the potent mix of too many bodies wearing too many competing fragrances. I didn't know where the maximum capacity level stood for the building, but the number attending likely exceeded the licensed amount.

Or it could be because I was waiting for my personal assistant and longtime friend, Cassie Dean, to crash the party and be my look-alike so I could break into the home safe of the party boy. Yes, besides an alibi, this party did double duty by letting me know the homeowners would be occupied and away while I slipped into their secured house. This was the first non-art related party I'd attended in some time, and ironically, I did so in connection to a pseudo-art crime. It wasn't something I allowed to be well known, but I wasn't a virgin when it came to such reclamation ventures. I wasn't technically stealing. The objective was to return stolen artwork to its rightful owner. Basically, the plan called for me to steal a stolen art piece from at least an accessory to art crime and possibly the instigator of said crime—if the Russian was the one who commissioned the original theft. The jury remained out on that last part of the equation, but I was still recovering stolen art.

Jack Hawkes whispered in my ear, "You look like you're contemplating a trip to the guillotine." He wasn't just my partner in crime this evening, but part of my team investigating forgeries and art heist activities over the past six months. He also doubled as our law enforcement tie with his connection to the British government and Home Office. He and I had begun our partnership suspecting each other as this six-month plot unfurled, until we realized it was nearly everyone else we couldn't trust. Lately, our partnership had turned personal as well.

"I'm almost wishing someone would cut off my head," I replied. "It's starting to pound as steadily as the bass." I tried to keep from elbowing the couple beside me as we all seemed to be allocated the same square inch on the crowded dance floor. After arriving fashionably late, we'd been at the party less than an hour and I had already been groped three times by drunken strangers. When another man stroked the part of my kicky little black Givenchy cocktail dress that covered my derriere, my elbow *slipped,* and the stranger's hand vanished. I raised my chin, motioned to Jack in the direction of a side wall, and said, "Let's see if we can find someplace marginally less crowded."

"But a table—"

"No table." Our plan depended on Cassie playing my doppelganger until I returned post-theft. That meant while I was in sight I needed to stay in the crush of the crowd until she arrived, so people could keep thinking they saw me across the room in the time period when they actually saw her. Tables didn't allow that kind of sleight-of-person trick.

Jack was a good head taller than I, and I'm no slouch at five-eight without the stilettos I wore for the party, so I let him lead through the path of least resistance. We ebbed with the flow, steadily dancing our way toward the spot I'd indicated. The location was a double winner in that it offered easier access to the hallway I needed to escape through when Cassie sneaked in and was pseudo-me in the short term.

As we gained the wall, Jack leaned down and kissed my ear, then whispered, "We can reschedule—"

"Shh." I put a finger to his lips then moved to straighten his midnight blue silk tie, letting my hand stay a second too long on his chest as I leaned in and replied, "Everything is in place, and we won't get a better chance. Besides, we have Cassie on board and she's kind of excited to be a part of this."

"I wish I hadn't had to involve you. I'd rather we were here to enjoy the party, not to toss you into an eleventh-hour art recovery."

"Frankly, a risky assignment is preferable to attending this shallow showcase of the rich and drunken. Though I do love that it gives you the opportunity to look so good." I ran a finger and thumb down the lapel of his fine Tom Ford jacket. "Nice."

"Not exactly slumming it yourself." Jack leaned down and brushed his lips with mine. "When this is all over, we're going to do some celebrating of our own. Maybe on a beach in Bali."

"Sounds exotic."

Then he frowned. "Maybe I should go with you in case backup is need—"

"Stop," I whispered. "Jack, I'm at my best when I work alone, and you can't get inside anyway. Don't try to make me into some Bond girl to follow your lead and has to be rescued. I don't fit the mold."

"Never. I have bigger plans for you—and all of them require that both of us stay out of jail."

I stretched as far as my Louboutins would let me tiptoe, kissed his chin, and whispered, "Stop thinking worst-case scenarios. It's a piece of cake."

"I wish you wouldn't say things like that when we're talking about something like this," he replied cryptically, but I knew exactly what he meant.

"We've planned every step. Our only concern was how to get a cover for the night and this party was a godsend. I already had an invite and you're my date. That's one of the benefits you get from sleeping with the glamorous Laurel Beacham, head of the Beacham Foundation London office," I teased. He chuckled.

Good, I didn't need an anxious date.

The birthday boy was a Russian oligarch who possessed a small Rodin bronze bust in his home-office safe. A work of art he'd either purchased illicitly from one of the more unscrupulous art dealers who looked the other way when a piece's provenance was questionable or missing, or the Russian took possession of the masterwork after hiring the thief himself. Either way, it wasn't in the English country house of a British noble where it was supposed to be residing and on exhibit to the public. The Russian liked running in art circles, and his new little wifey was cultivating all his money contacts. Officially, the Russian collected Chagalls. At least his Marc Chagall works were the ones with an official provenance to match. Unofficially, he collected everything that struck his fancy, so it wasn't a stretch for me to believe he sheltered an absconded Rodin.

To Jack and his coworkers in the Home Office, the problem was how to get back the bust. When six months of careful social and diplomatic channels couldn't restore the piece to the true owner, Jack was assigned the task of retrieving the masterpiece through unconventional channels before the oligarch and the Rodin left for Russia at the end of the week. No one in the British government said, "steal the damn thing," but that was the unspoken edict.

Despite the rushed schedule, Jack investigated every point of ingress and egress, tried every avenue of gaining access through subterfuge, and even consulted my Italian geek extraordinaire, Nico, and myself—because though it's only known by a limited and very small circle of individuals, Nico and I had quite a lot of experience in these types of challenges. With my tech wizard gathering confidential information and gaining necessary pass codes, and me actually "reclaiming" previously stolen works and returning the art to the true owners. However, because of the particular safeguards this household employed, the only viable channel of escape if the bust was burgled required exit through a small window several inches too narrow to accommodate Jack's broad shoulders. Strong and steady shoulders I'd leaned on any number of times in previous predicaments, leading me to persuade him to let me return some favors and handle the retrieval myself.

The only challenge was how to create an alibi without having to wear my Lycra catsuit to the party. Jack became my plus one for the event, and Cassie my plus one-half alternate.

Unfortunately, the expression he currently wore on his handsome face looked like he was reconsidering the decision, and the way his dark brows furrowed made him looked thunderous. This would never do. People remembered stormy faces at parties.

"Smile, Jack. Relax and flirt with me."

Instinct took over, and he flashed that cheeky grin I knew so well. But I recognized concern in his teal eyes. It was that control problem he had. No big deal if he was taking a risk and running a play, but when he had to give up control to...well...me...

The doppelganger part was probably overkill and wasn't something I'd ever done before in a retrieval situation. However, I'd recently been caught on a security cam while working a similar operation to this one and wanted extra insurance for reasonable doubt. Not that the earlier video was enough to convict me of anything, but it was confirmation that gave proof to someone who had harbored suspicions for years about my role in many such robbery reversals. Making me wonder how many other people of the criminal and/or law enforcement persuasion suspected I had hidden talents.

In particular, being on video in the previous project furnished evidence to an art crime mastermind who was known to the world as Devin Moran, real name Phillipe Aubertine, and whom I wanted my secret kept from about my extracurricular activities. Not the best outcome when such intel was revealed to a man I'd been trying to put behind bars for years on art theft charges. I bluffed when Moran tried to out me on one of my previous reclamation projects, but I didn't want to add to his cache of provable Laurel Beacham activities either. While I wasn't as concerned about Moran taking such evidence to the police, because too many of his own customers would be compromised, for continued self-preservation tactics it seemed prudent to avoid providing additional ammunition that could quash any upper hand I gained over him. His grandson, Rollie, the heir apparent to Moran's criminal enterprise, was another wildcard in the mix because of his desire to avoid my gaining a foothold in the family enterprise. Not that I wanted one, or even had the option yet—we'd need a DNA test to know that. But letting Rollie have any leverage over me was out of the question. For now, I was holding to the Beacham name and the mission of the foundation, something my reckless father lost after generations of Beachams kept the torch burning bright.

Both Moran and Rollie held key spots on Jack's and my personal top ten list of people we wanted incarcerated, so not giving anyone new ammunition was critical. I couldn't risk being the cause of any inopportune deal-making.

"Think of this as a character building exercise," I told Jack, focusing on the matter at hand. Without asking directly, since it would just tick him off, I'd circuitously asked enough questions to know I was far more experienced in one of these cat burgling maneuvers than him. But saying this would just start an argument. I tried calming him instead. "You know I can do this, and I'll be careful. So, smile and network, and I'll be back in record time."

"Take no chances." He cocked a dark eyebrow, but the grin remained fixed in place. Kind of like a grimace, but he was trying. When I thought about all the times I'd followed his lead or adjusted to one of his last-minute changes of plan, or got blindsided because he... No, I needed to get off this train of thought.

"I promise to stick with the plan. It's solid and workable. We've covered every minute detail." I smiled up at him and rubbed his cheek.

He caught my hand with his and nodded, then straightened and reached into the pocket of his handsome charcoal-colored jacket and withdrew his phone. Given the way the sound system pounded through my veins, I was surprised he could even feel the cell vibrate. He turned the screen my way, so I could read the text, then leaned down and pretended to nibble my ear as he said, "Cassie is in place. Take care."

I pretended to giggle and kissed his cheek, close enough to whisper, "Right. She'll text you when she needs to be let in the club's side door, and I'll text when I'm ready to return so you can let me back inside. She's carrying a burner for me to use."

Because too many unscrupulous people were suddenly interested in my whereabouts, Nico had used his techno-wizardry skills to the max on my personal phone, somehow working his magic to make any transmission from my smartphone appear to come from someplace halfway around the world. Despite that cloaking ability in regard to GPS, however, we didn't want my cell number appearing on Jack's mobile that evening, since I was supposed to be with him the whole time. Hence the need for the burner.

A sudden cloud of Obsession perfume overpowered the other scents around us, reminding me of a recent bad experience. I backed up a half-step to pivot and head for the hallway to meet Cassie—and slammed into a blonde who suddenly zagged into my path.

As I began apologizing, the blonde in the scarlet Vera Wang sheath laughed. Then she stopped and fought to get her long hair out of her face. Even under the club lighting, I could see the manufactured tan I knew stayed in place three hundred and sixty-five days a year. I stifled an oath as she sobered enough to recognize me. Melanie Weems, former museum director of The Browning, a small museum in Miami. Precisely the person bad memories of Obsession had already conjured. We'd been trying to find her since she hit Germany in January because she was tied to an art crime hood who'd been killed in Rome in one of our previous adventures. She also appeared entangled with another, bigger art criminal, Ermo Colle, who'd disappeared as solidly as she had. Now she'd snuck into the U.K. despite all of Jack's safeguards. Another hole in the system to plug. Again.

I reached to grab Jack's arm and assumed as light a tone as I could manage when I shouted, "Look. It's Melanie. What a surprise."

His eyes widened, and he leaned closer. "Unexpected...surprise."

"Oh, Jackie!" Melanie walked fingers up his wool covered bicep. Yes, they had history before Jack knew better. "Are you still slumming with Beacham?"

"What—?" I choked.

Jack cut me off with a small shove toward the hallway. Smart man. But Melanie grabbed my arm and pulled. I would have fallen off my high heels if Jack hadn't caught hold of me at the waist.

"Dammit, Melanie. Let go," I cried.

"I was stopping you from hitting me," she shouted. The smell of alcohol competed with her perfume.

"I was moving out of the way, not trying to hit you." Why was I arguing with a drunk? I needed to get away.

Then the bitch slapped me!

"What the hell?" My right hand automatically moved back to strike, but Jack caught my wrist and held tight.

"Dammit, Melanie, what was that for?" Jack asked. "Are you pissed or crazy?"

Okay, I knew Jack meant drunk when he said pissed, but the American version of the phrase was rapidly applying to my current mood too.

"Just letting you know you can't get anything by me this time, Laurel Beacham," she yelled, her nose millimeters from mine. "You're such a liar, and I'm not putting up with it."

I hadn't been Melanie's favorite person since we were all in college, and the summer I successfully scored on a revenge plot to counter one of her nastier schemes, which cost a good professor his job. She claimed it was nothing more than a summer school prank, but it foretold the full range of her mean girl persona. Her comeuppance put me firmly in her crosshairs from that moment forward, and she never missed an opportunity to diminish me in public. The fact I was presently with Jack upped the ante, and she presented a definite risk to our plans that evening.

I was feeling secondhand drunk from the alcohol fumes coming with her words. "Melanie, I think you've had enough booze for the evening. Maybe you should—"

And she slapped me again!

"You bitch! I'll—" I couldn't say anything more because Jack clamped a hand over my mouth and used his other arm to cinch me tighter around the waist, pulling me close against his body. "Laurel needs a little air. Right, love?" he said as he pushed us through the crowd and away from Melanie.

That's when I realized it looked like half the packed house was apparently following Melanie's and my exchange. Wonderful. I wanted to stay lowkey tonight, so Cassie could double for me, and now I was center of attention. Not to mention my face hurt from the damned slaps.

I pushed his hand away from my mouth, but he tightened his hold around my waist. Couldn't really blame him. I wouldn't have trusted me either. When we finally got into the hallway and away from the crowd he let go.

"Keep her away from Cassie," I warned. "Melanie could blow everything."

"I know, don't worry. I'll keep her occupied."

"How did she even get into the country without someone notifying us?" I fumed. "What's the point of having a means of flagging miscreants if they can just waltz through border security like they have an engraved invitation?"

"I'll check," he said, grabbing me by the shoulders and holding my gaze. "But now, you need to center. Forget all of this and go meet Cassie for the quick change."

I nodded. "Got it. I'll—" His lips met mine and my stomach gave a little flip-flop that tamped down the adrenaline I'd had surging just a few seconds before. I reached up and ran my fingers through the curls on the back of his head, and he pulled me closer and deepened the kiss.

As our lips parted, he said, "You're sure you don't want to abort the plan? Things are kind of—"

"Going sideways already. I know." I smiled, leaned against his chest, and looked up as if whispering sweet nothings his way. "Tonight is our best bet, skeleton crew in the house with most of the servants off, and our only chance since they're heading back to Russia next week. We're heading for New York tomorrow, remember."

"If anything looks risky, get out of there."

"I will." I patted his chest over his heart. "I promise to be careful. Besides, it's going to be fine. Within a few minutes, I'll be in my element."

"Your element..." He shook his head.

I pulled his tie and leaned close again. "My assignment for the rest of the evening is much safer than yours. I'm not the one who has to keep Melanie occupied." Smiling, I backed to the exterior door and blew him a kiss before I slipped into the brisk London night.

TWO

By the time I made it into the coffeehouse two blocks away, Cassie was wearing a path in the tiles from pacing. We'd chosen the site because it offered a single occupant bathroom. My assistant slid out of the dark jacket and Lycra cat suit she wore and held out a hand for my dress. As I donned the all-black suit and soft soled ebony boots, she slipped on my Givenchy LBD and Louboutin red soled heels. She'd kept the loose hood of the jacket up when she'd arrived, covering the blonde wig that approximated my curly tousled 'do and hid her own blonde and pink spiked style. While I had a mirror I first pulled up the tight hood that doubled as a collar for the inky suit and tucked every curly blonde strand into total confinement. I couldn't risk leaving DNA evidence. Once the looser jacket hood was pulled up too, it would lessen the cat burglar impression.

"How do I look?" Cassie asked, fluffing the curls in her wig to get the style back in shape.

"Terrific." I pulled my lipstick from the gold-chain purse I carried that night and held it out to her.

"Thanks, I'd forgotten. I do need to wear the same shade." She traded the lipstick tube and tiny purse for the black backpack she'd hung on a hook by the door. "Everything you need is inside. Escape rope, black gloves, mini flashlight, sensors, and that electronic gizmo your wizard in Zürich messengered to you today."

That electronic gizmo was a magic little device that would open the safe for me. My source had to move heaven and earth to get the gadget constructed and delivered in time, for which his bank account was greatly rewarded. The night wouldn't have a chance of success without the lovely apparatus. The backpack would also carry away the bust. The art piece wasn't large, only about a foot tall, but it was heavy, and the black canvas pack would improve transport and concealment.

"Thanks, Cass." Then I told her about the Melanie debacle.

"How did she get into the country without our knowing?" she cried.

"Exactly what I asked Jack. I swear the only information that comes to him on flagged passports is mine whenever I try slipping out of the U.K. without him." I pulled on the black gloves, then shrugged into the straps of the backpack. "But don't worry. He'll handle all care and feeding of the Melanie-monster at the party until I get back. And the place is absolutely packed. Just circulate constantly and stay free of any interference."

"What about the security cameras?" she asked.

I shook my head. "Won't be a problem. They're all ceiling mounted and wide angle. They won't get a full shot of you unless you look directly into one of the cameras. Keep your face tilted down and stay in the crowd dancing and they'll mostly get your hair. Not enough for facial recognition software. People will absolutely assume you're me. And if Jack is ever free of Melanie, go do some close talking with him. That will make it look like he and I are talking too."

"Got it. College all over again," she said, grinning as she pulled open the door.

"No kidding." At Cornell, we really had looked alike, with the same hairstyle, body type, and aquamarine eyes. The fact we were roommates made switching places even easier when one of us— usually me—was too hung over to attend a class that couldn't be missed. Officially, she was my assistant and the restoration expert for the European arm of the foundation we worked for. However, our history and similar physical characteristics meant her talents went far beyond what was written into her official job description.

We parted on the sidewalk, with her texting Jack that she was on her way and needed to be let in, and me heading to the Knightsbridge area and my assignation with a certain Rodindesigned head.

I took several long, centering breaths as I set a jogging pace. It was time to get my emotions in check and push all anxiety into the back closet of my brain. The jacket helped a bit with the early March temps, and the movement soon warmed me. I took the circuitous route we'd determined as having me on-camera the least, and I made sure the black hood hid my profile as much as possible from CCTV. Sure, my outfit looked suspicious to anyone who peered closely at me on the sidewalk, but I hoped with the jacket and luck that the hood would be attributed to the chilly evening air and the Lycra leggings were confused in the dark with skinny jeans.

My objective obviously wasn't as famous as Rodin's *The Thinker*, or as big either, but much like the Victor Hugo bust the sculptor completed in 1883, it was dear to the family of the subject and needed to be returned. I loved the idea of family art, kept available to the ones who shared the art and the stories of the work with the public. However, in cases like this one I had to admit it made more sense to let such works reside in secure locations like the Musée Rodin in Paris, as did the Hugo bust and *The Thinker*. So many private collections and small museums—sometimes large ones too—didn't have the security required to protect easily transportable masterpieces from thieves. No one had yet figured out when this bust was stolen. Jack and the Home Office were just focused on getting it back before the bust left England for good.

Oh well. It keeps my talents sharp, I thought, grinning. As I race-walked toward my destination, I tugged on the front of the suit's collar so it covered my mouth and most of my nose, then I stretched the top edge of the Lycra hood so it almost reached my brow line. I probably should have brought a scarf to hide behind instead, but the maneuver was necessary to keep hidden from cameras en route and in the house. However, I did make sure to duck my head anytime I encountered another evening stroller along the way.

Night air and exercise calmed my nerves. Within ten minutes I'd reached the tall wrought iron fence surrounding the house and made my way to the rear gate. I was loose and ready but took a second to scan my surroundings for unexpected traps. Nothing.

Jack made sure the prep work was done when he'd still had hopes of pulling this off alone. I stayed low and in the shadows as I picked the lock on the gate. The hinges were well-oiled and noiseless as I eased it open and crept onto the grounds, keeping to the shrubs and trees until it came time to cross the garden. I raced up to the terrace that ran the width of the house and fell into a dark corner near the door.

Lights filtered from the kitchen. I sighed in relief. The alarm system was zoned and wasn't activated so long as anyone was up and active in the house, which is what we'd counted on tonight. Yes, it was risky breaking in when someone was on-duty and awake, but even one servant was enough to keep the system silent as I entered. I needed that edge. Overnight or when the house was empty, lasers babysat the halls leading to the next floor. None of this would help in leaving, however, as all the doors and windows below the third floor were highly sensitive to metal passing by the sensors, programmed to reduce the risk of armed entry and active twenty-four seven. Meaning if I tried to escape carrying the bust with that much metal, the bronze would trigger alarms, and I'd have the London Metropolitan Police on my tail. Planned departure was via the top story, rather than the ground floor.

The service door had an electronic keycode, and I used a second handheld device to flirt with the lock and let myself in. As I slipped into the back hallway, I returned the device to the backpack and grabbed the first of the many ultrasonic alarms I left like electronic breadcrumbs along my route. Not so I could find my way back safely, but rather to alert me should anyone decide to follow in my footsteps. I poked the earbud in my left ear that would ding if a sensor was passed.

Keeping to walls and shadows, I crept down the servants' hall and ducked in time to avoid being seen by the couple talking and watching television in a lounge area. He wore sturdy gardening chinos and she was a maid. I heard pans in the kitchen, so there were at least three people inside. A little trickier, but doable.

I homed in on the area I knew held the servants' staircase. It was a closed box style with railings along the wall, so once I'd made it successfully up several risers I was invisible to anyone who wasn't standing at the top or bottom of the stairs.

No lights on the next floor, but before I moved into the open I used a dental mirror to surreptitiously check around the corner and make sure the hallway was empty as well as darkened. The way was clear. I also had night vision goggles in my pack but preferred to work without them if possible. It was too easy to be temporarily blinded if a light came on unexpectedly. I moved to the southwest corner of the floor, staying near the wall to reduce the risk of the floorboards giving me away to the occupants below. I knew better than to move too quickly, but I wasn't dillydallying either. Any sound I made needed to mirror normal house settling—not footfalls. I took another couple of centering breaths when I felt my nerves working against me. After I passed the danger zone above the servants and finally made it to the oligarch's office, I picked the lock and eased open the oak door. A second later I had the door relocked for insurance. It wouldn't keep anyone out who came to investigate, as I assumed there was a master key in the house, but at least it would slow down discovery.

The room was freshly cleaned, or it hadn't been used since the maid was in earlier. I breathed in a heady mix of scents that included lemon oil, beeswax, fresh flowers and lots of leather and expensive furniture. The intricately carved antique mahogany desk alone was nearly the size of a New York apartment. A thick, patterned Moroccan rug laid over the wall-to-wall carpeting and not only cushioned my step with expensive ease, but gave me more assurance of soundless movement. Box flats leaned against the window wall, in preparation for their departure later in the week. I didn't envy the crew who packed up this place. Oversized and solid seemed to be the bywords in what few furnishings I'd seen in my short travels through the house.

I opened the thick drapes about an inch, allowing enough

street light to aid my work. The bust was heavy, yet only about a foot tall. It could easily fit into the safe I found hidden behind a hinged painting from the school of Rembrandt. The safe was state-of-the-art, with an electronic locking mechanism, and a keypad I knew offered just three tries at the right combination before the digital lock would act like an iceberg and "freeze" me out of any further attempts. I couldn't chance it. Hence the eleventh-hour order to my Zürich wizard for the perfect open-sesame gadget. My new gizmo wouldn't need three attempts to gain entry.

A second later the safecracking treasure was out and ready for use.

The readout on my watch said three minutes ahead of schedule. I hoped I wouldn't need the extra time. I thought about texting Jack with the burner phone, knowing he'd appreciate an update. But that wasn't part of the plan, and we didn't need any digital footprints tying phone pings from this area to him if the FSB or SVR—or whatever the KGB called themselves now—and whomever they trusted in London later investigated this break-in. The burner stayed put.

In less than a dozen seconds my mighty electronic safecracker successfully breached the defenses. Only one try needed. Encased in the wall, the safe wasn't a walk-in, which had originally surprised me. However, it did possess an exceptionally large space inside, even with the Rodin taking a good third of the opening. Stacked metal drawers along the right-hand wall held trophy wife's jewelry.

This bust resembled the more famous Victor Hugo bronze in size and weight. Hugo refused to pose for his bust, and Rodin had to design on the fly using a technique he'd learned and perfected from Lecoq de Boisbaudran. The gentleman who'd matched this British bust, however, was a friend and fan of Rodin, and though he'd sat for one sitting, the artist's only available timeframe had been during the Brit's favorite hunting season. So, again, due this time to the nobleman refusing to postpone his hunting schedule for the required number of sittings, Rodin had to utilize the same exercise of drawing from memory to quickly sketch the impressions he wanted to reproduce in the clay model. But the artist had dined exquisitely while he was there.

Once the sculpted clay received the master's touch, it became a living work that everyone, including the busy nobleman, deemed a true likeness. Then it was sent to be cast in bronze.

I reached into the safe and pulled out the bust. The piece looked like the real thing, but I'd been fooled before. I turned it over, saw the mark and groaned softly.

This work had been placed to fool the public too. I traced a small circular mark with my gloved finger. I couldn't read the figures in the near dark, but I knew the mark shouldn't be on the bottom of the piece. The tiny torch clipped to the backpack gave me the light I needed to confirm my suspicions. The bust wasn't a Rodin. It was a forgery.

So, did the Russians know they had a fake? Or did they commission a forgery to spirit the real one out of the country by showing papers that they'd purchased a duplicate? However, if they wanted to cross borders with false papers, why have a fake made? Why not just say the bust was a copy that matched the papers?

I shook my head. No, they thought this was the real thing. My team had been following copies like this for months, forgeries of all mediums of art that had one important thing in common: they carried the small, often hidden, marks of forgers along with all the normal authentication codes. I wondered how many other fake Rodin busts matching this one were out in the world and presumed real. If experience meant anything, at least four more. Was the original actually stolen in the last year from the country house of the English lord? Had it already been swapped out and this forgery taken instead? Or had the Russian gained the original work initially but someone beat us to the theft?

Sighing, I dropped the light and hefted the bust in one hand, wondering what to do. If I left it, the piece could be resold over and again. If I took it, the theft would likely set in motion actions that wouldn't be worth the mountain of problems it could create. The Russian couldn't go through official channels, of course, but diplomatic channels could be hurt for nothing more than a fake bronze.

As I waffled on a decision, a card of photos that laid on the floor of the safe, which had been hidden under the bronze, caught my attention. I gasped.

It couldn't be.

I hugged the Rodin to my torso with one arm and grabbed the large postcard, then placed the bust back in the safe. I hustled over to the break in the curtains, letting the street light fall on the card.

Unbelievable.

Displayed were three paintings that disappeared after I saw them in the Miami office of a crime boss in October. Until that sighting last fall, these three masterpieces had been missing for a decade and a half. A grouping known in the art world as the *Portrait of Three*. In particular, the middle masterpiece was a painting Jack and I both hoped to find again. Me, because I loved it more than any other painting I'd ever seen. Him, because it was a brilliant study of his late-mother by the artist Sebastian.

The card was a business/event type mailer, used to promote special art items scheduled for auction. There was no date or auction house listed on the card, just a notation about the event being by invitation only to select members.

Members of what? A group? Consortium?

The card helped me firm up my decision. The bust stayed. The mailer went into the backpack. If I took the fake Rodin, the disappearance of the mailer would be noticed too. If I left the bronze, we had a better chance of getting on the trail of the *Portrait of Three* without whomever was in charge of the auction learning and possibly going underground again with the masterpieces.

I rotated the bust to replicate the way it sat when I'd first opened the safe, then closed the door and reset the lock. Not having to escape with the hunk of metal meant I could leave the way I came. Much easier. Shouldering the backpack, I pulled the drapes closed again and hurried across the room. My gloved hand was almost on the doorknob when I heard the distinctive scratching sound of picks in the lock.

Someone was coming in. Why hadn't my sensors warned me? My options were down to one. I dove into the dark kneehole of the desk and curled into a black Lycra ball.

After a full minute, the door finally opened. Obviously, someone hadn't been practicing their lock-picking techniques. The long fumbling seconds gave me almost enough time to get back my normal heartrate and breathing. Still, I kept my hands folded over my mouth and nose, as much to muffle any sound of my breathing as to further hide my face behind black gloves.

The intruder hurried across the room, offering me a glimpse of legs outfitted a lot like my own. The hurried walk was graceful, the legs thin but muscular through the tight leggings. A dancer maybe? Gymnast? Interesting.

Carefully, I uncurled my body and laid on the floor. The tiny dental mirror again helped me secretly spy around the corner of the desk to check out the scene and see what else I could learn. All black, full mask with night vision goggles resting at the eyeholes— and definitely a woman. Tiny waist, but full breasts and narrow shoulders. Couldn't tell hair color under the hood. Using the top rim of the safe as a gauging point, I figured she was a couple of inches shorter than I, but realized my perspective was in question since I was making my guess while crouched on the floor.

She used an electronic device much like my own and opened the safe a second time. She gave a breathy little squeal, then pulled out the Rodin forgery and lowered it into a drawstring black bag. The jewelry drawers were too tempting, and she took several precious minutes pulling out and returning different pieces. Eventually, a handful of rings, several bracelets, and a heavy dark necklace followed the fake bust into the bag. I wished I hadn't closed the drapes, so I could better see what she was absconding with. Not that it really made much difference in my case, since I'd come to recover rather than steal.

Yeah, that sounded like a circular error as I thought about it too.

She closed the safe door, and I slid back into the kneehole's depth. Leaving the door half open, I saw her head the opposite way down the hall from how I'd come in. She must have used the main staircase, which explained why my sensors didn't go off. After giving her a few seconds head start, I scrambled out and moved to the door.

Suddenly, klaxon alarms blasted from the direction in which she'd disappeared. She apparently tried to exit the same way she'd come in, setting off the security system with the metal forgery. Whether she escaped or not, the system would have already sealed off the ground floor. I had no choice but to use my rope and take the sky route out one of the tiny upper windows.

The top floor was mostly open attic. She could have been hiding, and there were a couple of closets and cubbies she might have hidden inside. However, I didn't bother checking because the attic floor was covered in a light sheen of dust, and when I used the mini flashlight to sweep the panorama, the only footprints I could spot were my own. I grabbed a fabric cover protecting a chest and used it to scatter my dusty shoe prints to the four corners.

The window was as diminutive close up as I'd figured. Since I wasn't carrying the bust, once I removed the braided line from inside the backpack, the bag laid relatively flat to my body. I also removed an eye hook from the front pocket and quickly screwed its sharp point into the exposed frame under the window. I said a prayer as I started raising the window sash; it was stubborn but practically squeak-free. Two other windows looked out on the south and western sides of the house, but the one I employed had better escape options, even if it allowed my escape to be readily seen from one street.

With a flick of my wrist, I sent the strong line through the opening, letting it dangle until I saw it did indeed end at a spot about half a floor above the bottom of the first floor—or second floor in the U.S.

Perfect.

A quick shimmy down the line, with the grip of my leather

gloves controlling the speed of descent, and I landed safely on the long carport that framed the front of the three-car garage like a dark eyebrow. I did a fast frog march toward the end of the overhang, trying to be as small and inconspicuous as possible. There were security cameras on this side of the house, but they were trained on the view below me to capture the images of thieves breaking in—not how one might escape from the top floors.

Nearing the end of the carport, I raised and sprinted toward the edge, then broad jumped across the narrow grass below, and over the wrought iron fence to do a tuck and roll. I landed on the side lawn of the property next door.

At that same moment, the bebop warning sound of Met police sirens grew in the distance. I ran from shadow to shadow as much as possible, and seconds later vaulted the much shorter fence protecting the back of this property.

THREE

Fourteen and a half minutes later I was a couple of blocks away from the coffeehouse again and turning on the burner phone for the first time. I texted Jack *buy milk on the way home*, which was our code for him to send Cassie back to the coffeehouse. He texted with the reply *need creamer too?* which I answered in the negative since he was asking if I had the Rodin.

I'd already freed my nose and mouth from the collar's masking, so the heavenly smell of ground coffee chased away my last bit of nerves when I opened the shop's door. It wasn't a great surprise when Jack arrived with Cassie a few minutes later. Despite the plan for him to stay behind and let me back in the side door, I'd had the feeling he wouldn't have the patience to wait. Especially since he knew I didn't have the bust. He would need to see that I was okay. I tossed him the backpack, saying, "Look inside and grab us each something warm to drink. Cass and I will be back in a minute."

He raised a dark eyebrow but didn't argue.

Cassie tried to pump me for information as soon as we were in the bathroom.

"I don't want to tell the story twice," I said. "Let's just get changed and out of here before Jack becomes antsier." Though I was fairly certain the auction card would hold his attention nicely.

We left the bathroom, once more in swapped outfits. He was at a table in the far corner. His back was to the wall and he sat in the perfect observation seat to view people coming in from any direction, but his attention remained riveted on the card in his right hand. As we approached, he gave me an expression of amazement and held up the mailer as I pulled out my chair. "Where did you get this?" he asked.

Leaning into the center of the table so he and Cassie could both hear me, I whispered, "Under the Rodin forgery."

"The what?" Jack asked, as Cassie added, "Forgery?"

I nodded. "It even had the faked mark of the Florentine forger that we found on the snuffbox copy."

"What happened to the original?" Cassie asked.

Answering with a shrug, I turned to Jack and asked, "Could the Rodin have been switched before it disappeared from the original owner?"

"Something I can ask, but obviously not something considered by my superiors," he said. "Why didn't you take it anyway? We might have been able to trace more from the copy. And we don't need additional known forgeries out there."

"I almost did." I tapped the card. "But since my bigger desire became a quest to not give them the heads up that I was taking the mailer, leaving the bogus bust sounded like a better idea. I was hoping they'd just think the mailer was misplaced. In the end, however, I had no choice."

"Why no choice? Were you spotted?" he asked.

"No."

The barista arrived with a tray of our drinks. We all stopped talking, except to give our thanks as she passed around our orders with her floral tattooed arms. I couldn't help but be mesmerized by the quality of the body art. Coupled with her chartreuse hair, I wondered if she was happier behind a garden trowel than a scone-filled counter. She left with her empty tray. Jack had tea, and Cassie and I pulled our coffees closer. I took a sip. Yes, heaven.

Again, I lowered my voice and leaned toward them. "Another thief came while I was still in the office."

At their collective gasp, I quickly detailed what happened after I slipped the auction card into my backpack. When I got to the alarms and how I slipped out by going up instead of down and how

I saw cop cars but didn't know if the thief was caught, Jack pulled out his phone and started thumbing his screen. Eventually, he shook his head. "Nothing yet regarding a capture. I'll follow up on it later."

"Carefully."

"Of course."

"Who do you think the thief worked for?" Cassie whispered. "Moran, Ermo Colle, or someone else?"

I shrugged. Given Melanie's surprise appearance at the party, and since before tonight she'd been last seen entering an establishment where Colle tried to kidnap me, it was natural for him to be on all of our minds. When we started this quest to stop the forgery ring, we'd thought Moran was our only real nemesis but soon learned there was a second player in the current art heist scheme and finally unearthed Ermo Colle. Only then to realize Colle was the man I'd known as my late father, despite the talents of an excellent plastic surgeon. Someone else died in the avalanche that Daddy Dearest let me and everyone else believe took his life. He disappeared again soon after I identified him—with Melanie two steps behind. She'd also dropped off customs' radar the same night. When we learned she'd resigned abruptly from her position as director at The Browning in Miami, and we'd already put her together with a mobster wannabe, Tony B, who worked under Colle, another puzzle piece fell into place.

"All I know is the thief was a woman, moved like someone who was young, possibly with a ballet background, extremely graceful movements. Based on what little I could see of her in comparison to points in the room, I'd guess she was about five foot six. Possibly inexperienced or cocky too, since she set off the alarms on her way out. She was definitely small enough to use the window I escaped from, but I saw no trace of her when I went up. She either hadn't done enough homework about the alarms or found another avenue of departure if it was a con for the cops."

"Could that have been planned?" Jack asked. "To double back and actually escape later?"

"Possibly, but I wouldn't try it," I mused. "Beyond the fact the zoned alarm system kicked on once the sirens blared, and the servants got sent to their rooms, extra security guards and an increased police presence are both likely from that point forward. Even harder to leave without being pursued."

"But you escaped without incident from the top floor." His gaze was intent on mine. I knew he wasn't just in discovery mode.

"Yes, by the barest of margins. Since I didn't have the bust there wasn't a need to lower the backpack first," I said. "I squeezed through the window and used the line I'd carried to lower myself to the side portico and carport. Then used the height to more easily jump over the fence and land in the next yard. I ran the diversion routes we previously plotted until I felt safe enough to pull down my hood and put my jacket back on in one of the CCTV dead spots to look more normal. I texted you when I knew I was a few minutes from the coffeehouse."

"You would have seen her enter the top floor?"

I nodded. "It's just storage up there, so all open. Mine were the only footprints in the dust on the floor, and I swept them away before I slid out the window."

"They won't be able to report the theft of the bust," Cassie said, leaning on her hand in thought. "Would the police do double duty if it's just a report of an intruder but nothing missing?"

"Good point," I said. "But the little thief left with jewelry too. The Russian may decide it's worth working with authorities to try to get those pieces back. Then he can send someone to try to get the bust back if it's learned who the perpetrator was."

"Any idea of value on the jewels?"

I shrugged. "Not my wheelhouse. I'm conversant in art, not gems. Plus, while she had night vision goggles, I didn't risk making noises to dig mine out of the backpack. Even with the night vision enhancement, however, I would only be able to ballpark a guess. Stands to reason she took the best pieces though, and I can't imagine the little trophy wife going for less than perfect sparkles. One necklace in particular, looked heavy with gold and gems, and several of the bracelets were impressive in the near dark."

"She didn't simply come for the jewels and see the bust as a bonus?" he asked.

"Doubtful. She lifted the fake Rodin first and squealed a little, like she'd met her goal," I said. "She put it into her pack, and almost seemed for a second to want to close the safe. Then she pulled out a drawer and grabbed a handful of jewels, but kept glancing down at the bagged bust as she checked some of the other stacked drawers. She didn't waste a lot of time on the jewelry. I think only half the drawers were opened."

He frowned. "This is something we need to keep in the back of our minds in case it becomes important later. And frankly, the timing of the crime leads me to assume this is the work of the mole or moles we already can attribute to Moran in either Westminster or Whitehall, or both. That would be the easy answer on how the information on the bust made its way to another thief's ear, and how the hit was made the same night we planned ours. But I can't see Moran hiring someone who appears to be inexperienced. Also, the purposeful setting off alarms to double back, while possibly a brilliant ploy, seems risky to me."

"Do we add another tick to the column fingering Moran as the one creating the fakes that use these forgers' marks, since you're saying it's less likely he employed this thief?" I asked. "Presuming he wouldn't bother stealing a fake. If so, that could mean she works for Ermo Colle, but would also imply Colle has as many moles in as many places as Moran in order to get this kind of confidential information about the bronze."

"Yeah, this is getting deep," Jack said. "I'll talk to my superior running this project and see what is sorted out in the follow-up. That way, if there is anything MI-5 learns, we'll learn it too, and we won't have to risk adding to our own fears about the long-term heist while we're still investigating. No point in letting the moles get all the information handed to them."

I couldn't help but think how nice it was that Jack handled the follow-up details on not getting the masterpiece and why, rather than me having to do so again.

Looking at my watch, I realized it was time to resume our normal personas, so I could keep my alibi solid. We finished our drinks and put Cassie in a cab. As we walked away, I waved at her through the back glass, and Jack set his jacket across my shoulders. Though it wasn't freezing, I was grateful for the warmth. I crossed my arms to pull the coat closer and got a stronger whiff of the sandalwood cologne he always wore, blended with the heady mix I'd realized was Jack's personal scent.

"Did Melanie give you any problems after I left? Or did she notice the Cassie switch? She was a year ahead of me and went to Yale instead of Cornell, so I only saw her during summer internships and workshops. But I'd forgotten she and Cassie met at a couple of the college art events we all attended. I should have—"

"Nothing to worry about. Melanie left right after you did. I was lucky to catch sight of her exiting the front when I returned from the side hallway."

"Wonder what her game was," I mused. "She's taller than me, which means she couldn't have been the second thief."

"I'd like to know who invited her since we suspect she's fallen in with Colle."

Oops. Grow up, Beacham. I'd been so busy with my adolescent revenge thoughts I'd forgotten about the bigger picture. "Uh-huh, that's what I meant." I thought for a moment then said, "Colle could be mixed up with the Russian. I still believe Melanie likely cultivated a relationship with him and Tony B to sell art on the side. We already know the Russian has no scruples about buying masterpieces with sketchy provenances. Or Melanie and Colle may be looking for a new way to liquidate forgeries on less than expert buyers like the Russian. Thanks to the directorship she held at The Browning, Melanie's resume has enough weight for her to bluff her way into expert status for anyone looking to scoop up shady art. She could be the front person for selling forgeries."

"Like we don't already have enough to consider with this bunch," Jack said, then sighed. "Forgot to ask how your lunch went today with the P.M. I meant to ask when I picked you up tonight."

"Well, it's not like you haven't had other things on your mind. We were both running what-if scenarios to make sure all the angles stayed covered."

"Still no excuse." He put his arm around my shoulders as we hurried across a crosswalk with the light. Street traffic was normal, but the sidewalk wasn't nearly as crowded as in the daytime. "How did your conversation with her go?"

"It was productive, I believe, and the prime minister had a good understanding already about the public version of what the foundation does," I said as we leaped up the curb and slowed our pace again on regaining the sidewalk. "We hadn't had a chance yet to meet and talk officially. And since Cassie and I are only allowed to live here because of our jobs, it's always a good idea to know people in high places and have them know me."

Jack gave a brisk nod, but frowned slightly when he said, "You and the Beacham Foundation might be patently American, but there are a lot of common interests between England and the foundation's mission."

"Exactly the kind of thing we discussed." We neared another zebra crossing and slowed to wait for the light. "It's nice walking London streets this time of night. We almost have the sidewalks to ourselves. Even if the cars still barrel right up to the crosswalks before braking."

The gray stone and trendy purple neon signage at the club entrance came into view. We angled that way since there no longer was anyone to open the side door for us. I couldn't really be irritated by the change in plan since I understood Jack's worries. Though I would file the instance away to use at a future date when I felt a need to deviate from agreed upon steps and wanted to avoid a lecture from Mr. Hawkes.

Jack took back his jacket to retrieve the invitation he'd shown to get us in when we'd arrived earlier. As before, the hipster gatekeeper checked the names on our invitation against the lengthy list on his clipboard and marked the time we reentered the premises. Luckily, he didn't ask how we'd exited mid-party—or couldn't have cared less because it wasn't in his job description. Either way, I was grateful. Despite the fact he'd varied from the original plan, Jack hadn't been out of the building long enough to worry, maybe ten or fifteen minutes. On video it would look like I left with him for a short stroll and returned—though the blonde on his arm during the exit was Cassie. Still, I let my brain run over any potential pitfalls and was glad the videos would be timestamped to coincide with the front gatekeeper's reentry list.

Our plan was to stay another hour, then give our best wishes and leave. We headed for the dance floor, making small talk with others as we rejoined the crush in the middle of the cacophonous beat. The birthday boy continued to hold court at his table, a waiter handing him another glass of clear liquid that I doubted was water. His spouse was nowhere to be seen.

I pulled Jack's ear down to my level and said, "Bet if I checked out my appearance in the ladies room I would find the trophy wife and her friends hitting a few lines."

He nodded and pointed. I turned and saw the wife and her posse stumbling out of the hall leading to the bathroom. Three of the women rubbed their noses in a suspicious way, and all were laughing uproariously.

"She'd better hope the servants don't call the cops."

"Too late." Jack pointed to the front of the club. Police constables and a plain clothes DI stood surveying the scene. One of the waiters pointed out the Russian and they held up their warrant cards to push through the dancing and drunken crowd.

Trophy wife had been chuckling her way back to the table until she saw the coppers homing in on her husband. She made an abrupt U-turn and double-timed it in the opposite direction. Instead of the bathroom, however, she disappeared down the hallway I'd used earlier to exit the side door.

"She must not be so high she's forgotten about self-preservation," I said. Jack nodded, then motioned toward the bar.

"Let's go get a drink," he said. "We probably can't hear

anything, but we'll be close enough for a better view of their body language."

Minutes later we were leaning against the bar. As the DI talked, the Russian's face grew darker. He finally rose to his feet and waved toward a redheaded woman in the group, pointing toward the bathroom.

"I think the missus is being sought," Jack murmured in my ear.

I raised my white wine to my lips but didn't sip. Instead, I said, "Notice the dance floor is emptying pretty quickly."

"The uniforms. Likely a good portion of the reason why the Russian is livid."

"Wait until his wife shows up and she's arrested for the coke up her nose."

Jack shook his head. "Look. The ginger is coming back by herself."

And indeed, she was. The redhead had her arms extended out and shrugging, signaling to the Russian and his entourage that wifey couldn't be located.

The Russian gave the DI a rude shove and barreled his way toward the redhead. The DI stumbled, then followed.

Jack set his untouched scotch on the bar. "Are you finished? I think we've probably seen all we need to see."

My glass went next to his and we headed for the coat check. I held out my hand. "Let me get my coat and you can work on getting us a cab."

He shook his head but pulled out my claim ticket. "We need to stay together. Then we'll take the Tube. Keep us more easily trackable on CCTV."

"Good thinking."

The dance floor was nearly empty by this time. I wondered how many people had been in the bathroom tonight since no one seemed to want to be scrutinized by the police. There were some holdouts, gawkers who stood on the sidelines or pretended to dance as they kept their attention locked on the little drama.

Jack put his arm around my shoulders as we walked, and he spoke softly into my ear. "I know Markham, the DI. We have friends in common. I'll try to connect with him later and see what I can learn."

"No, let's go by there now," I said. "We'll say hi. You can give him your card. See if he has any questions. Let him put faces to our names."

He didn't answer but steered us in that direction.

Markham was tall, even taller than Jack, and wore an expression of growing irritation. He recognized Jack and offered both of us a card. The Russian stood ten feet away, voluble in his angry confusion and ordering everyone within earshot to find his wife. He yelled at Markham that she may be a victim of kidnapping. Jack caught Markham's eye and shook his head slightly, handing over one of his cards and suggesting a phone conversation later. I stepped over to say goodbye to the birthday boy just as someone behind me finally got wifey on a cell phone. The Russian pushed me into the arms of one of the uniforms and ran toward the person with the phone.

The constable and I apologized to one another, though neither of us did anything wrong. Markham shook hands and said goodbye, telling Jack they'd talk soon. Jack took my elbow and we finally headed for the coat check. That seemed to be the end of all the excitement.

It wasn't the first time we'd been wrong that night, or the last.

FOUR

The subway ride was populated with the normal weekday night selection of interesting characters. I loved riding the train for precisely this reason. The nuances of my job required I keep as firm a grip as possible on my surroundings, which also meant observing exactly what groups and individuals were encompassed in those environs. Yet, there were times like these, when I was on a high after finishing a challenging task that ended more challenging than expected, and it was a bit of a mindless release to tally the distinct personalities surrounding us on public transport no matter the time of day. From tats to tube tops to tank coats, and even a couple of nice suits like Jack's, the subway displayed its distinct runway style.

The only available seats were beside a silent woman with shopping bags and quite a lot of cat hair on her sweater. Neither of us wanted to crowd her or her bags, so Jack and I grabbed one of the silver support poles, jostling along with the other standing riders. Once we hit my stop and exited from the Underground to the sidewalk less than a block from my hotel, Jack looked at his watch and said, "It's only half past ten. Markham did tell me he was there for the break-in."

I stopped and turned to look him in the eyes. "What are you up to?"

He gave me his shocked face. "I'm just thinking."

Like I believed that line. "About what?"

"Maybe..." He waggled his head side to side. "I'm thinking I could text Williams and try to get a look at the house. See which way the other person went. If the thief was spotted running away."

Danny Williams was Jack's wunderkind source in British intelligence for access to London's entire CCTV system, reporting to all arms of U.K. law enforcement. The two of them were almost like human face recognition software, and both could waste whole days in Danny's video cave following criminals on the multi-screen monitors employed there. I'd been floored by Jack's ability to recognize people who hoped to remain incognito. Danny's talents proved even better, and he had the additional face recognition software to increase efficiency against any disguises. I understood the draw of getting that kind of information, and I'd actually worked with Danny myself to keep tabs on Moran last month when he popped back unexpectedly in London and left before I'd even realized he was local.

Despite the appeal to gain an opportunity for Jack to see if he could identify the phantom thief, or even learn how and when she escaped the house, I knew I needed to rein in this idea. Too many hazards loomed.

"You don't think he might recognize me because of you asking to see the digital files?" I raised my brows.

His expression fell. "Ah, yes."

Poor guy. I patted his arm and pulled him down the sidewalk with me, saying, "Wait and see if Markham calls us. Danny can pull the files up later if we really need to check."

"True. And it's not as if we don't already have enough on our agendas," he said. "Are you packed for the morning?"

Morning. Right.

Jack and I were booked on an eight a.m. flight to New York to meet with the retired detective who had investigated my mother's fatal car accident nearly twenty-five years ago. A crash we were more and more convinced hadn't been accidental.

I'd been putting this off as long as I could, despite the fact I'd been the one who asked Jack to nose around and ask questions in the first place. I think the four-year-old inside of me still worried that hearing any information would make me heartsick again. Not to mention the way my family history had been jumbled up lately since we started delving into the past. Leaving me unsure who I was actually fathered by, and what name might ultimately be linked to my own.

Like peeling the layers of an onion, new truths of long ago years brought the kind of tears that couldn't be willed away, no matter the effort. I not only feared the man I'd known as my father all my life wasn't just a master criminal we now called by his alias of Ermo Colle, but I believed he had also caused my mother's death. Except we needed proof, and we hoped a trip to New York would provide said proof by letting us connect evidence that went cold a couple of decades ago.

If that wasn't enough turmoil, facts gained in the past few months pointed to the possibility the man wasn't even my father. Instead, my paternal parent might as likely have been the late brother of master criminal, Moran. The same master criminal I'd been chasing for years. I'd only learned this kernel of scandal when I began receiving anonymous gifts of jewelry and photos that had belonged to my mother. Through diligent sleuthing, I learned they'd been safeguarded by Moran after my mother's death. And after Nico and Jack did their own digging, the full story of my mother's affair with Moran's brother was revealed as clearly as the focus of those photographs. More investigation by Jack, and a conversation with a friend who had known my mother well, exposed the distinct possibility my genetic DNA could as likely be tagged to the Aubertine moniker as the Beacham surname.

Moran's brother, Paul-Henrì Aubertine, died in a fiery one-car crash in France similar to the accident that took my mother's life a few months earlier. Both crashes happened after Paul-Henrì and my mother had secretly carried on a decades-long affair, and my mother had finally said she was leaving Beacham and wanted a divorce. Coincidence? We thought it stretched credibility too far.

The plan was to meet with the retired detective, go over his case notes and files with him, maybe view the scene of the crime, and basically shake the trees to see if anything fell loose a couple of decades after the fact. We thought we had most of the dots located.

Now we just needed to get them all connected without more interference.

I wasn't optimistic.

We'd made it into the lobby of my hotel before Jack's phone rang. It was his Home Office superior, Cecil. I wondered if Cecil already heard about the break-in, or was just impatient like my boss, Max. Despite their government versus nonprofit careers, the men were two of a kind in the boss realm—and not in a good way. Even if an ocean separated them.

"I'd better take this," Jack said, frowning at the screen.

"Come back later if he lets you free," I said.

"I'll walk you up—"

"No. Answer your phone before Cecil gets an ulcer. He's not going to like what you have to tell him anyway. Making him wait will makes things doubly worse."

The ringing stopped as the call went to voicemail, and Jack leaned down to give me a kiss that promised much more in the future.

Then the ringing began anew.

"Go." I gave him a little shove toward the revolving door. He gave me his "I'm sorry" smile and answered the cell.

A quick sidestep by the front desk, and I learned the only messages I had were from my boss, who expected me to come by the New York office as soon as possible tomorrow. And call him. And email him. And text him. And call...I wadded up the pink notes and handed them back to the desk clerk. "Please file these in the trash for me, James."

"Yes, Miss Beacham."

I wasn't worried about Max getting an ulcer. He was too good at giving them to people.

For once, the elevator was sitting on the first floor when I hit the call button, so I was at my hotel room in less than a minute. I opened my door and was puzzled as the aroma of Obsession cologne immediately hit me. My first clue something was off. I figured there was trouble when I found the bronzed-skin woman in the red Vera Wang lying on the floor, the mauve carpeting and her mess of long golden hair covered in blood. However, I knew trouble was my shadow when I recognized the dead woman as Melanie Weems, the woman I'd argued with in public earlier this evening, and who had bitch slapped me twice before I could get away. Oh, and I also assumed the telescoping baton beside her, the one that probably cracked her skull, was likely the one I'd had in my possession a few months ago. The telescoping baton which happened to also be covered in blood.

The baton concerned me. Moran gave me one exactly like it the night I shared my last nearly lethal tête-à-tête with Simon Babbage on the outside ledge of a Baden-Baden hotel as he tried to kill me. Simon originally had my job with the Beacham Foundation, until I discovered he was also working for Moran. Around the same time Rollie, Moran's grandson, got suspicious and learned Simon was double-agenting on both of our organizations and aligned with Colle too. I hadn't killed Simon with a baton, just used the weapon to trick him into losing his footing and falling several floors to the pavement. He was still alive, if battered when I escaped. Before I could decide what to do next, Rollie, up-and-coming criminal mastermind legacy that he was, had Simon retrieved and killed.

That night, Rollie returned everything I dropped except the baton confiscated by his henchmen. I couldn't prove they had it, but since the other things I'd dropped with the baton made it back to me, I'd presumed they kept the baton for themselves. I had no qualms about them taking it at the time. It was Moran's property originally, and I was heading back to England and couldn't possess that weapon in the U.K. without getting into trouble. Except here I was in London and so was a similar—if not the very same—baton. Along with a dead woman whom everyone at the party knew hated me as much as I couldn't stand her. Dead in my room.

If I was a betting woman—which I was—I wouldn't have been surprised if at least one of my fingerprints was still on that baton. Mine, and no others.

Damn. I was being set up. Was it Rollie? Or someone new?

Finally, I was positive I was in trouble when I heard the be-bop of Met Police sirens for the second time that night. Because of the strobing lights filtering through my curtains, I knew they'd parked in the circle driveway below.

I stepped into the bedroom of my suite and looked at my packed suitcases, ready to grab for the a.m. flight, and equally ready for my flight right then from the room. A second later, I decided to travel light, with just the essentials. I yanked open the closet door and grabbed my Prada purse, which had the night off for the party, and scooped up the locked case of gizmos I couldn't live without. With the gadget case in the big bag, I pushed the strap high on my shoulder and raced out of the suite. I stood for a second in the hall, contemplating my options. Then I heard the ding of the elevator. Before the doors completely opened I'd pushed through the stairwell entrance. The door's automatic close routine continued making its slow progress as I flew down toward ground level.

Then I stopped. What was I doing running away? I'd be helping whoever was framing me. I chewed my lower lip and pulled out my phone to call Jack.

I heard a stairwell door open high above me and wondered if it was a cop or a killer.

FIVE

I dashed out the door to the lobby and raced to the front desk. Flashing lights filled the paved circle outside the front doors, at least two Met police cars and one ambulance.

James looked dazed, and his eyes widened even more when he saw me. "Miss Beacham, the police—"

"There's someone hurt in my room! Or...worse." I tried to keep my voice down, but panic was setting in. I didn't have to exaggerate my response. "Can you get the police to my room?"

James waved and a young uniformed constable who had been left at the elevators hurried toward me.

"I ran down the stairs," I babbled, grabbing the officer's arm. "The elevator dinged and I thought it might be the..." I dropped my voice again, "You know, killer, coming back."

Actually, I figured the elevator held the police all along, but I hadn't been ready to talk to them on my floor. I'd been in flight mode. My anxiety was genuine, and I really wished I'd let Jack walk me to my door like he'd suggested.

Someone led me to one of the chairs in the lobby, and someone else brought me tea. A minute later, a Met official in plain clothes got off the elevator and came my way.

"Miss Beacham."

"Laurel," I said, shaking his hand. He held out his warrant card, but I waved it away.

He was stocky and practically gray-headed. He sat down in the chair next to me and offered one of his cards. "I'm Detective Inspector Timms. It's my understanding you entered your room and found the body."

I nodded and pulled my keycard from my purse. "You might need this."

"Thank you." His eyes held a wary look. I was a suspect, obviously. He took the card by balancing the thin sides between his thumb and finger, then asked, "Can you tell me when you returned to the hotel this evening?"

"A minute or two before I entered my room. You can get the time from the key card. Also, James, the desk clerk, and I spoke very briefly when I came home." I remembered Jack looking at his watch when we came out of the subway. "We exited the Underground around half past ten."

"You live here in the hotel?"

"I travel a lot with my job. I'm in charge of the London office of the Beacham Foundation. Living here makes more sense when I'm in the city," I said. To be truthful, it probably didn't, but I hadn't had the time—or really the inclination—to do any house hunting. The board promoted me into the position after I'd outted Simon Babbage, the previous London head of Beacham Ltd., as a crook and a spy for criminals that he truly was. We suspected he gave away art entrusted to him for the foundation.

"You're American," he said. "This is your family's business?"

I didn't want to go into details. "My grandfather was the driving force behind the foundation, but after he passed away the nonprofit organization was sold for shares. An executive director and board run things from the New York office, but the London office handles the daily challenges of European concerns. I'm just an employee."

"I see."

No, he most likely did not. I decided to speed things along. "The person in the room. Was she—?" But before I could finish, the elevator dinged, and a gurney came out loaded with a zipped-up body bag. Instead of going through the lobby, however, they disappeared into the back hall. I checked out the windows and realized the ambulance was no longer in front. So, the body was going out the service bay. Even though I truly couldn't stand Melanie, it made me sad this happened. But knowing she was in my room, and likely killed there to frame me, left me angry.

"Did you know the woman?" he asked.

I nodded. "Yes, she was Melanie Weems. We're old acquaintances. She's American, like me, and we have both been connected with the art world since college. But she shouldn't have been in my room at all, nor her killer. The hotel has cameras on every floor—"

"It seems the ones on your floor were temporarily disabled."

"Then I do hope there are fingerprints. Maybe the killer left some DNA." I was babbling again. I bit my lower lip to stop.

"Yes, the crime scene unit will look for evidence of another person with her."

"I'm sorry. I was just thinking out loud. I wasn't trying to suggest how to do your job."

He smiled, but his dark gray eyes carried a calculating look that unnerved me. "No need to apologize. I think all the detective shows have made everyone tend to sort out crimes automatically." Then he switched back to the situation at hand. "Does anyone else have access to your lodgings?"

"No, I should have the only keycard to my room. Other than the service people with master keys of course."

"Of course. We'll need to get your fingerprints and the fingerprints of anyone who frequently visits. For elimination purposes, you understand."

"You can get that information from Superintendent Whatley of Scotland Yard. He can give you my prints and those of the people who work with me. We had a break-in at our offices the first of the year, and he oversaw the investigation. You should also be able to get the prints of Jack Hawkes. He's a frequent visitor here. The superintendent can vouch for him as well and give you further information."

"And this Mr. Hawkes couldn't have been in your room—"

"No, he and I attended a big birthday party at a club this

evening. The party broke up around ten when police came to tell the host and hostess there was a robbery at their residence in Knightsbridge."

I chewed my lower lip, contemplating whether to mention that Melanie had been at the party too. But if the inspector was worth his salt he should be able to get that information from the guest list, and I didn't want to have to explain Melanie's long harbored dislike of me and why she slapped me twice. Time enough for that later.

Besides, my head was pounding by this point. "Inspector, unless there's anything else, I need to see about getting a place to stay tonight. And I'm scheduled on an early flight to New York, so if I could get my packed bags from my room—"

"I'm afraid it would be preferable for our purposes if you postponed your trip."

I knew this was coming and probably welcomed the opportunity to avoid New York without it looking like I didn't want to go. But it also wouldn't look good if I played things too easy for the inspector either. "I understand, but I will have to call and see what arrangements can be made. Appointments have been set up, and several were difficult to schedule with all the individuals in question."

"I appreciate the effort," he said. One of the constables stepped up and whispered something to him. "Okay, thank you," he answered the constable. "Tell them I'll be right there." Then he turned back to me. "I think we've covered what is needed presently. I would like you to go back into your suite and look around once the crime scene people are finished. Just to see if there's anything that should or shouldn't be there."

"Will I have to do it tonight?" I asked. "I'm not feeling too chipper. I might spot things better in the morning."

"I quite understand. And morning would be preferable for our people as well."

I gave him one of my business cards. "You can reach me at the cell phone number listed on the back. Or if you call the office number it will be forwarded to my assistant and she always knows how to reach me."

"Very good." He slipped the card into a pocket, made sure I had one of the cards with his contact information, and joined the constable.

Once they were both in the elevator, I called Jack. My call was sent to voicemail after several rings, so I assumed the debriefing was still in progress with he and Cecil talking strategy as well. A text was more likely to get his attention faster, so I typed *Melanie dead in my room. Police here* and hit send.

Fifteen seconds later my phone rang.

"Are you okay? Where are you?"

"My hotel lobby."

"Stay there. I'm on my way."

In an incredibly short time, a government car pulled into the circle outside and Jack barreled through the door. The driver waited in the car.

"Come on," Jack said, extending a hand. "You're staying with me."

"Since you're here, the inspector might want to talk to you."

He rubbed the back of his neck with his hand, then moved to the window and gave the driver a sign to move on. When he turned back to me, he said, "I'll go up, but I don't really want to leave you here."

I held up the DI's card. "You can call him. Tell him you're here and see if he wants to come down again."

"Good thinking." He pulled out his phone. Timms returned to the lobby a minute later.

"I realize you'd like to keep Miss Beacham in your sights and all," Timms said, after shaking hands with Jack and introducing himself. "But I prefer to conduct this interview in private." He waved over the constable manning the elevators. "Jenkins will be here."

"I understand," Jack said. He squeezed my shoulder and I

touched his hand with mine.

"I'll be fine." I pointed toward the bar. "You can probably find a quiet spot in there. Unless you'd like me to go in, so you can use the lobby."

"No, you're settled here," Timms said. "Mr. Hawkes, if you'll follow me."

Several people came in the front door after gawking at the police cars outside, and Jenkins stopped them to make sure which floors they were staying on. My floor was apparently off limits. I figured they'd let me in to get clothes sometime the next day, but I didn't relish the idea of leaving Jack's place tomorrow looking like I was doing the walk of shame in my party dress.

I texted Cassie. *Are you still up?*

Yeah, why?

Wondering if I can borrow some clothes.

Sure, but why?

I can't get into my hotel suite.

Why?

I sighed. There was no easy way to say this. *Found Melanie Weems dead on the floor. Police are gathering evidence now.*

WHAT!?!

Yeah. All my stuff is off limits until they're through processing the crime scene.

Do you want to stay here tonight?

Jack said I'm staying with him.

No surprise there. Is he fully in his white knight persona?

I chuckled. *He hasn't had time yet. The DI is interviewing him.*

Why leave Melanie dead in your room? Do you think it was Rollie?

I chewed my lower lip. My subconscious had been working on these same questions, but I hadn't figured anything out yet. *Maybe*, I answered. Then I expanded. *My first thought was that I was being framed by him, or even Colle. But the security cameras in the hotel will show when I entered and hopefully will show who* entered with Melanie. *The cameras were messed with on my floor.*

It couldn't be suicide?

I shuddered. *Not unless she was capable of inflicting multiple blows to her head with a telescoping baton before she died.*

Multiple implies passion.

Yeah, I'm thinking someone really didn't like her. Besides me, of course.

After a beat, she texted, *You don't want to say anything like that around the police.*

Which is exactly why we're texting, I answered. *Besides, you and I both know I didn't kill her.*

Jenkins was heading back, so I ended with, *Have to go. Jack and I will stop by later.*

Okay. I'll put on coffee.

SIX

In about an hour, we were lounging around Cassie's historic and well-secured flat. Well, I was lounging. Jack was trying to set a time with Danny to check all the CCTV feeds leading to my hotel, and Cass was back to her pink, spikey-haired self and offering snacks and drinks none of us really wanted, but we accepted because she was in mother hen mode. Her flat was the real estate equivalent to my friend, crisp navy and white kitchen, as well as monochromatic shades from medium blue to robin's egg in the bedrooms and bath. Beyond the calming colors, the flat always carried the scent of either lavender or vanilla. A place to be cocooned, to go for backup, something to count on—just like Cassie.

I was still in my LBD, but I kicked off my heels. Cassie had already swapped my Lycra cat suit for velour sweats in a slightly hotter pink than the tint in her hair. Jack's coat and tie were history, and he'd rolled up the sleeves of his white dress shirt. We were ready to work.

I set my cup on the table when Jack finished his call and Cassie headed back to the kitchenette. "Okay, let's see where we stand on information and leaps of logic."

"I was just going to make a pot of decaf," she said.

"Forget it. I doubt we'll get any real sleep tonight. We may as well keep drinking the good stuff."

"I'll take a beer," Jack said.

"Be right back."

He gave me a cocky grin as she disappeared.

I rolled my eyes and pulled a pad and paper from my Prada.

"Before we go any further we need to figure out what we know and what we need to do."

Cass returned with his beer.

"Since we can't leave London," Jack said, "I'm meeting Williams in the morning to scan street views. Want to come with?" He twisted off the bottle top and dropped it onto the coffee table.

"You can leave London," I said. "I'm the only one who can't."

"Be sensible. You know I'm not going anywhere."

I ignored the thoughtful jab and scribbled on my pad. "We need to cancel both our seats on the morning flight, Jack needs to connect with the retired detective from my mother's case and explain why we aren't coming, and Cass has to call Max and get me off the hook for not appearing in the office for multiple command performances."

"Cassie has to?" Jack grinned and took another sip.

"Yes. She can tame the Max Monster much better than I."

Cassie had a pad by this time and was making her own list. "I'll take care of the foundation call to the boss, and I'll contact the airlines too. I can also connect with the detective if you'll give me his number since it's just regarding timeframes and explanations rather than case info. The two of you might be awfully busy by tomorrow afternoon when you'll need to reach him."

Those five-hour time differences really did impact plans.

"You're right." Jack pulled out his phone. "I'm texting you his number."

"Good."

I pulled one of my curls straight. "To jump ahead to hypotheses, was Melanie tied to the other thief at the Russian's house? Or was she simply some kind of potential frame to get me into trouble? I mean, come on. I go to a party to fake an alibi for a recovery job, then I find a dead woman in the lounge of my hotel suite. We have history. She was at the party earlier. Yes, the events appear completely separate and coincidental, but can we afford to look at them from that angle? Do we look for a connection or leave this as two separate events?"

"If Melanie left because she saw that you were gone, maybe she thought you returned to your hotel alone?" Cassie suggested.

"Worth considering."

"I did learn one thing of interest from Williams," Jack said. "Apparently, the cameras on your floor and throughout the stairwell went on the blink for a short time tonight—exactly the same timeframe when Melanie and her killer would have entered your suite. A time that came soon after you and I reentered the club."

"Timms told me the ones on my floor had been disabled," I said. "Who could have pulled that off? And why just one floor?"

"The working theory is in-house cooperation. My personal hypothesis is having just one floor go dark made the sabotage look like a system glitch."

"Sounds like I need to move again," I said, frowning.

"Brilliant observation."

"I was really starting to feel at home." I got up to pour more coffee, and Jack raised his empty bottle and his eyebrows. I held out my hand. "Yes, I'll put it in the recycle bin."

"And fetch me another?"

"I'll bring you coffee. You want high octane or decaf?"

"Tea?"

"Okay, but don't get used to this kind of service. It isn't a regular talent I cultivate."

I heard him chuckling as I walked away. When I returned from brewing his cup of tea, I found him and Cassie on their phones. She was clicking on the airline's site and Jack was speaking to someone, talking in a very loud voice. After a couple of seconds, I realized he was speaking to the detective in New York. The man was hard of hearing, and Jack always spoke louder and slower when they conversed.

"Yes, that sounds workable for us too. Yes, absolutely." Jack listened a minute or so and said, "Give your computer man my number and we'll get it sorted out. Brilliant. Cheers."

Yet despite how agreeable his words sounded, his face looked uneasy.

"I thought Cass was going to call him in the morning," I said.

"I was, but he called Jack," she replied, finishing up her phone clicking and tossing the cell onto the tabletop. "There. Neither of you has a seat on the flight to New York tomorrow and you each have a credit. I'll work to get the tickets reassigned when the trip is rescheduled."

"That may not happen anytime soon," Jack said. "I wasn't thinking about it still being early evening there. He called because his doctor wants him to come in for some tests this week, and he wanted to be sure he wasn't tied up when we were available. He implied they could take several weeks."

"How thoughtful." I set the teacup on the table. I hoped the detective wasn't looking at cancer. "If I was anticipating medical tests, I'm not sure I would be thinking about scheduling time with someone on an old accident case."

"I've had the feeling from our conversations his medical problems have become a bit of his daily fare," Jack said, leaning forward to get his tea. "Couple that with the fact there's new interest in a frustrating case he still views as open and untried after his superiors shelved it as 'closed' and 'an accident,' and the old boy is naturally excited about helping us."

"You mentioned his computer guy. Are we Skyping instead?" I slid next to him on the sofa.

"He wanted that as a backup since our trip is postponed." Jack blew out a breath and shook his head. "Just when I think we're getting somewhere on something, we have the rug pulled out from under us again."

"It's not like we don't have enough to keep us busy." I turned to Cassie. "Okay, to-do list is done except for Max. Cassie, you can choose when you want to call him."

"Tomorrow. He's at the ballet tonight."

"Max attends the ballet?"

She raised an eyebrow. "You'd know that if you ever spent any time with him talking non-business things. He speaks about ballet like a religion."

"Wow." I shook my head. Better her than me. "I guess I always pictured Max in a suit, focusing on whatever missing art piece has his attention. Or complaining—loudly—because I spend too much money."

"He talks about your spending too," she said, grinning. "Endlessly."

"I'm ignoring that, and if you keep it up there won't be a gift on Personal Assistants' Day." I scooped up my pad and pen. "As crazy as this sounds, which crime do we start with first?"

"I vote for being framed for murder," Cassie replied. "That sounds personal and could lead to future problems since this attempt didn't pan out. Second tries, third..."

"At least we have to hope not."

Jack shook his head. "From what I picked up from Timms when he interviewed me in the hotel bar, and later from Williams's input regarding the fact they know the hotel's cameras were tampered with, I don't expect the police to consider you a suspect for long. But they can make it uncomfortable for you in the short term, and they will have to keep tabs on you until they get a better suspect. You did find the body, after all. Also, when you mentioned we'd attended a party that broke up because of a home burglary, Timms used the time between when he spoke with you and when I arrived at the hotel to get details about the break-in and briefed on when the police arrived at the club. Your instincts were well founded about us speaking to the inspector in charge before we left. So, Timms knows we reentered the club about half-past nine, and he said he was getting the incident report sent to him from Markham, the DI we met at the party. If they interviewed anyone at the party who knew Melanie, it will likely be widely reported she slapped a certain blonde. And when they check the digital files, which they will, Timms is likely to spot you're the blonde who was slapped. It's also going to look suspicious that she left almost immediately after she slapped you. All of this is conjecture on my part since Timms seemed to just want information from me and didn't offer much in the line of quid pro quo. He didn't ask a lot of questions about you, as if he was focused on you for the murder and wanted confirming details from me, but he is obviously following up on the information you gave when he interviewed you."

"Lucky me." I chewed my lower lip, thinking. "Which means we're back to trying to decide if this murder was carried out by Rollie, Moran, or Colle. There are only three reasons for her to be left in my room. It was either to frame me, shake me up, or show me I can be reached at any time. None of the reasons thrill me."

Cassie leaned over and took my hand. Her fingers were cold. "What does instinct tell you?"

"My gut says Rollie, simply because of the similarity to him leaving Miguel for me to discover dead in Barcelona," I said and rubbed her fingers with my thumb. "Plus, the fact a baton was left behind."

"Scotland Yard is still investigating internally how Rollie escaped from custody in early February," Jack said.

Rollie had disappeared in Barcelona after Jack and the Spanish police captured the guns Moran's grandson had been attempting to appropriate. A day later, after we returned to London, he somehow slipped into the country and orchestrated a move to kidnap me at gunpoint. I'd been shot before we left Spain, so I was hurt and on crutches. Jack arrived in time to take down Rollie and turn him over to Scotland Yard. Within twelve hours, however, Rollie was again nowhere to be found, and I later received confirmation from his grandfather, Moran, that one of their confederates was responsible for the successful escape from police custody.

Moving on to my next questions, I read from my abbreviated list, "Can we link Melanie's appearance at the party tonight through a connection to the second thief who came in behind me and took the fake bust? Or was Malicious Melanie at the party because we were on the guest list? And was the fact she slapped me the reason her killer decided to leave her in my room—so was an attendee at the party too? Or was she at the party because the killer wanted her to interact with me, and she went overboard?"

"Or was her appearance at the party a coincidence?" Jack asked.

"You don't really believe that, right?"

"No, only talking out loud. Money and power and art were like aphrodisiacs to Melanie. Her being on the Russian's guest list makes total sense, except she isn't supposed to be in the U.K."

"Thank goodness we did our twin trick," Cassie said. "We thought we were covering your tracks in case Moran learned about the Rodin theft, and now you're covered for the time of the murder as well."

"Hopefully."

Jack took my pad and pointed as he spoke, "I get what you're saying about Rollie and why he could have set up the frame. And we know through video evidence from The Browning event he was at least acquainted with Melanie, but Ermo Colle could have easily tried to frame you as well. And the evidence more strongly supports Colle doing the forgeries. The mark on the Rodin points to a probable connection there, based on the evidence we have to support our theories."

"Yes." I took back my list. "But if Colle is responsible for the forgeries, why would he send in a thief to steal a fake he commissioned?"

"He wouldn't. I was just covering bases. Unless Rollie or Moran commissioned both crimes, we can assume Colle killed Melanie and Team Moran hired the second thief," he said.

"You thought Melanie had thrown in with Colle," Cassie said.

I nodded. "Yes, when I left the Baden-Baden casino after recognizing Ermo Colle as my long-dead father, Melanie showed up soon after. But killing her would mean Colle is murdering his own side. Why would he kill Melanie?"

"Maybe she found someone else with more money and traded sides like Simon did when he moved from being Moran's spy to Colle's?" Cassie suggested.

"Possible. She was always one for cozying up to bigger money." I'd originally had her pegged as being a Tony B collaborator, so it wasn't a stretch when I found I could tie her to Colle. But while Jack was right about her loving power, I hadn't known Melanie going for the older sugar-daddy-aged crowd—money or otherwise—so Colle had surprised me. Though art circle gossip told us she'd had longtime ties to Tony B, another thug who tried to kidnap me last fall, their decade difference in age kept him close enough to his prime to not surprise us that Melanie threw in with him. Especially when he probably held a rank somewhere around second lieutenant in Colle's entourage. Until Tony B was killed in Rome two months prior, which might have left a door open for Rollie, since he was younger than her and had new potential from Moran's enterprises. Except for the bigger question, which ultimately was who had the most money and power. That award tied back to Colle, since Moran still kept the keys to his own kingdom. Shaking my head, I held up a hand. "There are too many what-ifs here. We need to wait until Jack and Danny can go over the street videos and see who can be recognized around the party, the house, and my hotel."

"Right," Jack agreed. "Since the Amazon is Rollie's hired gun, we'll know it was him if I see the redhead on any of the CCTV views leading to the hotel prior to the time we think Melanie was killed. We know some of the men employed by both Moran and Colle, so if it was anyone other than the Amazon, hopefully I'll get a good enough look at the killer or killers to recognize them and know who employed them."

He put his arm around me. "I have to tell you, though, the frame attempt concerns me for an entirely different reason. We know Moran and Rollie have confederates in the London police system, and there's no evidence to assume Colle doesn't as well. I have to wonder what kind of small welcoming party you might have encountered if you had been hauled to jail."

"I mentioned to Timms he could get our prints from Superintendent Whatley," I said. "Perhaps I need to connect with Whatley myself to make sure he's apprised of the situation. I know we can't use him as our personal watchdog, but he's probably the one person in Scotland Yard who has the best idea about what's going on with our project. Even if a lot of what he knows has to be conjecture."

"Agreed," Jack said. "I need to talk to him on a connected matter anyway, so I'll mention our concerns. I'll also do a little double checking and see if I can give Whatley a bit more of the picture. We've kept everyone outside of our group on a need to know basis, but since we've seen no attributable leaks come from Whatley's direction after he learns something from us, I think it's worth taking a chance."

I put my head on his shoulder. "Well, after that scary supplemental hypothesis, and all the *good news* you had about how the police probably won't think I'm a suspect but certainly could once they see the videos, I hope Melanie wasn't killed during the timeframe when I was breaking into the Russian's safe. Or if she was, that everyone truly believes Cassie was me in the club. It's not the best kind of alibi when you can only say 'no, I wasn't killing the nasty bitch in my hotel room—because at that exact moment I was trying to decide whether or not to steal a fake Rodin bust from the safe of the couple throwing the party.'"

SEVEN

We traded ideas until Cassie was ready to pass out on the sofa. She rose and walked to the keypad by the front door, set the alarm, said the guest room was ready, and padded off to bed. Jack decided to stay. My watch read 3:23 a.m.

Almost exactly three hours later I woke to my phone nearly vibrating off the nightstand. My eyes had difficulty focusing, but when they opened enough to see "Lincoln Ferguson," my brain shot into the rage zone. I turned off the phone and threw it across the room.

"Who was that?" Jack pulled me close.

I snuggled to regain the warmth. "No one. Go back to sleep."

His phone began a clanging ringtone. "It's your pet reporter," he said.

"What? He's calling you because I hung up on him?"

"Guess so." Jack grabbed his phone and answered in speaker mode. "This is Hawkes, Lincoln. You better have a damn good reason for waking us up."

"Laurel's with you?" Lincoln Ferguson was an up and coming investigative reporter who had gotten on my trail in January and never really slowed down. He knew there was a story to be gained, and despite all of Hawkes's and my dissuading tactics, he had only stopped stalking me after I broke his nose and promised him an interview if he stopped following me all the time. Except he didn't really think of what he did as stalking, and I couldn't tell him what he really wanted to know anyway, plus he had probably saved my life last month because he wouldn't leave me alone. So, he kept my number memorized, and I pretended to ignore him. This, however, was borderline unforgivable. Sleep was precious.

"Yes, I'm here, Lincoln. I turned off my phone because I didn't want to talk to you." I covered my eyes with my arm.

"There's a report that ties you to a death overnight," he said.

"And you want a confirmation? Okay, I'm not dead."

"I can get all the information I need from the police. I'm just checking that you're okay."

Ah, now I felt about three inches tall. But I was still irritated. "I'm fine Linc. Or I died. Take your pick but let me go back to sleep."

"Sorry. Should have thought. Called without thinking. Sorry."

That'll be the day, I thought.

"And I wanted to see if I could get you on record about finding the body."

There. The response I actually expected.

"No, Linc, no comment. Detective Inspector Timms would be the best person to contact for a statement."

"The public would love to hear—" His voice disappeared. I moved my arm and saw Jack putting the phone back on the nightstand.

"Did you turn it off?"

"Oh, yeah."

We staggered into the kitchen a couple of hours later, and our first argument of the day started before I'd downed my coffee. Never a good idea. He naturally wanted me to stay in the flat until he could bodyguard me everywhere. Cassie and I finished off the pot, then I set the small coffeemaker brewing another round and headed for the shower. In the privacy of the bathroom, I took the opportunity to text Inspector Timms and set an early appointment for going over my hotel room. When I came out I found Cassie had left her dark red wool dress on the bed for me to wear. She knew it was one of my favorites.

She was flipping channels between morning news shows when I entered the lounge.

"Everyone has covered the murder," she said.

"We know," I replied, moving into the kitchen and refilling my mug. "Lincoln called for a sound bite at six thirty this morning."

"I've only heard your name mentioned a few times. Usually, they just say Melanie was found by the person checked into the hotel room, or words to that effect. Mostly they're reporting a dead woman was found in the hotel room of another guest."

I looked at my Twitter feed, swiping the screen on my phone to see dozens of tweets that included my Twitter handle. "Well, the news programs may be keeping me incognito for the moment, but that damned blue bird on the internet isn't."

"Another reason you should wait until I can go with you to do the walk through of your hotel suite." Jack picked up where our arguing had left off. "Too many people know it happened in your lounge, and the space is still a crime scene anyway. You'll only be allowed in to give your impressions and possibly grab a few things. They don't need you there first thing."

"Except I want to get that part of the day out of the way as soon as possible," I said. "Cassie has already volunteered to go with me."

She hadn't, of course, but she picked up the cue instantly and nodded. "Absolutely."

Jack pulled out his phone. "I'll call Timms, and see—"

"No." I put my hand over the screen. "Please. Let us take care of this while you work on the angles we can't. I've already contacted Thomas Banks and he'll drive us there." Thomas was a cabbie we'd met and been impressed with several weeks ago. His observation skills and military experience had made him my go-to driver ever since. "Cassie will be with me the entire time, as well as the police. I'll text you when we're ready to leave and we'll regroup. Besides, you need to go home and change clothes before you head into the office to match wits with Cecil."

He sighed and looked down at his wrinkled shirt. "Are you going with me to check out videos with Williams?"

"Again, I think that might be risking detection. You can get him to skip ahead to the second thief a lot faster if I'm not there to make him think the first one looks familiar."

"I get it. But something tells me you need to see the files too."

"Can you get Danny to email them to you? Use Dropbox or whatever? We can all watch them together later."

He nodded. "Brilliant. I'll get it sorted with Williams. If not, I'll schedule time with you and have it set up to begin right at the flight of the second thief." He scratched his right eyebrow with a thumbnail. "Are you sure you didn't notice anything distinctive?"

I shook my head. "Just that she moved gracefully. And the more I think about it, the more I'm convinced she was very young. Early twenties at the most." I shrugged. "Remember, I didn't have the best observation post, and my handy-dandy dental mirror offered limited scope."

Thomas arrived, and Jack spent a few minutes bringing him up to speed while Cass and I filled to-go cups and armed the alarm. We'd just slid into the backseat when Jack's cab arrived.

Morning traffic was stop and go, but Thomas pulled into the traffic circle outside my hotel within half an hour. I didn't see any unmarked Met police cars I'd noticed the night before, but we were a few minutes early.

"We'll wait in the lobby until the inspector arrives," I said. "Thomas, I'll give you a call—"

"Jack already paid me for the morning," Thomas said, turning to look at us as he spoke. "I'll find a place to park and be waiting for you."

"Good enough. Thank you."

Timms stood by the elevator when we walked into the lobby. So much for my arriving ahead.

"Good morning, Miss Beacham." He extended his hand and strode closer.

"Good morning, Inspector." I took his hand, then said, "This is my associate Cassie Dean. She's come to help me look things over today and lend a little moral support."

"I called for the lift when I saw you come in," he said, just as the elevator arrived. We stepped into the brass and wood box, and the DI added, "Your room is still a crime scene, I'm afraid. But if you'd like to take some of your personal items, we can work with you on that sort of thing."

"Thank you," I said. "I already have luggage packed for the postponed trip. That will likely be enough for me. You're welcome to look through the bags before I leave."

"Very good." He held out latex gloves. "If you wouldn't mind...the rooms have been dusted for fingerprints, but we don't want to add any new ones."

Cassie and I nodded, each taking a pair of gloves.

Two uniformed constables were in the hallway of my floor. The shorter one opened the door to my suite as we neared. I smiled my thanks and led the way, then halted in my tracks.

"Laurel?"

I registered Cassie right behind me, and an arm going around my shoulders. "I..." Shaking my head, I came out of my daze. "Sorry." I offered a light laugh. "Something came over me."

"Take your time, miss," one of the constables said.

"Yes," Timms spoke up. "No hurry."

Cassie kept her arm around me and we took a slow turn through the first room. A police photographer was packing up equipment, and another crime scene tech was busy with some type of meter, but the room was a huge mess with fingerprint powder everywhere. As I walked, the DI spoke up again, "Take us through what you see, Miss Beacham—"

"Laurel," I said.

"Laurel," he corrected. Then he followed up with, "We'd like to know what is the same and what looks different. Let us know if there's anything surprising for any reason."

The first surprise wasn't one I knew they wanted to know. I felt violated. This is the second London hotel I've lived in for the last six months and in the near term I'd be changing places again after living here less than three months. I was sure for appearance's sake that the hotel would be happy to change my room, but coming home to find someone dead on your floor—someone I knew, even if I never really liked her—tended to be a deal breaker for me. And beyond the murder, this was exactly like the first time I had to change hotels because I feared Rollie, or someone equally bad, had found my personal space. Where I lived. No, that's not completely correct. I knew Rollie could have known where I lived because in late January and early February his grandfather, Moran, stayed in my hotel incognito for several days and I'd only noticed him as the man behind the newspaper in the lobby reading. I wasn't convinced Moran gave Rollie the information, given the old man's chivalrous nature toward me. However, finding Melanie in my room was different. On so many levels. Whether it was Rollie or Colle, there was more motive to dig out before we knew what, and who, we were dealing with in this incident.

I couldn't know the message for sure, only assumed the murder and leaving the body in my room was a way of showing me I could be gotten to at any time. That was the scariest possible message, and the fact I couldn't even be sure who the messenger was made the situation more unsettling. One part of me believed Colle had Melanie killed because it made more sense. She'd been with him in January—I knew that even if I didn't understand it. He would be more likely to know where she was last night. Yet I absolutely couldn't rule out Rollie and/or any of Moran's team. I'd been after them for so long, and my information had put so many of the thieves in prison over the last half-dozen years. The problem with this thinking was I still believed Moran had to be the one who hired the second thief last night. Too many angles to consider without real evidence.

"Relax and look around," Timms repeated behind me, and I realized I'd let my mind wander too long. He kept his voice at a Zen-like tone. "Look carefully for anything changed, for anything different. Obviously, anything missing."

What I immediately noticed missing, of course, was the dead body in the middle of the room. The carpet was marked to show where the body had laid. Something told me, though, that wasn't exactly what Timms had in mind when he said to look for anything different. I scanned this lounge room carefully, but I still didn't feel like I was concentrating on anything. Lists continued streaming through my brain of everything but what I was supposed to focus on. Silly lists not worth mentioning.

"I'm...I... Could I get a bottle of water from the refrigerator?" I asked, hugging my Prada closer.

"Jenkins, would you please," Timms ordered. The uniformed constable I remembered from last night hurried to the tiny fridge, then brought the cold bottle to me.

"Just take it easy, Laurel." Cassie grasped my left arm and moved her right hand from my shoulder to rub up and down my back. "Take your time."

I focused on the liquid traveling down my throat, then took a steadying breath. "I'm okay. Let's do this."

Keeping well back from the marked spot on the floor where I'd last seen Melanie, I circled the room. Cassie stayed right beside me.

The furnishings, of course, were the property of the hotel, and it was kind of embarrassing how small a personal stamp I'd put on the place. A few pens and a notepad were on the table-cum-desk, but my tablet wasn't where I'd left it on an occasional table near the loveseat, plugged into the charger.

"A ten-inch tablet was charging here when I left for the party," I pointed at the table.

Timms looked at the crime scene tech, who nodded. The DI said, "Anything electronic in the room was taken away for evidence testing. I'll make sure it's returned to you when the team is finished."

"That's fine," I said. There wasn't much on the tablet. I mostly used it for books and articles, and since I'd had a laptop stolen last fall I hadn't let the device vault my passwords for email. My searches might be interesting, but nothing damning. Nico usually did all that kind of digital snooping for me.

I resumed my reconnaissance. The entertainment center wasn't open, chiefly because I didn't watch a lot of television. I'd left it closed, and that was how the unit stood now. A couple of magazines, London entertainment issues, peeked out from under the loveseat. I started to pick them up, but Timms stopped me.

"We'd prefer—"

"Of course." I stepped back. "I'm sorry. I don't need them or anything, but they were on the small table when I left. They apparently fell off, slid underneath, I suppose."

"Did you write in them?" Timms asked.

I shook my head. "I don't think so." I motioned toward Cassie. "We've been planning to see a couple of plays and upcoming museum shows. I got those to remind us what restaurants and things were around each venue. Nothing important."

Timms looked at the crime scene tech. "Go ahead and bag those, just in case."

We moved into the bedroom, and that was when I had a surprise moment. "My luggage is gone."

"For your trip?" Timms asked.

I nodded and pointed to an area along the wall between the dresser and the door. "I packed before the party. I figured we'd be back late, and we had an early flight. I didn't want to take a chance on forgetting something."

"Did you have your passport inside?"

"No, I carry that in my purse. But I did have my ticket printout in the side pocket of the carryon bag. Otherwise, it was just clothes and shoes."

"What about jewelry?" Cassie asked.

"Nothing important. Some costume pieces I like, but I can live without them. I have some jewelry of my mother's, but I left those in the room safe."

"Why don't you see if everything is still in the safe," Timms suggested.

"Okay." I walked back to the entertainment center that looked like a standard piece of furniture but was actually unmovable, both bolted to the floor and affixed to the back wall. I opened the double doors, then pressed the point for the tension lock on the smaller door inside, next to the television, revealing the safe hidden behind. I caught myself chewing my lower lip as I punched in the code.

"Oh good, the box is still there," Cassie spoke for both of us as the steel door opened.

I turned to Timms. "I was going to ask to take these anyway. Is that okay?" I opened the big jewelry box. "You're welcome to catalog anything. And the smaller case just has bracelets."

He nodded. "Yes, I don't see any problem with you taking these. I can't see where they have any bearing on the investigation. But do check to be sure nothing is missing before proceeding."

The jewelry box and the items inside were relatively new treasures to me. Until a few months ago, they had been with Moran since my mother's death. They were keepsakes my mother had left with Paul-Henrì, jewelry she wore when she was with him. When he died, Moran kept the items, intending to return them to me, he said. These pieces, and the photographs that were enclosed, were my first inkling about the reason for my troubled history with the man I'd been raised to believe was my father—or at least the man who always purported to be my father, despite keeping a distance between us almost as wide as the Atlantic. Something else Jack and I were intending to look into in conjunction with returning to New York to investigate my mother's death. Though I had no idea how to prove one way or the other since we didn't have any comparable DNA for either of the two men who could have fathered me. All I knew for sure was that I looked just like my mother.

Everything inside the big box was untouched, and I opened the clamshell case I used to store the jewel toned bangle bracelets my mother loved to wear. I also made sure the photos were in place, but I moved the large one quickly, so DI Timms couldn't get a good look at it. The smaller one still held the creases where it had been folded for some time in my mother's compact, but it was still safely on the bottom of the case where I'd left it.

"Everything is here."

I looked around the room, but nothing stood out as different. Cassie moved to my closet and pulled down one of the large heavy paper shopping bags I saved on the top shelf.

"Set those in here so you don't have to worry about dropping anything," she said.

"Thank you." Now that my luggage was gone, it looked like I'd be using the rest of the stored bags to carry away any clothes I had left in my closet. I joined her and opened the doors wide, perusing the meager fare left behind on hangers and a small shelf. "Most of my good things were packed in my suitcases. Should I take the rest of my clothes? Or do I need to wait for the all clear?"

Timms walked closer, saw how little encompassed my wardrobe, then gave a brisk nod. "I don't see any reason we'd need your clothing. But if anything else is missing, please let me know immediately."

"I'll pack up these things for you, Laurel, and you can check the bath," Cassie suggested.

"Thank you."

Naturally, it didn't take long in the tiny bathroom. I grabbed up what few things I had in there with Timms's continued approval, and by the time I exited I saw Cassie bagging up the last of my shoes. I was once again carrying my belongings around in shopping bags, exactly like this London adventure started in September. Six months and too much of my life was still transient and unchanged—except back then my belongings were winging their way to Lake Tahoe for a vacation I still hadn't had time to take. I had no idea where my AWOL luggage would land this time.

I felt a migraine starting and didn't know if it was due to not enough sleep, too much stress, or way too many surprises. Probably a combination of all the above. There likely were more items that belonged to me in the suite, but I didn't feel up to crawling around to look under the bed or checking the narrow crevasses between furniture.

Since I'd given what little input I could about the room and retrieved enough of my own things to keep me marginally clothed, I mentally crossed fingers and asked DI Timms, "I can't see anything else to mention, but I will call if something comes to me later. Do you need us here longer? Or would it be okay for Cassie and me to leave?"

Timms nodded. "Absolutely. You've provided us the information we need. I'll let you know if we need you to come by again. I spoke to Superintendent Whatley early this morning, and he assured me that yours and Miss Dean's fingerprints are safely in the system. As long as you stay in London, Miss Beacham, I think we're finished for the time being."

But when we headed for the door, he added, "I do need contact information about where you'll be staying. I spoke to the hotel manager and she's eager to help you relocate to another room if you'd like."

I shook my head. "I'll be staying with friends for a few days at least, Inspector. When I know a location for sure, I'll send you a text with all the contact information. In the meantime, feel free to call me at any of the numbers on my card."

"Very good. Thank you."

I texted Thomas when we were in the elevator and told him we'd be in the lobby momentarily. He texted back he'd be waiting for us.

"Why do you think they took your luggage?" Cassie asked.

"Maybe they saw my ticket printout and thought my passport was in there as well."

"I didn't want to say anything in front of the inspector, but..." She dropped her voice to a whisper. "The locked case you keep in your closet with all your special devices was gone."

I shook my head. "That's the only thing I took after I found Melanie dead on the floor. Well, that case and the Prada. I honestly thought about grabbing my luggage, but figured I needed to travel light. I ducked into my closet, scooped up the purse and case and lit out."

The elevator dinged to announce the lobby. The floor seemed empty of uniformed police. I assumed everyone was finishing up on my floor.

"So, you have these clothes and everything electronic." She

raised the shopping bag in her right hand. "Guess you're kind of getting used to losing your packed bags, right?"

"I don't think I'll ever get used to it," I said. "I am getting resigned to it, however."

Then she asked the bombshell questions. "But did you not notice your luggage was already gone last night? Or didn't you look?"

I was in mid-stride, heading toward the front desk and suddenly my legs didn't feel strong enough to support me much farther. I hurried to a chair, and Cassie followed at my heels, close enough that I could whisper, "Omigod, my luggage still sat grouped in the bedroom when I was in the suite with Melanie. I distinctly remember seeing the packed bags when I came out of my closet after grabbing my gadget case and Prada purse. But I'd heard the police sirens and panicked, walking past the luggage because I wanted to be able to move quickly."

Cassie made a kind of strangled sound, then asked, "You know what that means, don't you?"

Nodding, I didn't trust myself to speak, but internally I was screaming—Hell, yes! It meant I was in the room with a murderer who left right behind me with my luggage.

I remembered the door that closed above me on the stairwell after I'd flown down several floors. Finally, I said, "That must have taken some nerve. The elevator dinged right as I headed down the staircase, so whoever it was had to have snuck out in the seconds between when I entered the stairwell and the lift opening. If the ding signaled the police arrival of course."

The lights strobed through my curtains only a minute or so before I heard the elevator. Once I thought about it, the arrival would have been close to the police's, but it was a viable fear either way. If it wasn't the police, and the killer exited directly after me, he or she could have been the one I heard open the stairwell door. Or the killer could have really had balls and boarded the waiting elevator with my luggage, pretending to be a guest ready to check out of the hotel. I huffed. "And who called the police and tipped them off about the murder? Was the luggage part of the killer's plan to get away or an improvisation?"

"My guess would be the killer took your bags and called the police," she whispered.

"I was just thinking exactly the same thing." I wondered if James would remember anyone leaving as the police arrived, but in the excitement, he easily might have missed such a departure. Since the hotel offered express checkout, it wouldn't have been unusual to see someone leave with bags without stopping by the front desk. I needed to remember to ask Jack to get the security footage to see if we spotted anyone with my luggage. "But why? It couldn't be for framing me, since Melanie was already dead when I arrived. Maybe the killer had an alibi somehow for when the time the call would have been recorded?"

"Do you want to go back and tell the inspector any of this?"

"How can I do that without admitting I went into my closet for my purse and case? Something I didn't admit before."

"Yeah, you're right. Maybe Jack could suggest that's why the luggage was taken."

"Maybe."

Jack always lectured me about my penchant for removing items from a crime scene. I figured I'd be in for another refresher when I admitted last night's transgression to retrieve the gadgets. Instead, I could call the inspector later. Probably denial on my part, but I felt rattled and didn't want to risk calling attention to myself again anytime soon. It would be too easy to say more than I should.

Thinking back, I couldn't be sure the door I heard opening while heading downstairs was even my floor. Which meant it might have been the murderer—or not. There were several floors above mine, and the person sharing the stairwell with me might as easily have been someone else from a higher floor heading down for a late night drink and a bit of exercise who had no correlation to what occurred. I knew I hadn't heard anything that sounded like my luggage banging through the door. The wheels alone would have made a recognizable noise if they'd been set down on the concrete landing. Besides, I'd already moved into flight stage by then, and everything seemed a potential enemy at the time. I would have noticed a sound out of place.

Not that I was currently very calm. Neither was Cassie, so she didn't argue when I said I'd call Timms later. I needed to finish my business with the hotel. When Thomas pulled up to the hotel entrance a minute later, I was at the front desk trying to thank the hotel manager for all the assistance and do my best to keep my options open. While I didn't close the door on returning to lodge there later, saying I was staying with friends in the short-term, I had no doubt she picked up on the anxiety ping-ponging between Cassie and me. The manager promised to collect any personal items I may have left in the room, and we agreed to talk again in a few days' time about my future lodging plans.

Thomas stashed all my shopping bags in the boot without comment, and Cassie and I stayed quiet as we pulled away. When he asked me where to go next, my brain had to catch up to the fact there was still so much to do.

"We probably need to check out the office," I said. "But I want to keep our schedule open in case we need to reconnect with Jack. How about if we go back to Cassie's first and drop off my things?"

"Will do," he said, turning at the next corner.

Admittedly, a part of me wanted back in Cassie's alarmed flat just so I could hide under the covers. I couldn't stop wondering how close I'd stood to the murderer.

EIGHT

When we arrived at Cassie's flat, Thomas stayed with the car and we promised not to take more than a few minutes. We raced up the stairs, and once we were inside she turned the alarm back on as I twisted the deadbolt.

"I know I'm being silly," she said, nodding her head toward the keypad. "But I'm kind of feeling heebie-jeebied right now knowing the murderer was with you in the suite."

"No need to convince me." I followed her into the guest room. Neither of us bothered taking off our coats.

Because the building was nineteenth century, and despite many modernizations, the owner kept the flats as close to historically accurate as possible. Cassie had even exchanged rent early on by doing restoration work to the historic plaster moldings and woodwork, and she had changed wall coverings to better suit the period. In all those changes, however, closet and storage space were kept to a minimum, so an antique wardrobe filled the bill in this room. She opened one of the double doors and grabbed a handful of hangers.

"It's kind of lucky we had our adventure last night," she said, hanging up a white Valentino I loved, and was so glad hadn't been in the absconded luggage. "Otherwise you'd be down two of your most worn outfits."

I laughed and started pulling out and folding the sweaters we'd tossed into another bag. "I don't know that I'd say my black Lycra suit is one of my most worn, but I would hate to have to replace it. Same goes for the LBD. Which reminds me, it should go to the cleaners since it's the only black dress I have."

"Also, now that you and Jack aren't going to New York, do you want me to see if I can get you a last-minute re-invite to Caro Taylor's event? You RSVP'd regrets while you were scheduled to be out of town, but it may be worth attending for the chitchat alone."

Caro Taylor was a society maven who held an annual arts luncheon and fashion show each spring. I adored the woman, now in her sixties, for her quick wit and patronage of art and artists. Her fundraisers were legendary for giving new artists the financial shot in the arm they needed from both the grants she bestowed and the attention she threw their way.

"It's a good idea. But let's wait and see what develops. I'd hate to beg for a last-minute seat, and then find I need to be somewhere else instead."

"Okay, just let me know."

She moved on to hang up my pants, and I dropped the shopping tote filled with shoes in the bottom of the wardrobe. Cassie had made sure each was in its own storage sack, so it wouldn't hurt anything for the shoes to stay jumbled together until later.

"Since you're staying here, shouldn't you text the inspector?" Cassie asked.

"Do you mind if I stay here a few days? I didn't really ask, and I can't promise safe—"

"Stop it. You know Jack will probably get police patrols beefed up in the area. My neighbors and I will be safer because you're here."

I grinned. There was no use arguing with sound logic.

Before I could finish the text, my phone buzzed. I touched the screen with my finger, putting the call on speaker. "Hi, Jack. Cassie and I are back at her flat and Thomas is downstairs waiting on us. The police let me take away most of my things."

"What did they keep?" he asked.

"Just my tablet, I think, but the luggage I had packed for the trip was gone, too, and Timms said the Met police didn't take it." I waited to see what he'd say.

"But you said you almost grabbed it before you ran."

Give the boy a gold star. "Yes, I did. It was there when I found Melanie in the sitting room."

His voice was low and measured, but the calmness didn't fool me when he asked, "Are you telling me the luggage disappeared between the time you left and when the police arrived?"

"Looks that way."

Cassie wrapped her arms around her torso. I completely understood the impulse. The line remained silent, and I waited for Jack to speak again. Finally, he said, "Makes the idea of a frame look all the more plausible since you weren't attacked and someone besides Melanie was likely in the suite with you."

"Yes, but maybe the murderer was just there to drop off Melanie's body for the frame, then search my room."

"Why carry Melanie into your suite? It would be much easier to get her to go there on her own and kill her onsite."

"I forgot to ask if she was killed there." I massaged my temples. "But you know how drunk she was at the party. She might not have even known where she was going if someone led her."

"Good reminder. Might be easier to spot her on CCTV in a drunken condition with someone else." Then he asked the question I'd been dreading. "What did Timms say when you told him?"

"I...haven't yet."

"Why not?" Though I couldn't see him, I knew he was squinting his right eye as he spoke those two words.

"I figured he'd ask me why I was in the bedroom, rather than running out immediately after spotting the body on the front room floor."

"And why didn't you?"

"I'd gone into my closet to grab my gadget case and my Prada." I caught my lower lip in my teeth and waited.

"You grabbed electronics, but not your clothes..."

I knew what he was thinking, and I wanted to slap him. Sure, I bought designer clothes, and he never failed to razz me about them, but Jack of all people should have known I'd gotten used to losing them at every turn. My custom devices were entirely different. "It was a priorities issue. The gadgets are more difficult to replace. Plus, I didn't think it was a good idea for the police to get a look in that case."

"Valid point," he said.

"I'd thought for a second about grabbing my carryon," I admitted. "Which is why I know the luggage was there when I left."

"But you didn't see or hear anyone?"

"Of course I didn't, or you would have heard me screaming all the way to Cecil's office. I do acknowledge, however, that I wasn't really looking around. I saw Melanie, I grabbed the purse and gizmos out of my closet, and I lit out."

"I'm not saying you should have done anything differently. Simply asking."

When no lecture came, I asked, "So you agree it's okay I took my purse and case?"

He sighed. "Why don't we leave things at saying it probably wouldn't be a good idea for London police to have seen inside that case while they were processing the scene."

That counted as a win in my book.

My phone received a call waiting chime, and I said, "Thomas is calling. He probably thinks we're dead up here." I looked at Cassie, and she had already pulled out her phone and was dialing. "Where are you, and where should we meet?"

"I'm waiting at Williams's video cave, but I see him coming down the hall. Why don't you get some lunch and we'll meet up at the office and trade information while we eat? And if I can get copies of video segments we can watch them there on the big screen."

"Sounds perfect."

We signed off. Cassie finished assuring Thomas we'd be down momentarily, then slipped her phone back into a pocket.

"Was Thomas irritated?" I asked.

"No, just worried, and he knew he needed a key to get into the building."

Choosing lunch options called for a discussion, and Cassie and I finally settled on Thai takeaway. An Asian restaurant occupied the ground floor below the Beacham Ltd. office, but we'd used that as a fallback too much lately when the weather was colder outside than we'd wanted to brave. Thomas knew of a good Thai restaurant on the way and headed that direction.

"We'd love for you to join us, Thomas," I invited.

He shook his head, and I noticed a bit more gray in his hair than before. "I texted my wife earlier, and we're going to meet. Don't always get the chance to eat together midday, but try to do so at least once a week. Gives us time to talk without the kids."

"How many kids do you have?" Cassie asked.

"Two boys. Don't know how Michelle managed while I was on duty. They're a handful, eleven and nine."

"Rambunctious, I'll bet."

"Understatement." He laughed, and I realized that was the first time I'd heard him sound jolly and almost carefree.

Traffic was more stop than go, so I asked Thomas the name of the restaurant and found their site on my phone. I picked favorites from the menu to work up an online order, and when I finished, I asked, "Any idea on an ETA for the restaurant?"

"Tell them fifteen minutes. It will likely be twenty, but they usually run a little longer than expected. It's a really popular place for lunch."

I added the expected time for pickup, paid with my currently working credit card, and shot the order into the cybersphere.

The food smelled wonderful, and I wasn't sure we were going to get to the office before I ripped into it.

"My mouth is watering, and my stomach is rumbling," Cassie whined.

"Tell me about it," I said. "How soon to the office, Thomas?"

"Probably seven or eight minutes."

"Can we picnic back here, or do you have rules?"

"I'll hurry, Miss Beacham." The hint of a smile appeared in his profile.

"Please call me Laurel."

Cassie and I used iron will to keep from diving into the bags, and Thomas helped us carry the food up the three flights of stairs when we got to the office. On the second landing, I heard his stomach rumbling and smiled. "Sure you don't want a quick snack before you leave?"

"Thank you, but I'm quite fine," he replied.

After we were safely behind the red steel door and the complicated electronic lock, Thomas took off for his date with his wife, and Cassie and I unloaded bags. Cartons of pad thai, panang curry, and jasmine rice made a beautiful presentation on the large conference table. Utensils and napkins were piled next to the paper plates I pulled from the shelf below the coffeepot.

"I'm going to be rude and not wait for Jack," Cassie said, opening the nearest carton and loading up her plate.

"Right behind you, sister." Then my cell phone chimed Nico's ringtone. My techno geek never liked doing field work, he was much happier living in his digital world. But when we learned one of the forgers we wanted to talk to might be in Italy, Nico agreed to take on the search duties if he could stop and see his grandmother while he was near Rome. Personally, I would have gone with him if I could have for the chance to eat her home cooking. I put it on speaker. "Hey, Nico, where are you? Still in Rome?"

"Milan," he replied. "But the bigger question is, where are you?"

"In the office with Cassie. Why?"

"Hi, Nico," Cassie called, then slipped another bite of Thai chicken into her mouth.

"*Ciao,*" he responded to Cassie.

"Chow is right, I'm eating," she said with a giggle.

He took a second then said, "So the fact you aren't in New York answers my first question. Is Jack there?"

"No, we're waiting on him. He's watching CCTV with Danny Williams but should be here soon."

"I take it things didn't go well last night."

I sighed. "I'm sorry. We should have called since you were involved in the planning, but everything started going sideways at the club and continued sliding the rest of the night."

"I heard Melanie Weems was murdered in your room. I wanted to check and make sure you were unharmed."

"Hell! You heard that in Milan?"

"*Sì*. I take it from your response that you are fine."

"As fine as I can be when I'm interviewed by the police and have to change places of residence because where I lived was a crime scene. Who told you?"

"Remember the source I came here to find?"

"Yes..." I left the word hanging. Nico was in Italy trying to locate a trail to a forger who made a sword that started this whole jagged journey, along with the snuffbox that led Jack on a fool's errand. Nico had shared a conversation with another friend last week and talk of metalwork forgers came up. This kind of thing regularly happened with the types of people he and I knew, so it wasn't as unusual as it sounded. Learning this particular nameless forger also knew Simon Babbage, and did jobs for him before he was killed, and because Simon was the person evidence pointed to as having absconded with the sword we assumed the forger duplicated, all led to Nico landing in Italy yesterday morning.

He explained, "We met for coffee, and he told me that he heard from someone, who heard from someone else—"

Lack of sleep always made me impatient. "How many different *someones* are we going to go through?"

He laughed.

"Spill it, Nico."

"You're the talk of the thieves and pickpockets of Italy."

"Did anyone say who ordered the hit? Or who actually killed

Melanie?"

"I said you were the one talked about, not anyone else." He was quiet for a second, then said, "Surely the Met *Polizia* couldn't think you had anything to do with the murder."

"I did find her."

"I'm sorry. Were you alone?"

"Yes. She was beaten with a baton like the one I had in Germany." Also, she slapped me earlier in the evening, and a packed house witnessed the episode, I thought. My legs were starting to feel a little shaky. I leaned against the table. "And apparently the murderer was hiding somewhere in my room when I thought I was alone with the body."

"*Mio Dio!*"

"But that isn't all." I took a few minutes explaining how and why the theft of the Rodin bust didn't happen as planned.

When I finished, he asked, "The same mark as was on the snuffbox?"

"Exactly." I combed the top of my hair back with one hand and changed the subject. "Have you discovered any lead on the forger, so we can see if he did the snuffbox and the sword, and try to get some insight into that angle?"

"I have a first name, Arlo, and I'm told he lives in Paris. I'm booked on an afternoon flight," he replied.

"Okay, great. See what you can learn. I'll have Jack call you—"

The loud *clunk* of the lock said Nico wouldn't have to wait for a call.

"Do I smell Thai chicken?" Jack asked as he opened the door. He looked at us and stopped. "What's come up now?"

"Nico, fill Jack in," I said. Walking to the coffee setup, I grabbed a couple of water bottles and carried them back to the table.

Jack listened quietly until Nico finished, then asked, "Any chance you'll hear anything more substantial about Melanie's death later?"

"I have a lot of feelers out," Nico said. "Many people know

Laurel and like her, so I expect to hear something."

"They just like her because they don't have to work with her," Cassie said, grinning at me.

I grinned back at her, but my heart wasn't in it. I finished putting enough food on my plate to look like I was interested in eating, and listened as Jack said, "For the time being we're grounded here. What little I've tracked down says they don't have any reason to hold Laurel, but it's early on and it makes sense the police want her to stay in London. So far, they've only labeled her as someone helping with inquiries. If you find out anything in Paris and need backup, call and I'll see if I can get something worked out. But until we have a reason to leave I don't want to push anything."

"I plan to keep everything low-key," Nico said. "Always meet in public places, that sort of thing."

"Good, Nico, stay safe," I said.

Jack took a swig of his water bottle, frowning as I spoke. I looked down at my plate and scooped up some curry.

"Was the baton the one Laurel had?" Cassie asked. "Did the police find fingerprints or anything?"

Jack shrugged. "I phoned a mate of mine who knows someone in the lab. There was a partial print, but it didn't match anyone they thought might be connected to this case. Meaning the four of us, of course. Doesn't rule anyone out either."

I nodded and kept eating.

"What about the video?" Nico asked.

"Williams is parceling the cuts off into smaller files and loading everything onto a flash drive. We figured it might be better if there wasn't a digital email trail. He'll text me when it's ready," Jack said. "We watched every available video of the escape of the second thief, as well as the views when everyone left the club and the entrances to Laurel's hotel. Nothing jumped out to help identify the killer. It looks like she exited through a long disused doggy door, by the way. Also, we found where Melanie was dropped off at the service entrance of Laurel's hotel, but the car drove off and she entered alone. Still staggering somewhat, so she might have been mugging it when she slapped you in the club, but she was definitely some degree of pissed. Then, she appears in the work areas of the hotel, wandering through to the elevator. She gets on alone and disappears from the video because of whoever tampered with the hotel's feed."

I clutched my throat. "That can't be very good for me since the video won't conclusively prove I wasn't with her in the suite."

"Except that Williams already has your movements cataloged to the minute, long before she arrived at the hotel, through your appearance arriving in your lobby, and even has the video highlighted that shows me running off when Cecil phoned."

"Good lord, I'm glad Danny's on our side," I said.

Jack set down his plate and walked over to put an arm around me. "Not just Williams. From what Nico said, you have half the underworld pulling for you."

"Come on, stop. You're making me sound like a hood. I just have an extensive circle of eclectic acquaintances."

"One way to phrase it," Jack said, grinning.

"You're just jealous I have more connections than you do." I patted his cheek and winked.

"Of course, that's what keeps me up nights."

Nico spoke again, "I'll call or text if I learn anything else from this end, but unless there's additional information for me to know or do, I should go so I won't miss my plane."

"Go," I said. "But be careful."

"Always," he replied.

Everyone said their goodbyes, and I tapped the screen to end the call.

Cassie dropped her empty plate into the trash and very deliberately said, "With lunch and the updates complete, I'm going to use the ladies room." She grabbed her purse. "Think I'll also run downstairs and see if I can get some rangoons too. I like my lunches multi-Asian. Don't worry if I'm not back right away."

As she closed the door, Jack asked, "Has she always been that subtle?"

"She's an art restorer," I said. "Not an actress."

He wrapped his arms around me and nuzzled my neck. "Is my kickass girlfriend feeling a little vulnerable?"

"I guess that's one way to put it." His lips moved to meet mine, and I felt a lot of the tension go out of my body. When we broke from the kiss, I rested my cheek against his crisp white shirt. "You know, you clean up pretty well after having to go home in the clothes you wore last night. Did Cecil appreciate the extra effort?"

"My boss just wanted to continue grousing about the bust retrieval being...well, a bust." He rubbed a hand up and down my back. "It's like when you talk to Max, and you try to explain the particular details rather than simply producing the item like magic, the way he really wants it done."

I took a step back to be able to look him in the eye. "How bad is this really, for both of us?"

"For me, it's over. I can't give them the authentic piece they were looking for since what you found was a forgery. At least with this new curve getting thrown toward the problem, Cecil can shift the purpose to when the original could have been switched for the fake."

"And someone in the British government is positive the bust in the Russian's safe was the same one originally at the real owner's country estate?"

"MI-5 is. I haven't learned specifics, but Cecil assures me the chain of events were complete as far as the Home Office was concerned as well. Says this new development will require a lot of double tracking in the coming days."

"But at this point, they're unlikely to find who swapped the piece out initially."

"There is that."

I crossed my arms and paced. "We should have pointed out to Nico the metal works forger in Paris could be a likely suspect for the creator of the Rodin fake."

Jack pulled out his phone. "He's probably already ahead of us, but it doesn't hurt to remind him for when he talks to Arlo." He sent a quick text and received confirmation the message had been received. "There. Done."

"I'm overthinking, aren't I?" I laughed and walked to the windows and opened the drapes.

Squinting at me, he said, "Yeah, you likely are. Maybe because you don't want to think about other things?"

"Hey, you're were the one who texted him." I laughed again and said, "Someday we both need to address our control issues."

"Pity. We could probably use them in many more creative ways." He waggled his eyebrows.

I smiled and resumed pacing. My brain wouldn't shut off and kept looping over old ground. "Look, I realize you couldn't really ask about the theft at the Russian's house. Were you able to work it in at all because it tied peripherally to the party?"

"Right, yeah." Jack shoved his cell into a pocket. "The Russian's making all kinds of stink about the jewelry. Never mentioned anything else according to reports. Williams did pull up all those perimeter cameras too, and I saw the second thief light out with one of the coppers spotting her and giving chase. She disappeared though. From the time stamp and the fact Williams didn't mention seeing anyone else drop out of the top floor, she had to have been ahead of you. But none of the camera views on the street revealed her actual exit from the house. I didn't ask to watch video showing the time around the house afterward, but I'm assuming if she hadn't been spotted and pursued you might have been seen as well. So far, no one's interested in the CCTV video coming after they took up her chase, leaving any cameo appearance you made ignored unless new evidence arises."

"I would have hidden myself somewhere if a police car had been outside." But I hadn't been watching closely enough for anyone on foot. Bad practice, Beacham. I'd heard the sirens and been lulled by the sound of their distance.

"And I would have had a heart attack in the club waiting for you to call," he said, grinning.

I slapped his shoulder. "If you had even half the heart attacks you claim are possible...*sheesh*. Just think of it as your daily cardio workout."

He caught me around the waist and pulled me close again. "I can think of a far better daily workout for my heart." The kiss this time was longer and hinted at the worry I knew he'd felt the previous evening.

Putting my hands on his chest, I pushed away and asked, "Did you learn anything else I need to be aware of about the investigation into Melanie's death? Am I on the hook even peripherally? Or totally off police radar at this point? Fingers crossed."

"To be honest, it's too early to know anything for certain." He sat on the end of the table and grabbed his water bottle. "But after following the party's multi-camera views...Oh, and Cassie did such a great job working the floor that even Williams didn't catch the switch. And with the working hotel cameras showing Melanie while we were still at the party venue watching the police arrive, I think anyone would be hard-pressed to build any kind of case against you unless they were trying to squeeze you for information."

"Meaning I just need to keep acting open and cooperative?"

"Best plan."

The door lock *clunked*, and Cassie poked her head inside. I slid up on the table next to Jack and picked up my plate to finish eating.

"Good." She grinned. "I'll quit worrying about you since you're eating."

I rolled my eyes. "What's on your agenda this afternoon beyond calling Max?"

"I have an appointment at the National Gallery," she said. "I'm doing some background research on a couple of restoration techniques, and one of their experts said he'd answer my questions. How about you?"

Jack's phone pinged, and he said, "Williams has the flash drive ready. How about we all go together? We'll leave Cassie at the National Gallery, then meet Williams."

Cassie glanced toward the window and said, "We need to grab

umbrellas. It looks like it's going to rain any second."

"You're kidding me." I stared unbelievingly. "It looked like the clouds were breaking a few minutes ago."

"Remember, you're in London," Jack said, wadding up empty cartons and bags and tossing them into the trash like basketballs. He only missed once. "This passes for a fair day this time of year."

"At least it isn't snowing like the New York forecast shows," Cassie added, as she stacked the cartons still containing food in our tiny refrigerator.

"Small favors," I groused and grabbed a to-go cup, filling it with coffee.

NINE

Since cabs are doubly hard to get in rainy weather, we hid under umbrellas and trudged the long block to the Tube. My Manola Blahniks weren't my favorite walking heels, but they were closed toe and the dark leather would look okay even if they got wet. Cassie used the opportunity to call our boss, using the road noise to distract Max while she told him I wasn't in New York and wouldn't be there as anticipated.

"No, Max, I have no idea when she'll be able to travel outside London," Cassie said in a normal tone, then held her hand over her mouth and quietly added, "The police are investigating a murder in her room. They're calling the shots."

Luckily, everyone was hurrying in all directions, because Max's responses were loud enough that they could have been on speaker. Cassie finished up the conversation saying, "I promise I'll call when I have more information, but I'm entering the subway, and I'd better hang up. Not a lot of good reception down there."

"Have Laurel call me," Max yelled.

"Will do, sir." Cassie grinned at me. "Have a nice day."

She pocketed her phone, and as we rode the escalator down Jack texted with Danny. We all used our Oyster cards to slip through the queue and as we neared the platform he said, "We're going to meet up again inside the National Gallery. His eyes need a break from the screens, and we should be able to find a place to talk in the museum."

Fine by me. I loved wandering through the National Gallery and did so every chance I could. We shook the water from our umbrellas, then entered one of the crowded train cars.

When we were back on the sidewalk again, Nelson and the lions welcomed us, glistening in damp air as they kept a weather eye on all visitors coming to Trafalgar Square and the National Gallery. Unless the boys disagreed, I planned to suggest we do any discussion in room forty-three of the gallery, where I could gaze on one of the four *Sunflowers* paintings that Van Gogh completed in 1888 immediately before he and Paul Gauguin shared the little yellow house in Arles, France. I loved how he wrote about the series to his brother Theo, saying "I am working at it every morning from sunrise on, the flowers fade so quickly." It was the kind of reminder I needed to seize every opportunity of the day—no matter how small—while I had the chance.

Danny Williams waited for us inside, near the Trafalgar front entrance. Like us, he was damp, his light hair darkened from the rain since he had no umbrella, but his grin was as bright as a summer day. He'd already been my partner in crime on one project, and I knew if there was anything video-wise to prove I had nothing to do with Melanie's death, Danny would find it. Unfortunately, I also worried if he spent too much time watching video around the Russian's house that he'd catch sight of me sneaking in or out as well.

"Cassie Dean, this is Danny Williams," Jack introduced them.

"Nice meeting you, Cassie."

As she shook Danny's hand, she said, "I've heard a lot about you. But don't worry, it was all from Laurel, so it was complimentary."

"Splendid," Danny said, smirking at Jack.

Looking at her watch, Cass said, "I hate to say hello and run, but I have an appointment in the Pigott Education Centre."

"We'll see you later," I said. "Call if you want us to meet you somewhere."

"I'll head back to the flat once I'm done here. I don't know how long this will take." She waved as she rounded the corner of the espresso bar to get to the ground level galleries and shortcut her way to the rear section of the museum and education center.

Jack raised an eyebrow. "You're going to continue to stay with Cassie?"

"My things are already there."

"But—"

"We'll talk about it later."

I slipped my left hand into the crook of his elbow and took Danny's arm with my right, steering all of us back toward the Trafalgar Square entrance and the stairs to the second level.

"So, Laurel, are you seeing anyone right now?" Williams quipped.

"I'll let you know if the situation changes, Danny. It's a moment by moment thing."

"Oh, funny." Jack glared at both of us.

We climbed the stairs and entered the nearest opening to The Wohl Galleries, a small series of connected rooms filled with enough reasons by themselves to visit the National Gallery, including an Impressionist room with works by Monet and Manet. My objective was the third room, beyond impressionism in both location within the museum and the artistic period. Room forty-three held the work of Seurat, Gauguin, and the sunny Van Gogh *Sunflowers*. The painting was as captivating as I remembered. Only two other people were in this gallery, one woman stood as I did near the Van Gogh work, and the other, a man, was drinking in Seurat's brilliance.

The guys moved to the farthest corner, to allow Jack to fill Danny in on what Nico had told us without anyone overhearing.

I happily forgot for the moment everything that happened the previous evening and took in Van Gogh's genius. Nothing like sunny art for a drizzly day.

He painted this series in early fall, 1888. Originally, the artist planned a full dozen panels to decorate Gauguin's room in the Yellow House in Arles, but ultimately just four were completed in his goal. Gauguin and Van Gogh parted company after only nine tumultuous weeks of trying to form their artistic community, the

"Studio of the South." A fifth painting, a replication of this London work, was completed in January 1889 at Gauguin's request, about six months before Van Gogh's death. That fifth painting, experts believe, is the copy hanging in the Van Gogh Museum in Amsterdam. The two men were ill-suited in this artistic partnership and living situation, but Gauguin knew the sunflowers were Van Gogh's seminal work and continued to say so. When he returned to Paris, leaving Arles only a few months after he'd arrived, he asked Van Gogh to send the copy for him to keep.

The sunny yellow painting I gazed upon, with its bright blue "Vincent" painted on the vase, was purchased for the National Gallery in 1924 through proceeds from the Courtauld Fund. This was why I did what I did. From finding lost art, to helping museums raise money to fund the acquisition of great works to offer free to the public, it made me continually count my lucky stars I could play even a small role in this type of good work.

I remembered seeing the painting as a child with Grandmamma and having to keep my hands behind my back so I wouldn't risk touching any of the exquisite works in the gallery. Even to this day, my fingers itched to touch the dying flowers, created on the canvas with Van Gogh's thick brushstrokes and heavy layers of paint, a process known as impasto, building up the texture of the seed heads. In August 1888, when he was in the middle of this painting, he wrote to his brother Theo, "I am hard at it, painting with the enthusiasm of a *Marseillais* eating *bouillabaisse*." I totally got that.

My fellow patrons moved on to another gallery. I continued my studies but could hear the low murmur of my guys in the background, a cue to continue losing myself in the art. It didn't matter how many times I studied a master work like this one, I always found new points to marvel over.

Suddenly, I was grabbed at the waist and lifted off my feet. I started to fight and scream, but my captor shoved something into my mouth and pinned my arms against my body. I heard Jack and Danny holler as we moved toward the side galleries. I struggled, but this guy was big. I couldn't turn my head enough to get a good look at him, but my peripheral vision showed he'd brought a couple of buddies along to entertain Jack and Danny.

TEN

The sound of fighting came from behind us, and I wondered who was landing the better blows. I tried attacking my captor's legs with my heels, but he pinned me tighter against him with one arm and raised the other to put my head in a modified chokehold. This wasn't the most unusual way anyone had ever tried to kidnap me, but it was close.

"Stop or I'll snap your neck." His voice was low and gravelly, his accent Slavic. I did as he said but wracked my brain for any other options. Another shock came as we exited into the hall, and I noticed uniformed feet sticking out of a door. I hoped the guard was just unconscious.

I'd been in the museum countless times, but never in a life or death situation. People screamed when they saw us on the stairs. As everyone pointed and yelled from below, he raised me effortlessly over his head and bellowed, "I will throw her, and she will die. Everyone, out of my way."

Halfway down the stairs, my stomach did flip-flops with each step he took, but being above his head meant I had a view back upstairs and could see Jack and Danny round the corner and start down. Both looked like they'd just gone three rounds in the ring. I shook my head in warning. Part of me wanted to smile in relief at seeing them, but I felt hot, angry tears instead.

Mentally measuring distance, I wondered if I could tuck and roll on the marble floor and not break my skull or back if I found a way to escape his vice hold and jumped to freedom. My mental exercises didn't matter, however, because when my captor reached the last step he looped me back around to my original pinned position. This time, the hold on my neck was tighter.

Police cars pulled up on the street, and officers bailed out, running across the long square. He watched through the doors, and repeated, "Back, out of my way. Don't try to stop me. Tell the police to let me go or she dies."

One of the guards headed out the door to intercept the cops.

I could see Jack peripherally. He was nearly down the stairs but stopped when he realized the new danger I was in. He signaled to someone, Danny, I assumed, and I tried to figure what he had planned. I was carried toward the front door. Everyone stood back while the police remained outside. I wondered if there were sharpshooters on the neighboring roofs.

Then from around the staircase, a guard raced toward us, wielding a taser. Would it even work on a guy this size? Thinking optimistically, I ran my hands between my neck and shoulder and his arm, hoping to be able to push away his thick lower arm if the charge affected him enough.

What I didn't figure on was getting caught in the charge myself. His body probably got most of the juice, but I suddenly wasn't sure where I was, who I was, or what my body was doing.

I kind of came out of it a few seconds later, realizing Jack's arms were around me, cradling me on the floor. But I still couldn't move, and my eyes wouldn't stay open. Between those long blinks, I saw the giant try to get up, but the guard zapped him again.

"I'm sorry," Jack whispered in my ear. "I tried to grab you quicker, but the charge was already going."

I think I said something like "my hero" but I wasn't sure. It was a good bet though since my first language in situations like that was sarcasm. Though I'd never been tased before, so who knew. What brain cells I did have working made me want to grab that taser and shoot the guard while someone had him in a half-Nelson hold. Except I probably needed to thank him instead. So many dueling emotions.

Jack helped me up, and I leaned on him, trying to walk. But he was having some problems too. I assumed he'd received a little taste of the taser when he pulled me away or suffered from the repercussions of the fight he'd had with the giant's cohorts. We were ushered into the small office to wait for the police. I was offered a water bottle, but all I really wanted was the nice soft chair. Danny came in a few minutes later. I focused on not falling out of the chair.

"They're hauling the guys away," Danny told me. I think I nodded. To Jack, he asked, "You recognized them?"

Jack nodded. "They're muscle for Ermo Colle."

"That's what I thought too," Danny replied.

"Call Whatley," I whispered, not yet able to get my voice to register correctly. I coughed and took another sip of water.

"On it already," Jack said, and I saw he was finishing a text on his phone.

"Your inspector at Scotland Yard?" Danny asked.

We nodded.

Danny pulled out his own cell and started flipping screens. "Amazing video of you and King Kong, Laurel." He punched his screen with a finger. "Hey, you're trending big time on Twitter."

"What?" I tried to grab his phone, but I knocked it out of his hand instead. Danny picked it up and set it on the desktop beside me.

"See? You've already been shared over three thousand times. You've eclipsed your mentions about having lived in the hotel room where the murder happened." He pointed to the RT icon, then flipped to Facebook and added, "Someone ran it live on FB, and here they're still rolling while the arseholes are getting thrown into the Met's cars."

"Why? How?" My phone started ringing in my purse. I looked at Jack. "That's Linc—"

"I'll take care of it," he replied. He called Linc and told him in no uncertain terms that I had no comment, and to not call me again today. Then he asked Danny, "Can you go and get Cassie? Bring her here for safety concerns."

"No," I shook my head, but that felt weird so I stopped and repeated, "No. She's safer where she is. If you bring her here, someone could start videoing her too. Leave her alone."

As I finished talking, I folded my arms on the desktop and rested my head. The last thing I heard before I passed out again was Danny saying, "She's right. Someone could connect them both being here and working for the foundation, and Cassie will follow Laurel to internet stardom. I'll go back and wait outside the door until her meeting is over. Then I'll get someone to show us out of here by way of an employee exit."

ELEVEN

The benefit of experiencing secondhand tasing is no one wants to wait for you to get your brain back up to speed, so all the tedious questions with the cops were handled for me by Jack and Danny. Plus, they knew the names of two of the bad guys already. All I could have told them was that a giant grabbed me and offered a very high chance of my death.

Of course, there were downsides, like still having no sense of taste or smell an hour later.

When I felt like I was functionally alert again, Danny was gone and there were a couple of new suits in the room with Jack and me. They made their introductions but didn't offer which government services they reported to. However, I quickly figured out the new guys were MI-5 and MI-6, and they were there to pick Jack's brain. While their conversation was probably half over already, I gathered from what I was privy to that Jack pretended to be accommodating, but wasn't telling them anything about the more important personal stuff we knew about Colle. Namely, that he was the man I'd grown up believing was my father—though recent facts that had come to light left my true parenthood in question. Also, he was likely the initiator of a forgery operation which put a substantial amount of high-end fakes into the market the past few years, affecting all of Europe and possibly the four corners of the globe.

"We learned from a source in early February that Colle did have additional plastic surgery, and most likely has a completely new name and persona," Jack said. "All the intel is hearsay of course, but I reported all of this information to my Home Office superior at the time, and I'm assuming it hit the radar in each of your departments as well."

What he didn't say was one of the reasons Colle had to refurbish his look and background was because I not only recognized him as my presumed dead father, but I escaped from his capture just after the first of the year by bashing him in the head with a baton much like the one that killed Melanie.

The new suits offered little in the line of quid pro quo, so I had to assume Jack had good reason for what he was doing. He usually did though. I'd learned firsthand that running the odds of any con was something he did naturally, and the little he let slip told me part of what he provided was to cover his ass. Like he'd said, information regarding the new identity was shared when Rollie was arrested in February. Because that information was used by Rollie to give me a jab when he thought he was leading me to the slaughter, we had to assume it was true.

Yet none of this explained why Colle's goons tried to kidnap me without any escape procedure beyond sheer muscle and nerve. It couldn't have been a sanctioned grab. Colle was too smart for anything so mundane.

That was something for us to discuss later. I didn't feel the need yet to share with my new acquaintances.

DI Timms knocked on the door, then stuck his head in. "Mind if I join you?"

"Hi, Inspector," I said, propping my head on one hand. "Welcome to the party. I feel like I already have a hangover."

"Sorry you had to get tased," he said. "Your first time, I take it?"

I nodded. "Hopefully my last too."

Jack made introductions, and all the men exchanged cards. Then MI-5 and MI-6 looked at their respective watches, decided they had other brains to pick and took their leave. Timms sat beside me in the office's other available visitor's chair, and Jack leaned against the wall.

"I realize you're not feeling top form at present," Timms said to me. "But a piece of evidence has come available that I felt needed to be followed up on immediately."

"Shoot." I waved the hand I wasn't leaning on.

"It's...uh..."

"Personal?"

"Possibly." Timms shrugged. "The crime scene unit found a strand of hair we think may be that of the killer. Since you, the victim, and your assistant all have blonde hair, I wondered if any of you naturally have...had...another hair color."

"The hair is from a woman?"

"Well, it's a long blonde hair, but it's been bleached, and the hotel assures me all their maids are brunettes."

"That's true, brown and black-haired maids are all I've seen. In answer to your question, Cassie and I are both natural blondes, but hers is much shorter than mine and has pink tones, and I do add highlights, so part of our hair has been bleached lighter than the natural color. I only knew Melanie as a blonde, and I'm positive she highlighted hers as well. To be sure, however, you might check with her family. We ran in the same circles in college and from what I remember she came from Hartford, Connecticut in the U.S."

"You never saw her as a redhead?"

I jerked up in my chair and looked at Jack. He circled the desk and took the chair behind it.

"Are you saying the hair you found was from a bleached redhead?" Jack asked.

"Or, the hair was one highlighted to keep the auburn color from looking flat?" I suggested.

"Affirmative," Timms said. "The hair shows a very small bit of auburn root."

I pulled out my phone and found the two JPEG files Roberto drew of the Amazon, based on the description of the police officer who saw her immediately before and after she killed Tony B in Rome. The colored drawings which showed her auburn hair and the highlights I suggested the artist add because that was how she wore it when I first saw her. I passed Timms my phone. "There's a high probability this is your suspect."

All evidence pointed to the Amazon working for Rollie and possibly Moran as well—but particularly toward the grandson. Besides killing Tony B, she was believed to have killed one of Colle's forgers in Germany and did the final wet work after an Italian military police officer and I were chased by three gunmen across rooftops in Barcelona in early February. We had another longer list of crimes we attributed to her with less proof, but firm belief. I'd tangled with her a couple of different times, never sustaining a debilitating injury, however, which always made me wonder if Moran had more control over her than we'd first thought. But she had nerve and skill as an assassin. While I had no idea how or why she killed Melanie in my room, I totally believed she was capable of getting in and out without leaving a trace. Only one other time— that of the murder of the German forger—had we learned evidence was found to possibly point to her, and it was again a strand of hair.

Jack picked up the explanation at that point, and I stayed quiet. I didn't trust my brain enough yet to not let something slip accidentally. He detailed what was already in the Italian police database and gave Timms contact names and numbers of both the detective we'd worked with in the *polizia*, as well as his friend in the military police, the *carabinieri*, who had also been onsite when the Amazon killed Tony B in the Rome hospital.

Timms made extensive notes and had me email him the drawings. When he closed his notebook, he said, "I will contact the Italian police and circulate these drawings as a possible suspect."

"Customs should already have the drawings in their system," Jack said. "But since I was supposed to be notified if she arrived in the country, we could be jumping to conclusions. Or she could have found...an irregular...route into the country."

"I've noted all of this." Timms slipped his pen and notebook into an inside coat pocket. "I'll be in touch."

We all stood, and I added, "We would appreciate any additional information, Inspector. We've had a few close calls with this woman and finding her is a priority of ours too. We won't impede your investigation in any way, but we prefer to stay a step or two ahead of her. Also, I would be particularly interested in the three men's motives for the incident today if that comes out in the interviews and you're able to share the reason why. Just counting on brute force seems a little illogical to me."

"I understand," he said, shaking our hands as he prepared to leave. "And I will definitely let you know if I gain any sharable information in either case. I never realized a job in the art field could involve interacting with such dangerous people. You truly have a risky occupation."

"Most often, it's pretty boring," I said, crossing my fingers behind my back.

"Anytime something is worth a great deal, and desired by unscrupulous people, risk and danger can go hand in hand," Jack said. "Art is no different than any other field in that regard. I once heard someone say, where there's a sea, there are always pirates."

He winked at me, and I felt my face warm. I'd said exactly that phrase late one night when we were sharing wine and reminiscing about recent jobs in Miami and Barcelona.

"Very good." Timms nodded and opened the door.

I cleared my throat and spoke up, "One other thing, Inspector. My job does require a lot of travel, and while I can put some things off, I never know when I really do have to leave London quickly. Have you gathered enough evidence to give me any idea when my travel restrictions will be lifted?"

Timms nodded, but he didn't look apologetic. "I'm sorry. Yes, for the moment we would appreciate it if you remained within the city boundaries. If anything changes, however, I will contact you immediately. The investigation is early on, and everyone is still under suspicion. I would appreciate knowing your whereabouts. In case I have further questions, you understand."

"Of course." *Sheesh!* What did it take to get off this guy's list? Oh, yeah, a suspect he could tie to the crime with evidence. The fact we didn't have a name for the Amazon, nor any information on how to locate her couldn't help either. Maybe he would change his mind after contacting the Italian authorities.

"And you're still staying at the address you texted to me earlier?" he asked.

Cassie's flat. I nodded without looking at Jack.

"Then that's all I need," Timms said. "Cheers."

"Goodbye, Inspector."

I didn't feel the least bit cheery.

TWELVE

Danny called as we were putting on coats. He and Cassie had left a few minutes before from the education center, and he wanted to know where to meet. Jack covered the mic and asked, "Are you hungry? You want to meet them in a pub?"

"I still can't taste anything, but a pub sounds fine."

They settled on one nearby, and Jack and I made our way back into the hallway. One of the directors met us and offered a less trafficked exit through a side door. We thanked him, grateful for a little anonymity, and left.

The afternoon had come and gone, and the sidewalk was filled with umbrellas sheltering the end of the workday crowd from the heavier rain now falling. I didn't bother opening mine, since Jack wrapped his arm around me as we walked, and one umbrella kept us relatively dry.

"I forgot to ask if you got the flash drive from Danny," I said.

"Good lord, that seems like three years ago," Jack said, laughing. "Yes, we can either go back to the office and watch it on the large screen or borrow Cassie's laptop when we get to the flat."

I smiled when I heard the last sentence. Sounded like Cassie had another houseguest for a while. Not that I thought she would mind having Jack and his muscle around, given the current circumstances.

As we neared the pub, several couples entered the door ahead of us. I worried we wouldn't get a decent table. Or any table for that matter. The good thing about the damp day was our eyes didn't have to adjust to the lighting in the pub. The bad thing about the drizzle was the place was as crowded as I'd feared. However, Cassie and Danny had secured us a place along the far wall.

"Hey, how are you?" Cassie jumped up from her chair and hugged me as I got to the table. "Danny told me what happened."

"I'm fine," I said, hanging my coat on the back of my chair. "Feeling better every minute."

Danny volunteered to go to the bar and order for us, but Jack said he'd take care of it. I took the opportunity to begin telling them about the hair Timms's team had discovered, but my peripheral vision picked up on the fact people at adjoining tables were staring at us. When a guy at a farther table said, "Hey, look, isn't she—?" and his girlfriend smacked his shoulder, I realized what was going on.

"How many social media shares do this afternoon's videos—plural—of me currently have?" I asked Danny.

He grimaced and raised his eyebrows. "Probably something north of ten thousand."

"Crap." My curse was quiet, but heartfelt. Add that to the local news story trending after Melanie was found dead in my room, and my status as an unwilling media sensation in London seemed unstoppable. Time to head off this latest problem. I jumped up, grabbed my coat and purse, and whispered, "I'm going to hide in the ladies. Tell Jack to get our order to go and we'll reconvene at the flat. Cassie, come and get me when we're leaving."

Jack ordered a cab, since we all figured I'd garner just as many stares on the subway.

"How long does it take for these kinds of things to die down?" I asked once we were safely behind Cassie's alarmed door.

"Until the next viral sensation hits social media," Danny replied with a shrug. "But you've had back-to-back opportunities, and there's no telling what it might mean. Your break in media attention could be any day. Or if you're lucky, any minute."

"Can't be soon enough," I groused. "Why aren't the

Kardashians up to something that gets the world's attention?"

"They'd probably kill to get the views you've gained by accident," Cassie said.

"I may kill someone if it doesn't stop soon." I checked my phone and saw two messages from Lincoln Ferguson. "And I have a pretty good idea who my first victim might be." I deleted the messages.

We shared the food, then Cassie brought out her laptop and the flash drive was plugged in for the CCTV viewing debut. I hoped Danny wouldn't have any reason to think about mentally inserting me into particular sections of the theft video. The views of the second thief at the Russian's house were run first, with her appearing out of neighboring shrubs and entering easily through the front door. I sat on the floor, nearly eye level with the screen and stared hard, looking for any way of identifying the person hidden under all the black.

As she left, this time apparently from an unfilmed side exit, Danny pointed at the screen and said, "We've confirmed she exited via a medium-sized doggie door installed by a previous owner."

"Did the current residents use it?" I asked.

Danny shook his head. "No, and it wasn't wired." He pointed at the screen as a shadowy image raced from the side of the house. "You can see the dark bag she's carrying. It looks a lot bigger than just some pieces of jewelry, but I spoke with one of the guys investigating and he says the owner is adamant only jewelry was stolen. Gotta wonder."

No, we didn't have to wonder at all. The only thing I'd been wondering was how she got the piece out of the house without leaving via the roof like me, but the doggie door explained that. Now I wanted to know how she knew about the unconventional exit, large enough to squeeze through, and why the security firm hadn't alarmed it in the same way as the doors and lower floor windows. Probably for the same reason they hadn't wired up the window I ducked out of—they didn't realize any adult could slip through without getting stuck.

Cassie spoke up, "She had to have had knowledge of her escape route before she went in. It's too unlikely she would have stumbled onto an out of commission dog door after getting trapped by the metal-attracted alarm."

"If so, why did she try exiting first through the door?" Jack mused. "She could have left without anyone even knowing she was in there if the alarm wasn't tripped."

I kept quiet and sent Cassie a look to warn her. We didn't want Danny realizing we knew as much about the alarm system as we did. Jack had enough contacts that Danny likely wouldn't question why he knew more. But Jack saw the look Cassie and I exchanged and gave a slight head nod, letting me know we were all on the same page. I could see from the expressions on Jack's and Cassie's faces that they had as many questions to throw out as I did, but we weren't going to try filling in the blanks while Danny was part of the group. We were supposed to only have an interest in the house theft because of the party.

A few scenes from the party were pulled up next. Everything seemed to substantiate the alibi I'd prepared. Cassie was as good as Jack had said, taking an opportunity to use my personal hand movements she'd perfected while we were in college. I'd teased earlier that she was no actress, but she was definitely a terrific mimic.

"Did you send these to Timms?" I asked, just being curious, and I rose to stand next to Jack's chair.

"Yes," Danny replied, sitting hunched on the sofa so he was close to the screen. He grinned at me as he spoke, "Timms stopped by right after Jack left, while I was loading up these files. I came off looking über efficient, since I didn't waste a second grabbing the views Timms needed to be able to follow you through the night. I left out the bit about the theft at the Russian's house, of course, but added where you and Jack stepped out for air and returned to the party through the front entrance about a quarter-hour later. Timms mentioned wanting to know where you went."

Jack nodded. "He called me. I gave him the name of the

coffeehouse we walked to. Laurel was fighting a headache and needed to step out for air."

"Pretty conclusive that you couldn't be at the party and murder someone at your hotel in the same timeframe," Danny added. I smiled at him and shook my head.

"It hadn't been enough for Timms to lift Laurel's grounding order," Jack said, wrapping an arm around my shoulders and pulling me close. "I had a few words with Cecil. He's not going to step in yet, but he is ready to if we need his help."

Given he knew I was breaking into the Russian's house at the time because Jack couldn't, I felt a little help from the Home Office was truly the least Cecil could do.

We hadn't yet told Timms about the luggage disappearing after I left. The longer we waited, the more I felt we should keep the information to ourselves. Jack would likely bandy around an obstructionist-charge argument if I mentioned it again. But he hadn't come up with a good way to tell Timms either, and I didn't fancy volunteering to implicate myself any further for a conclusion that currently seemed to be bringing everyone into agreement.

Since the Amazon was suspected of being the murderer, it left me puzzled about how I escaped unscathed. She'd never hesitated to attack me in the past.

Danny finally loaded up the files showing Melanie's journey into my hotel. I'd gone to the kitchen for coffee, and when I returned I grabbed a better view by balancing on the arm of the chair Jack occupied. I held my cup with one hand and hugged my torso with the other as we watched her stumble into the back door of the hotel. Jack pulled me into his lap and whispered in my ear. "You want us to stop this?"

I shook my head. We needed to know all we could. So far, the videos didn't show anything we hadn't already known, but without studying the scenes we'd never be sure we had all the available evidence. "It's fine."

But when we'd finished all the files, Cassie asked to see them once more. "I think there's something there my subconscious is getting, but I'm not sure what it is."

"Which files?" Danny asked.

"I'm not sure. I got this feeling when the party scenes were running. I don't know, though, if it's because I saw something at that time, or I subconsciously realized something earlier, and my brain got around to reporting on it as the party file played."

I pushed up from the chair and faked a yawn. They could rewatch everything until dawn if they liked, but my day was done, and I needed a break. "Hope you all have fun, but I'm whipped. I'm going to turn in early. Sorry for being a party pooper."

"Heavens, no." Cassie jumped up. "Go get a good night's sleep. You must be dead on your feet from the stress alone."

Jack stood. I hugged him and bussed his chin with a quick kiss. "You don't need to come too. I can tuck myself in. Stay and watch with everyone. I know you want to look for more clues."

I smiled at him, and he raised a questioning brow. Patting his chest, I said, "Don't worry about me."

He still followed me to the bedroom and gave me a much better kiss good night. After I sent him back to follow the CCTV evidence, I grabbed my night things and headed for the bathroom. A long, warm shower was exactly what I needed to help lessen the tension in my neck and shoulders. I couldn't control the internet, but I could do everything possible to relax enough not to care so much. I brushed my teeth and used night cream on my face, letting its familiar scent remind me that things were going to be normal again. Of course, in my case, what was normal? I was so used to sleeping in various hotels in as many countries and cities, it didn't bother me that I was at Cassie's instead of my own digs. The surroundings didn't help me de-stress, but the regular nightly routine did.

As I crawled between the sheets, the auction card on the *Portrait of Three* hit my thoughts. It was still in the backpack I used for the aborted theft the other night. It had affected Jack as strongly as it had me when he saw it at the coffeehouse, but we hadn't had the time to investigate the card at all. He'd watched me slip it into the bag, but he hadn't said anything since. No other works of art were pictured or listed on the auction card, only the *Portrait of Three*, and that alone raised all kinds of red flags. While we hadn't discussed it since then, we probably needed to see if anything could be learned about when the auction would be held and where. Or if it was already a past event. And if the event featured more paintings, were the other works originals or as fake as the Rodin? In the meantime, in case the Amazon wasn't enough of a suspect, we needed to give the authorities other persons of interest to consider to keep me out of jail. Until I fell off the "best bet" list, I'd never get my travel restrictions lifted. Using Cecil needed to be a last resort, but getting out of London was becoming my dearest wish since social media seemed to think I was a trending personality.

I thought about checking my feeds to see what the count was up to, though I knew the number was probably higher than what I was imagining anyway. I punched my pillow instead, deciding it seemed safer to snuggle under the covers.

If my story was still viral in the morning, however, I planned to camp out at Cassie's until the next internet sensation hit.

How hard is it to start a competing viral event, I wondered.

THIRTEEN

I woke at half-past seven in the morning, starving. Easing my way out of bed, I grabbed my robe and headed for the bathroom. Jack was awake when I went back in to dress, and we spent a good while saying good morning. My senses of smell and taste seemed to be normal again, and when the aroma of fresh brewing coffee wafted in from the kitchen, the day was officially started.

"Morning, Cass," I called as I entered the kitchen. She responded by handing me a cup of coffee. "Thank you so much."

"I went out for croissants," she said. "There are eggs in the refrigerator if you need more, since you went so light on lunch and dinner yesterday."

"Good point." I grabbed a small skillet and started the process for scrambled eggs. I wasn't much of a cook, but I had mastered that dish at least. Jack came in soon after and I added a couple of eggs for him as well.

"What's on the agenda," I asked, as we sat around the table sharing croissants and butter. Jack's phone pinged with a text.

"Sorry," he said. "I need to take care of this."

I thought about adding no-phone-at-the-table rules, but neither of our jobs truly allowed that.

"I have a full schedule," Cassie said, giving me an apologetic smile. "I loaded up when I thought you'd be in New York. But I can postpone some of my research if you need me for anything."

"Don't be silly. It's fine."

"What did you decide about Caro's event?" she asked. "Should I call her?"

I grimaced. "Given my new internet status, I might get more attention than the fashion show. No sense in going anywhere that throws me near reporters and cameras—fashion or otherwise. Plus, I don't want to worry about impacting their fundraiser in a negative way."

"There is that too."

Jack finished his text and said, "I need to go interview someone at a company in the Docklands. Possible financial fraud with external ties to a couple of people we've dealt with before. MI-5 is taking the lead. I'm strictly backup to make sure the Home Office stays in the loop. Shouldn't take more than the morning."

"Guess I'll stay here today and see if I can find out anything from sources," I said. "I don't want to hide away, but it seems like the best alternative under the circumstances." I couldn't stand not knowing and pulled up the current video shared stats. The numbers were staggering. "Everyone still seems to be interested in following the aborted kidnapping story." I saw a version with music added that focused on the tasing and wasn't the least bit flattering to me or my giant kidnapper as we jerked and flopped around. "I also want to connect with Nico," I added. "See what he's learned."

"He called last night after you went to bed," Jack said. "He still doesn't have a last name on Arlo, but that isn't so unusual for forgers."

I nodded, smiling. "I always think of the Middle Ages, when it was Seth the blacksmith and Jed the miller. All these years later and forgers are still known more by their craft and talent than their full proper names."

Jack finished eating, then headed back to the bedroom for his tie. I stacked up the dishes and helped Cassie carry everything to the sink.

"By the way," I said, running the sprayer over a plate to knock off crumbs. "When I went to bed you were going to rewatch the videos to see if you could spot something gnawing at your memory. Did you figure out what it was?"

She shook her head. "I was hoping my subconscious would

figure it out while I slept, but no luck."

"We're all running on a diminished charge," I said, grinning. "Well, I got a booster yesterday, but I don't think it necessarily helped in that regard."

"Can you describe what getting tased felt like?" she asked.

"Like something I never want to experience again." I shuddered. "But try not to think about what you're wanting to remember, and it'll come to mind easier."

"That's what I keep telling myself, but I'm not much better than you when it comes to patience for that kind of thing."

"I hear you."

After Jack and Cassie left for their appointments, I texted Nico and received word back echoing what Jack told me earlier. My gorgeous geek was staying in the Montmartre area of Paris and was hopeful about making contact with Arlo today. I told him to be careful, and he said for me to do the same. Then he sent a link to one of the YouTube videos to remind me not to try hiding anything from him. I didn't even have to see him to know he was laughing as he typed the message. At least it wasn't the music video version where the giant and I were caught in an endless loop of twitching until Jack's arm pulled me away and the loop started up again with the music running ad nauseam.

Moving on from that bust for new data, I tried to be good and work my contacts like I'd said. After a few texts, I used the laptop to email several more, asking in a roundabout way for information on fake Rodin bronzes anyone had seen popping up anywhere, or real Rodin works making a surprise appearance, as well as new female cat burglars working the U.K. and the European continent. Nothing came back, but I knew email wasn't always as instantaneous as texts.

At that point, all the inertia hit, and my brain rebelled. There was no way I could spend time alone in a flat simply waiting for electronic responses and for Jack or Cassie to come back and talk to me. Viral videos or no viral videos, I needed to expend some energy and suddenly knew exactly where I needed to go and what to do when I got there.

I texted Thomas. He didn't respond right away, so I figured he had a fare. He called back inside of seven minutes.

"Hi. Can I hire you for the rest of the morning?" I asked. "I need to go to Chelsea, but there's some shopping to take care of on the way."

"Of course. Are you at the flat from yesterday?" he asked.

"Yes."

"I'll be there in about twenty minutes."

"Good. That will give me time to make a list." Before I began, I changed into jeans and a long-sleeved ice blue colored t-shirt. Looking in the mirror that hung behind the door, I smiled. This outfit said I meant business. And with a few more accessories I'd be unstoppable. Rummaging through Cassie's bathroom, I found a hair scrunchie and slipped it on my right wrist. My watch and my GPS charm bracelet stayed on my left hand.

True to his word, Thomas texted me twenty minutes later and said he was outside the building. I grabbed Jack's bomber jacket and my Prada before heading out, making sure the note I'd written was still squarely in the middle of the coffee table and the alarm was on guard when I closed the door. Thomas stood leaning against the cab, smoking, as I exited the front door, but he threw away his cigarette and opened the back door when I drew near. I slid across the seat, so I could see his profile as he drove, then pulled out my list.

"First, I need to buy a pair of work boots and heavy gloves," I said. Through the rearview mirror I saw him raise his sandy eyebrows, but he didn't say anything. When he parked ten minutes later we were in front of exactly the kind of store I was hoping for.

"I'll be quick," I said, opening the door and jumping out. "I know what I want."

The atmosphere was definitely function over fashion, and my designer jeans were out of place. I found a helpful clerk, who recognized me right away from seeing yesterday's videos but didn't push the connection, and he walked me over to the kind of boots I wanted. We found a pair that fit me perfectly and located rawhide gloves to give me a good grip on tools used in colder temps, as per my request. He even suggested a large canvas hat that covered most of my face and shielded my eyes from the sun—or the curious public. I was sold immediately. My impulse buy was a brown canvas vest modeled by a headless mannequin. There wasn't a need for the vest, but it fit my mental picture at the moment, and I loved all the cargo pockets running down each side of the front panels. Inside of ten minutes, the shoes I wore into the store were sacked with the gloves, the vest was off the mannequin and on my torso, and I was feeling pretty pleased as I walked back to the cab in my new work boots. No glass slippers for this modern-day Cinderella.

"Next stop," I said. "I need a home store that sells tools. Specifically, I'm looking for an ax."

Thomas turned in his seat and looked at me, but again gave no commentary, just said, "Unusual hat."

I smiled. I was enjoying this opportunity to spend time with a man who kept his opinions to himself. I wondered if his wife knew how lucky she was.

The ax purchase took much less time than the boots, and I even found some girly safety glasses. I think the clerk recognized my name from the credit card, because she looked at me with a little more interest as she wound a PAID sticker on the handle of the ax and gave me my receipt. Thomas shook his head when I reentered the cab, but we were soon on our way to Chelsea. As we pulled up to the huge warehouse building, I fished my keys from the Prada and said, "Feel free to go get yourself some lunch if you like. I'll be all locked in, so no worries."

"But yesterday—"

"Was a fluke," I said firmly. "Obviously you've seen the news reports or the YouTube videos, but it had to be an isolated act. I'm still waiting to hear what kind of cockeyed reason those three had for pulling a stunt like that in the National Gallery, without any exit strategy whatsoever."

"Still, I think it might be best if I wait here. Or I'd be happy to accompany you, miss." This was the first time I'd ever heard Thomas argue with any of us about one of our crazy requests. It made me feel a little guilty.

I pulled the outside door key off my ring. "How about this? You follow me to the door, and when I get it opened, I'll give you the key in case you need to get in before I return. The outside door locks automatically."

"And where will you be?"

"I'm going to number eighteen." I set my Prada on the floorboard. "I'm leaving my purse here since you're staying. It would be in my way if I take it inside."

He nodded but didn't meet my gaze. I couldn't tell if he was agreeing with me or reconciling himself to the situation. Either way, he followed me to the outer door and took the key as I entered.

The head of the ax weighed down my shoulder, balanced and ready as I turned the key in the lock to number eighteen. I slipped the key ring back into the bottom right pocket of the vest and opened the heavy steel door, then flipped the light switch and used the doorknob to hang up the bomber jacket. I took a second to remove my watch and charm bracelet and slipped them into one of the vest's pockets for safekeeping. I pulled on the tan work gloves and felt the resistance that came from their newness. These gloves would be much better than my black stealthy leather ones for helping maintain a grip on this weapon and not leave behind fingerprints. Not that fingerprints would be much of a problem, but it had become standard operating procedure for me to think about such snags by this stage in the game.

A bland fluorescent fixture buzzed from the middle of the ceiling. The open doorway revealed a first look at my objective. Sitting in the middle of the space and surrounded by castoff minions, a coatrack, a chair, and a warped filing cabinet.

Smug, tightlipped, continuing to hold onto the secrets I knew could be laid bare if I had an inkling of what to say, what to do, or what to punch, this was the perfect answer when I needed to strike something today. One frustrated evening last month I'd even begged—pleaded—for a tiny clue. A single secret to calm my frustrations and whisper the answers I needed. Nothing. So, the door was locked again, leaving the prisoner behind, and I walked away to plan another try later.

This time, I wouldn't leave without answers. I came prepared.

Through the walls I heard the be-bop sound of a London police siren and wondered how near it was.

"Can't save you, anyway," I said, taking a moment to size up my adversary and reaffirm where to strike first. I'd had a lot of enemies, but this was the most frustrating one I'd recently had to try to outwit. Well, besides the viral videos anyway.

I took a moment to drop the ax head to the cement floor and hold it upright between my boots. Finger combing my blonde curls, I used the scrunchie band on my wrist to hold my hair in a messy ponytail. Safety glasses dangled from the hot pink cord around my neck. I flipped out the earpieces and set the frames on my nose. Dressed in my jeans, the long-sleeved blue t-shirt and my new brown canvas work vest heavily accented with the cargo pockets, I was prepared for whatever flew my way with every strike of the weapon. The heavy work boots and gloves had been mandatory purchases. The safety glasses made sense once I'd noticed them on the rack. And the vest was just my celebratory buy for the occasion.

Hefting the ax again, I swung in a tight arc toward the ground, missing my adversary by inches. A test run to check balance. I gripped the handle tighter, so the head wouldn't strike the cement floor. The ax head swung slightly, like a pendulum. Not enough to hit anything yet, but to show my mind and body were ready for the job.

"You had your chance." I spoke in a quiet voice, biting off the end of each word. "I measured you, I coaxed you, I prodded and pushed every potential button I could find or imagine might get you to give up the secret. You gave me nothing. I don't even know what secret you're hiding at this point, but I know one's there. Probably a big one. Something that will most likely impact me and my group. But especially me, because you did Simon's bidding."

I stepped closer and swung the ax back into attack mode.

"Time to take you apart. Piece by piece."

The fluorescent fixture buzzed from the middle of the ceiling and in the harsh light, I took a hard look at my objective. Again. One last time. To see if any light reflection revealed a fleeting clue or offered one last prospective tip.

Silence. Nothing more.

I braced my feet and let the ax again hang toward the floor. I wanted the first strike to be a full circle for maximum impact. A deep breath and a shake of my shoulders released any tension. Ready for the follow-through, I stomped one foot forward to compensate when the shock of impact arrived. I felt the smooth movement as the arc of the tool swung behind me to begin its cyclic climb. But as the heavy triangular head rose to the apex of the swing, the ax shuddered to a stop, the momentum of unused energy nearly knocking me off my feet.

Then the ax was plucked from my hands.

I whirled to deliver a roundhouse kick. The ax clattered to the floor and my leg was grabbed mid-movement.

"Dammit, Jack!"

"We've done this dance before, Laurel, I recognize your moves."

"You could have at least made a noise, so I knew you were there."

"What would be the fun in that?"

He stared at my boot and his eyes widened. "These are steel toed. Do you realize how much that would have hurt?"

"Safety first. Besides, it wouldn't have hurt me at all. Just you."

He grinned and cocked a dark eyebrow. "At least this time I didn't send you on your arse."

Unlike the last time when I was wearing a designer gown and stilettos at a high society art fundraiser. "Yes, you've become quite the gentleman, Hawkes."

Laughing, he let go of my ankle and picked up the ax from the floor. "This really can't be the tool of choice. You're looking at an antique hand-carved rosewood desk." He shook his dark head. "You know the pedigree of this piece."

"I know it has some kind of super-secret trap holding information Simon secreted inside that I can't find," I said. "He always held information back he believed he could use later. I can't count the number of art-related coups he accomplished simply because he knew something no one else was privy to. When he broke into the office on New Year's, it had to be to find something hidden in this desk. Don't forget, at the beginning of this little adventure, I found the flash drive he'd hidden in the waterproof coral cache decorating his aquarium. Simon always used eccentric methods to hide things."

Jack waved a hand toward the desk. "I get your point. You think it has another trap still to find. But we've found two already. They were both empty. There may not be another."

"Remember, he didn't stop with the office break-in," I said. "When we were in Rome in February, just days ahead of his death, Simon broke into this storage unit for some reason and the break-in was discovered by the guards before he had time to get out whatever he came to steal. This desk was his. This is the only thing stored in the facility we can point to that he used as head of Beacham London, which could have held something he felt was valuable. Just because we haven't found anything in our previous searches doesn't mean there's not still something important to uncover. This rosewood desk was his for more than ten years before we learned he was a traitor. Whatever he wanted when he broke into my office must be inside. Something which could help us as we're looking for our next big break in this case."

"So instead you're going to break the desk and find—"

"Yes, Mr. Obvious." I sighed. "I'm going to find a break in the case by breaking the desk."

He grinned, then looked down. "The vest is a bit over the top."

"Jack, I'm not validating my fashion choices with you, so don't try to change the subject. Give me back my ax."

"You have a little pulse...right here." He touched my neck.

"That beats in your throat."

I slapped away his hand. "What did you do, follow my bracelet?" I peeked into the vest's left breast pocket and saw the silver tattletale nearly hidden in its dim environs. The brief glare of the overhead light seemed to make the wondrous tiny camera with the GPS wizardry hidden inside wink at me. Great, a smart-ass charm too.

"No, someone was a little concerned about your choice of shopping meccas for the day and texted me that you were ultimately heading for Chelsea," he said. "I figured you decided to bang your head against the desktop again. Thought I'd see if I could come and take you to lunch instead."

"I can't believe Thomas ratted me out! No wonder he stayed so quiet. He'd already used his thumbs to shoot off his mouth to you. But in answer to your offer, no. By the time I'm through today there won't be anything to use for head banging, and I'll likely be a little too sweaty for a lunch date." I stood with my fists on my hips. "Can I please have my ax back?"

"Give it one more close scrutiny or x-ray—"

"No. Negotiations are concluded. The desk isn't talking, and I think chopping it into kindling will do wonders to relieve my current stress levels."

He leaned the ax against the far wall. "I can think of better ways to relieve stress," he said. Then he took off his black leather jacket and moved closer to me.

I held out my hands. "Uh-uh, no playing around. I mean business."

"Then hold my coat. The poor doorknob can't take any additional load." He tossed the jacket lengthwise over my arms and swiped my safety glasses at the same time.

As he walked back to retrieve the ax, I investigated the lining. Hugo Boss. And very new. "Is this to replace the bomber jacket I keep forgetting to give back to you?"

"Yeah, you keep forgetting." He smirked, but the effect looked comical with the glasses and the pink trim. Then he raised the ax into position.

"I take it you've decided to do the demolition yourself," I said.

"Have you ever chopped up a piece of heavy furniture, or even a small tree?"

"Can't say that I have." The coat was a good weight. I pulled off my right glove with my teeth and brushed my palm across the black leather. Nice. About a month until spring. I was going to miss the chilly London days and seeing Jack dressed like this. I added, "A saw seemed like much more work. I figured the ax was the best way to go."

"Your back might not think so in the morning." He loosened his tie, undid the buttons on his sleeves and rolled the cuffs up his arm, then hefted the ax. He waved, making a "step back" gesture with one hand. "Get clear of me. Not sure how far splinters may fly."

Obviously, I was just going to be a coat rack. Not that I minded. He couldn't say I finagled him into doing the work for me, but just because I wore the right clothes for the job it didn't mean I couldn't step aside for a more experienced player. I'd already been contemplating the probable necessity of a long soak afterward, before Jack hinted at sore muscles. I moved into the far corner to watch, happy to let him have the workout.

Since I was only five-eight and the fluorescent light hung down from a warehouse-high ceiling, I hadn't worried about hitting the fixture, but with his longer reach Jack had to step back or swing from an angle. Anything less and he risked hitting the dropped light fixture and plunging us into darkness. He took a few practice swings and adjusted his stance. I watched his shoulder muscles bunch under his shirt, and I tensed for the sound of contact.

Whack! Dead center of the rosewood top.

I thought I heard a soft snick.

Jack wiggled the ax head out of the wood's grain, while I circled the desk looking for what might have made the tiny sound.

"What is it?" he asked.

"Not sure." Nothing on the short side. I tossed his jacket and my glove onto the end of the desk and walked around to the kneehole. Eureka! I had heard something. The veneer on one side of the kneehole expanded out, open at the top, and I could see a file inside. "I was right!"

Kneeling, I reached into the tight space with my right hand and worked the file out of the secret cubby. There was also a pink tinted sheet of thin colored plastic, like some type of single sheet protector. I stretched to feel my way down the space with one hand to see if anything lay at the narrow bottom. Nothing more.

I slapped the file and plastic sheet onto the desktop. "When you hit the top, the impact triggered the opening mechanism."

"Must be why Simon had the cricket bat when he broke into your office," Jack suggested, moving to stand the ax against the long wall of the storage unit. "It wasn't just to knock out the camera and use as a weapon."

"No, I think Simon used the cricket bat for exactly how he'd planned to use it," I said. "Well, for half the reason. He shattered the security cameras with one strike of the bat, but I imagine he'd planned to at least threaten using it on me as well."

The file was thin, but I kept my hopes high for some clue to help us with the heist plot we'd been working on for several months. I flipped the cover and my heart leapt to my throat. Nothing prepared me for the contents."

"Is that—?"

"What my father looked like before he became Ermo Colle," I finished. My hand shook, and I could have easily cried, although I didn't want to think about why.

A metal clip at the top of the file held the interior stack of pages. Since I still had a glove on my left hand, I used it to flip through the sheets of paper. The first pages were color copies that showed a small collection of photos taken against a light blue background. Beyond the full-face, there were profile shots, and close-ups showing detail of specific facial and ear features. Farther in were pages of sketches of proposed plastic surgery and patient details. For us, the crème de la crème of this evidence was the last page. Again, a collection of color photos, but this time a couple of photos after bandages had been removed.

"There's still some swelling in these last views, but a very good likeness of the way he looked in Baden-Baden," I said, flipping back to the name of the plastic surgeon and the Swiss clinic, then stepped back from the file. "I'll get Nico on this after he finishes his current search for the forger in Paris. Simon likely stole these files or paid someone to steal them, but if Daddy Dearest's current likeness is in the facility's digital storage, my gorgeous geek will be able to easily hack in to download any new photos."

Jack knocked the edge to skew the folder in a half-circle and better see the contents. "If Colle is still alive. And despite what we told the security forces yesterday, what Rollie said last month could still have been a way to confuse the issue or bug you. Face it, I've never seen you in action with an expanding baton, but I've little doubt of your expertise. Your blow against Colle's head had to do some damage."

"I'll take that as a compliment. Kind of creepy, but still a compliment."

"Moran was obviously impressed by your prowess. I've never known him to give someone accolades they didn't deserve, despite his legion of ethical shortcomings in regard to absconding with things that don't belong to him."

Yes, after gifting me with the weapon in Baden-Baden, the old conman-thief did flatter me with reminiscences of how I used a similar model to break his assistant's wrist years ago on a job in America.

"Rollie may have been focused on kidnapping me last month, but one thing he did admit was Colle is already rebuilding for new enterprises," I reminded. "As long as Colle is competition for Moran's and Rollie's organization, they're going to keep tabs."

"Granted, as long as Rollie was telling the truth. He has this tendency to prefer when people are off balance, and the information he leaked was primed to leave you significantly shaken." Jack didn't look at me as he spoke, focusing instead on the pages of the file.

"Have you not told me something I need to know?" I asked.

He shook his head and raised his gaze to meet mine. "I simply want to remind you not to think Nico will be able to pull another digital rabbit out of the internet hat. Until we know the rabbit isn't an illusion Rollie wants us to believe."

"I agree, except I'd likely be dead now if you hadn't arrived in time to tackle Rollie. What would he gain by making me believe I hadn't killed Colle?"

"I can think of a few things. People who play head games often can't help themselves." He shrugged and used a pen to lift the last page of pictures. "What's this?"

A clear envelope laid flat, stuck to the back of the file with a kind of adhesive. Inside, several hairs shone under the buzzing light. Hairs dyed blonde, but which showed a tiny bit of silver at the root. Roots that each included a follicle.

Jack's gaze met mine. "You don't think—"

"I do." I nodded, then put my right glove back on so I could open the zipped envelope without leaving prints. Not easy with the thick rawhide, but doable. I teased an individual hair away from its brothers. The hair and follicle looked healthy. "Simon broke into the office to get the sample of Colle's hair he secreted in this desk trap."

"To prove Colle was—or was not—your father?"

I frowned. "That would be my first guess. Or maybe to identify him later in case Colle had to change appearances again—even without running into me and my baton." Returning the hair to the envelope, I asked, "So what changed? Simon obviously had the hair for enough time that he hid it in this desk. Why suddenly break into the office on New Year's to try to get it again? Remember, when Simon was trying to find this file Colle still thought he was hidden from all of us. We didn't know who Colle was until after we went to the casino in Baden-Baden, and Simon didn't learn we knew until hours afterward."

"Maybe Simon didn't know for sure the information was still

available to him." Jack sat on the desktop and shifted so there was room for me to sit beside him. "We know he took off suddenly in September. We know he ran to Moran's chateau in France. We also know just a short time after you talked to him the Amazon was ripping apart his office looking for something."

"And the Amazon—we think—works for Rollie," I prompted.

"Exactly. Rollie. The person who likely believes he has the most to lose if you are not the blood relation of Ermo Colle," Jack finished.

Something I didn't really want to think about. I wasn't thrilled about the thought of being the daughter of Ermo Colle, but if I wasn't it meant I was most likely Rollie's cousin. And I was apparently a threat to Rollie because his grandfather wasn't turning the empire over to him and retiring as expected. Worse, Jack learned Moran had kept Paul-Henri's architectural firm crime-syndicate free, with the head position of the company still open all these years later. Talk about a tangled family web. Everything seemed so straightforward a few short months ago.

"Maybe Simon just cached the hair in the file right before I arrived in London to retrieve the sword?" I mused. Logically thinking through everything that happened made us believe he was likely in Italy the evening before the office was trashed. However, he'd been working that morning in London, playing the part of a good Beacham Foundation employee, trying not to let his mask slip so we and the two criminals he also worked for—competing criminals no less—wouldn't know all the things he was up to simultaneously. "Once I took off for France and the police started working the case of the break-in, he had to bide his time."

"Then you were awarded Simon's position when his duplicity was discovered, and you tasked Cassie with a complete restoration that ultimately sent this desk into storage," Jack added, patting the top with one hand.

"Well, not completely. If it had been up to Cassie the desk would still be in its normal position in my office," I said. Call me shallow, but I hadn't wanted to work at the desk of a traitor who not only tricked me on the professional front, but on the private side as well. I took a deep breath to get all my emotions in check and said a little brusquely, "You have your phone?"

"Of course."

"Take a picture of the clinic info and a few of the early and later pictures. Send them to Nico. Tell him not to get sidetracked but let him know this is waiting when he has any time open." I jumped up and walked over to the boring gray metal wall of the storage unit and leaned against the cool steel, suddenly wanting to get away from the contents. "Explain we need him to cyber dig for any photos showing what Colle looks like now, and to start by hacking this clinic."

"Yes. If Colle trusted this doctor once, he likely went to him for a new face," Jack said. He pulled his phone, typed on the tiny keyboard for a few seconds, then said, "If you'll turn the pages again, I'll grab an image on each one."

"My prints will already be on the cover," I said. "I'm not sure I could have grabbed it from that skinny opening if I hadn't been barehanded. But we don't need to add any more. Simon must have used tweezers or a thin grabber of some sort to pull things from that trap."

When we got to the final page, Jack emailed Nico and attached the images.

I began pacing, unable to stand still. "Take the file to whichever law enforcement sources you think best. If they need a charge, give them an attempted kidnapping charge when he made me go with him against my will at the casino and held me at gunpoint."

Until I flipped out my weapon, struck Colle in the head, sent his gun sliding across the room, and had run like I'd had demons after me. Amazing how adrenalin and a telescoping baton could even out bad odds.

"What about the hair? The follicles?"

Yeah, what about that? I paced faster. "It's DNA. It could help a conviction."

Jack stepped into my path and took me in his arms. "Of course," he said, speaking low and into my hair because I wouldn't raise my face. "But I'm asking what Laurel Beacham wants done with it," he said, hugging me closer. "Do you want an analysis run, so you know for sure if you share any genes with the man?"

"If I don't share his genes then I'm not really Laurel Beacham," I said. My stomach dipped for a moment. "I...I think..."

I pulled away and took another long breath. I met Jack's teal gaze. "I'm not sure what I want to know yet. I know it's silly, but while I don't want him to be my father, the alternative doesn't sound thrilling either. And while I thought I lost everything when my grandparents died, and the family fortune disappeared, I still had my own identity. If I'm not a Beacham...well..." I placed a hand over my heart. "It would be kind of like starting broke all over again, but this time my history would become the stolen false security."

"Not exactly."

"But I'm not sure I'm ready to strike out as a new nobody."

"You'll never be a nobody."

I started to argue, but it was like he read my mind.

He lifted my chin with his finger, and all I could see was the caring on his face. My gaze locked on his and I focused on the gold flecks in his eyes. "I may not know exactly what you're feeling right now. However, I do know what it's like to not know precisely where I fit into quite a number of different situations—societal or otherwise. Or, for that matter, which family lineage I should admit to."

While I'd known for several months Jack was raised by a single mother, it was only a few weeks ago when I learned who his father was—a married British lord. Strangely enough, I'd met Jack's half-sister years ago in finishing school, and later she and I had raised our own kind of hell one college summer. All without my even knowing she had a slightly older brother. He went by his mother's surname, but he and his father and half-sister were close. His stepmother, however, was another matter altogether, and preferred Jack not be considered part of the family.

Stepping closer, I wrapped my arms around his waist. "I'm sorry. I didn't mean anything—"

"No apology necessary. I simply wanted you to know..." He shrugged. "I understand. Whatever you want."

Standing on tiptoe in steel-toed work boots isn't the easiest thing in the world, but for every inch I stretched upward, he bent two, and our lips met. As we parted, I said, "Thank you."

"You never have to thank me for kissing you."

I couldn't help it, I laughed.

"Mission accomplished," he said, grinning.

I slapped his arm, still smiling. A couple of steps and I grabbed his jacket. I wiggled a finger toward the file and asked, "Did you get finished with your email to Nico?"

"Yes, boss, I did." Jack grinned. I picked up the closed file, slipping the plastic sheet in too.

"What do you think the pink thing is for?" I asked.

"Don't know. But Babbage hid it, so we're taking it with us." He rubbed the scar in the middle of the desktop. "One blow. Not as much damage as it could have been. You can likely get the top rehabbed. Maybe ask Cassie—"

"Knowing my art restoration assistant, she undoubtedly will come nurse it back to health as soon as you tell her about it, no matter if I say so or not," I said, switching the file between hands as I shrugged into the bomber jacket. "But don't be in any hurry." I pointed the file in the direction of the ax. "I'm not positive I won't be resuming my kindling job on the desk. I'm leaving that heavy little wonder here for now, but I like your idea about x-raying the piece before another strike."

Jack put on his coat and shrugged it comfortably onto his shoulders. "Then my work here is done. You approved my suggestion, we found a secret file, and I didn't even break a sweat."

"You bragging, cowboy?"

He grinned. "I do nearly every day."

"Don't I know it." When would I learn? "So, you came to take me to lunch, huh? Where are we going?"

Chuckling, he said, "It was my plan, but I didn't know you'd be decked out like a lumberjack."

"You have a problem with lumberjacks?" I considered for a moment. "Or maybe I'd be a lumberjill."

"I've been around you too long, because that actually makes sense." He looked toward the wall with the walk-through door. "Where's that magical carpetbag you call a purse?"

"I didn't bring the Prada. Left it in the cab with Thomas." I wasn't sure about the magical carpetbag crack, but it was true I carried an assortment of unusual items. "It didn't really go with my lumberjill look. And I have enough pockets to carry what I needed for this job."

Jack shot me a surprised look. "I had no idea you could go anywhere without your purse."

"Yeah, it's kind of like your ego. Hard to keep it packed away, but sometimes it doesn't fit the situation."

He grinned. "You want to head to Cassie's first to change?"

"You really do have a problem with my working woman outfit, don't you?"

"I think I did most of the work," he said, cocking a dark eyebrow.

"I was ably prepared to do what I came to accomplish. You just took over, and I let you." I pulled the key ring out of my pocket and motioned him through the door. "Tell you what. If you promise to take me somewhere nice we can go back, and I'll change. I'll even carry the Prada, so you won't think you're with a strange woman."

"Deal."

"Besides, Thomas is probably getting worried about us by now."

"Nah, I texted him before I sent the photos to Nico."

"Wow," I said, grinning. "Cassie better watch out. I may make you my new personal assistant."

He stepped close, his teal gaze holding mine. "Doubt you could afford me."

"Maybe we could negotiate for additional compensation," I whispered.

"I'm always open to negotiations."

FOURTEEN

We had just rejoined Thomas in the cab and asked him to drive back to Cassie's flat when my phone rang. It was Nico. "Must be about the files you sent," I said, hitting the speaker option. "Hi, you do know you don't have to work on those files right away."

"*Sì*, that's not why I called."

"Okay, what do you need?"

"You, here in Paris," Nico replied.

"Me? Why?"

"I found Arlo—"

"Please don't tell me he's dead," I jumped in. After everything that had happened in the past couple of days, this would be too much.

"*Non*, he's alive, but in hiding. And he'll only talk to you," Nico explained. "He knows who you are, and your reputation. Says he won't talk to anyone else. Said it is important he speaks directly to you."

"You're not going alone," Jack warned, giving me the look I knew meant he wouldn't compromise. Not that I would either at this point.

"I already told this to Arlo," Nico said. "He understands. He is afraid."

"This sounds like a trap," Jack said.

"I don't think so," Nico said.

I stopped them before an argument started on the phone. "Nico, I can't come to Paris right now because I can't get permission to leave London. I tried again yesterday. Does Arlo know about Melanie being found dead in my room?"

"*Sí*, that's one of the reasons he says he will only speak to you. He says Melanie is a part of this."

"He worked with Colle?"

"I don't know. He won't tell me anything more than he has to speak to you."

"We need to move slowly on an ultimatum like this," Jack said.

"I agree." To Nico, I asked, "Can you make contact with him again? Is he waiting to hear about a meet?"

"He calls me by phone, but it's always a burner, and I cannot tell anything when I trace it except that he's always in the Montmartre when he calls."

"When he phones again, tell him that we're working on getting me permission to leave, but we have no idea when it will happen. He has to understand this is an active police case, and until they narrow down a suspect I'm as viable as anyone else for the murder."

"Wait," Nico said. "Back up a second. The plan was CCT—"

"Nico, I'll call you back in a bit," Jack said, hitting the end button before cutting his eyes toward the back of Thomas's head as the driver moved the cab through traffic. I nodded, getting his meaning since I'd been about to do the same thing. While Thomas had been completely trustworthy the month or more we'd known him, and he knew our business wasn't just charity affairs and lunches out, neither of us wanted to test his ethics by letting him know too much too soon. It was one thing for him to be aware we ran after bad guys; another for him to realize I did some off-the-books reclamations when there wasn't a legitimate way to recover stolen property.

Jack and I stared at one another for several seconds. I finally spoke because I didn't want Thomas getting suspicious. "When you take in the file from the desk, can you go by and talk to Timms, or maybe call and see if he's spoken to the Italians yet?"

"I could get Cecil to contact the Met brass, something we've already talked about, but doing so might look like I'm going over the inspector's head."

"Which is probably premature at this point. We should save any option like that as a last resort."

"Agreed." Jack rubbed the back of his neck, and I wondered what kind of tension load he carried. He said, "I'll go by and feel the inspector out as best I can, then decide what to do afterward."

I nodded, more to signal I thought our ruse was over than anything else. "Call Nico back and talk to him, but don't put him on speaker. I'm going to close my eyes for a minute and see if I can get rid of a headache before it gets stronger. I'm not up for any more questions for a while."

He smiled. "Fair enough."

I pushed redial on my phone and handed it to Jack, leaning my head against the seatback. He rested his free hand on my thigh, and I covered it with both of mine. Then I closed my eyes.

The headache wasn't a complete fabrication, and the line I gave about no more questions was absolutely true. I'd had my fill lately. When Nico answered, I followed Jack's one-sided conversation, knowing what he was cryptically saying about the video we'd counted on for my alibi regarding the theft, and were now counting on doubly to put me in the clear to Timms regarding the murder. No way Thomas could catch the clues without knowing more of the story.

They moved on to Arlo, and Nico spoke more than Jack. Mostly Jack gave orders about getting more info on Arlo, so he could be checked out. I finally knew the conversation was wrapping up when Jack said, "We're on our way back to Cassie's flat. Sounds like you and I are on the same page about this. Laurel or I will call you again soon. And thanks, Nico. I know this wasn't an easy job."

I smiled hearing him say the last bit. When we first met, Jack had come across as such a cocky bastard I would never have expected him to acknowledge Nico's contribution in that way. I still wasn't sure if he was maturing, or if the first impression had all been part of his act, but I liked how things were changing. This wasn't the only such incident I'd noticed lately.

"You know," I said, opening my eyes. "The office would be better than Cassie's place. We can make copies there of the paperwork in the file."

"Good idea," Jack replied. "I work off images most of the time anymore, but having a physical backup is safer."

"Thomas, can we reroute to the Beacham office, please?" I asked.

"Already doing so," he replied.

Our copier in the office was relatively slow. However, it did terrific full-color images and was worth the draw on my store of patience. I'd used my gloved hand to turn the pages when we were in the storeroom, and I used the gloves again to make the reproductions. When the copies were completed, Jack slipped them into a new file folder.

I removed the work gloves and asked, "I guess the next question is do we pass along the new file and copies, or the original pages from Simon's master file?"

"The originals," Jack replied. "Your prints are only on the outside of the file, but everything inside would be Simon's and whoever got the information for him. Turning those pages over to a police forensics lab makes more sense than us doing it ourselves and distributing the information later. Better for sweeping with a larger net."

"But we'll have no control over the way the information is disbursed. What if someone holds out on us?"

"I appreciate your concerns, but I'll make certain I have assurances. And I'll be very picky about whom I turn the file over to initially. That will make a lot of difference."

"What about keeping a strand or two of hair?" I asked.

"Agreed." Jack used a pen to open the original file folder, then caught the pages at the bottom with the pen and flipped them all back at once to reveal the short blond hairs. "Looks like three strands have better follicles than the others. Let's keep one good one and a couple of the not as good. Pass along the rest."

"I have tweezers in my purse, and Cassie keeps small zippered plastic food bags in the cabinet over the coffee pot." I rummaged through my Prada while Jack got the box from the cabinet.

It was still difficult opening the small zipped bag with work gloves, but the tweezers made the job a little quicker this time. Seconds later, I'd removed three strands from the first bag and dropped them into the second that Jack held open. He added the plastic baggie to the folder we'd just made, and I placed the original file inside a second file folder, to allow Jack to handle it without adding new prints on the outside. Then I removed my gloves.

I pulled my watch and bracelet out of the vest pocket and put them back on. "It's practically noon, though the morning has been so packed it's nearly flown by. I'm going to heat up leftovers from yesterday. You want some?"

"Sounds good."

We each loaded up a plate of the panang curry and Thai chicken and veggies. While waiting for the food to get thoroughly nuked, Jack said, "You know, you're welcome to go with me. I can't promise a fun experience, or that someone won't ask you questions you don't want to answer about all that's happened or about the players in this farce, but you don't have to be alone all afternoon."

"As long as I'm internet fodder, I prefer to stay behind locked doors with cameras pointing out instead of in. I've already sent dozens of calls from reporters to voicemail today, and I have four unread text messages from Lincoln alone."

"You could wear that sexy black wig you showed me in Spain." Jack raised an eyebrow and shot me a half grin. "Change your look and change your identity."

"Are you saying you don't like my new hat either? First my vest, now my bucket hat."

"Let's just say sexy wig trumps dumpy fishing hat any day."

The microwave dinged, and we removed our plates. We were both too lazy to make coffee or tea, so we grabbed water bottles from the refrigerator.

I jumped up to sit on the table and answered his question about disguises. "Wigs get hot. They're fine short-term for a job, but I'm not comfortable relying on them all day and night. Whether we decide to meet up with Arlo under his terms and conditions or not, I'm hoping my grounding restrictions get lifted soon so I can get out of London. Figure I'll be less recognizable by the public if I'm not in the place they expect me to be."

I dove into my food, loving the way the flavor of the spices was enhanced by the overnight refrigeration. But something still bothered me.

"If you turn this file over to your people at the Home Office, they're going to share it with everyone connected to any Colle investigation. Right?"

"Yes, exactly. We want to get him locked up to reduce any new threat toward you."

"But who's to say one or more moles in the government or Whitehall won't get the information as well? You and I banding together started because of the likelihood of a mole in one or more parts of British law enforcement. And once we knew who Colle really is we assumed there was a mole or moles in the Beacham Foundation too. Even if you limit this to people interested in Colle from a non-art heist angle, just the import/export investigations, I'm seeing a risk."

"You're thinking Colle could get tipped off."

"Yes. And if he's had additional plastic surgery he'll likely have the doctor's records stolen, order a hit on all the personnel at the clinic who can identify him, and we'll lose our best opportunity for finding him before he finds us again."

Jack ate in silence for a moment. I waited while he thought through options.

"What about removing all of the pages from the file except the ones with color photos of Colle's face that matched how he looked in Baden-Baden?" he asked. "There wasn't any doctor or clinic identifiers on that page, just the pictures you can confidently say are Colle."

"Well, I can positively state the man who others knew as Colle was, in fact, the man I knew as my late father. Are you saying I have to admit that now?"

He blew out a long breath. "No. Not yet. Maybe never. I don't know, but don't worry, I can spin this. I'll keep to the Colle ID based on our learning he would be at the casino that night. I won't mention a possible family connection to you. Then the follicles can be tested for DNA matching if an arrest is made. Won't be as likely since we won't be telling them everything we know, but you're right. If one of the moles learns about the file's data and reports to any of Colle's organization, the clinic option will get shut down immediately. This will buy us time until Nico can start hacking for the new ID, and we can regroup afterward to see what to do next."

"Sounds feasible," I said. "Why don't you call Cecil before we change our minds."

He set down his plate and pulled out his phone. Less than a minute later he hung up, stared at his screen and said, "Bollocks. Low battery. Forgot to put my mobile on a charger last night."

I wiggled my fingers. "Give it to me. We have a charger that'll work for your model. You can take mine when you go." As I plugged it in, I asked, "When are you meeting Cecil?"

"As soon as I can get to his office. He has a full afternoon planned and isn't sure how much can get initiated today, but he'll handle things from here."

"Good."

While he ate, I put my gloves back on and reopened the original file. Two metal fingers that ran through holes at the top of the pages kept the paper secure. I opened the clasp, removed all the pages and returned the colored photo pages we'd discussed. I pushed the silver fingers back into position and closed it up again. "Are you going to mention anything about dusting for prints?" I asked.

"I'm simply going to say you discovered the file with some Beacham property, and since we've learned Simon was affiliated with Colle's organization while still working at Beacham, we assume it was how he got the information in the file. Cecil already knows a bit more about this anyway, since he and I both discovered the high probability of a mole in our organization at almost the same time. But he doesn't know your connection with Colle as Beacham."

"Sounds good." I set the file beside him on the table and pulled my phone from the Prada. "Okay, take this and you're set to go."

"Yes, I'd better leave." He shoveled the last bite of curry into his mouth and chugged down the rest of his water.

We walked to the door, kissed goodbye, and he disappeared down the stairs.

I grabbed another empty folder and, since I still had the gloves on, set the pages I'd taken out of Simon's file inside and wrote "Original Simon" on the tab. The gloves came off next. I tossed them on the floor near the window, then decided to walk over and open the curtains. I caught a glimpse of Jack hurrying along the busy sidewalk as he headed for the underground station, before he disappeared into the crowd. Glancing in the opposite direction from the Tube stop, I noticed a tall auburn-haired woman crossing the street and heading for the restaurant's front door. I automatically reached for my phone to check the app for the security cameras, then remembered Jack had it. His wasn't charged enough to help me, so I scooped up Cassie's tablet and logged in to the cameras to try for a clearer identification of the woman. I pulled up the shot from seconds before when she opened the restaurant's public door and the zoom nailed her profile.

Oh, shit. The Amazon. For real.

What to do now? I tried using a Skype call to get Jack, but there wasn't an answer. Could he have gotten a train that fast? I tried sending an email-to-text message in case it was just a limited service issue, but he didn't respond. Even if he got the message as soon as he surfaced from the Tube, he couldn't get back here in time to do anything. I could run for the fire escape on the other end of the floor, but she was probably already on the staircase—unless, of course, she just came there to eat Chinese food in the restaurant.

Oh, who was I kidding?

I checked the video cameras covering the staircase and saw she was halfway up. In one hand she held what looked like a small black box. Her right hand held a gun. The only possible weapon I saw to use was the fire extinguisher that hung out in the hall. Something told me blasting her with foam from above wouldn't do anything but make her angry.

Our door stood strong in all its steel glory and Jack trusted our keypad. But I didn't have the luxury. I owned enough whiz-bang gizmos—most not for legitimate sale—that could get me into places other people tried to keep me out of. I wasn't about to think the Amazon couldn't get similar gadgets if she needed them.

With the stair cams showing she was already on her way, I had no conventional way down. I could run to the other side of the floor to use the fire escape, but I'd be completely visible to her the whole way, since the hallway was open to the staircase. I grabbed the short end of the heavy conference table next to me and pulled to swing it around, so the length now paralleled the doorway wall. I shoved it tight against the wall, almost grazing the knob, with the door centered in the length of the table. Then I did the same with the second table, giving the extra shove needed for its long side to buddy up tightly against the first table. Not an elegant fix, but trying to push that kind of double obstacle would slow her down if she managed to make it past the keypad. At least I knew she couldn't shoot me through the door.

I took a quick second and sent another email, this time putting Inspector Timms's contact info in the receiving line and typing a quick SOS.

Next, I pulled up the camera that sat in the keypad outside the door and my heart sank. She was holding up the small black box, and it was exactly the kind of device I'd been concerned about. She wore a grim smile as her electronic gadget worked magic on our keypad. It wouldn't take long for the gizmo to find a way to coax the lock open. She'd have trouble pushing the weight of those two tables, but from experience I knew the Amazon worked to meet her objective. I didn't know if she wanted to kidnap me or kill me, but I had no intention of finding out. While I did have questions that I wanted answered about the night Melanie was killed in my room, I figured I'd wait and ask her when I had Jack around as backup.

My gaze raked over the items in the office space. Nothing to use as a weapon or escape route. Why couldn't I have thought to at least bring a rope? We'd talked about getting a long rope ladder but hadn't followed through during the past month. Three stories down. This is precisely the kind of trap Nico gave me the mini-chute to avoid, but that lovely yellow wonder was packed in the luggage that disappeared with my clothes forty hours ago.

I stared at the drapes.

Moments later, I heard the lock *thunk.* I raced over, leaned across the tabletops, and manually reengaged the door lock. But I knew it wouldn't last long. An oath filtered through the steel door, and the Amazon kicked it for good measure. I hoped she broke a toe.

Leaping from the tables, I ran to the first extra-long drape. Thick curtain rings held it to the rod. I tugged the material repeatedly until it completely separated from its holders. Then I moved to the next curtain. On my last mighty tug, the second curtain filled my arms and the lock again disengaged.

The curtains fell to the floor as I raced back to throw the bolt another time. I heard a double fist pound, signaling her frustration at my maneuver. She never spoke, so I didn't know if she realized I was inside thwarting her successes or if she thought the lock was automatically doing the deed. She may have heard me slide across the tabletops to reach the lock each time, but I had to think the steel door blocked out a lot of interior sound.

I went back to my craft project as she redoubled her efforts. I got the two curtains tied together well enough to risk the chance they would hold, then I looked around the office for something to use as a brace. Our war room primitive décor offered few options.

The lock *thunked* once more, and I sailed across the slick wooden tops. But she was faster this time. She pushed the door into the room. Just an inch or so. Not enough to show a crack of light at the frame, but I couldn't simply lock the door either. I leaned into the task and pushed from my side, but she was stronger. I jumped off the tables and shoved the wooden tops against each other to push the door, leaning to use my weight and that of the tables as leverage against her superior strength. The level loop carpet and the tread on my steel toed boots helped my feet gain traction as I dug in. Eventually, our stalemate made her sigh and step back for a moment. It was almost a shock when I saw the door close. I zipped back on top of the tables and shot the bolt in the door.

Now she knew someone was definitely inside.

I punched the email icon of the tablet. Nothing showed from Timms or Jack. Couldn't count on the cavalry. But even if one of them did send help, the Amazon would get in before police backup had a chance to arrive. Bailing remained the best option.

All the files around me in the room, the prints Cassie hung on the wall, the tablet that slid off the table when I started this siege, the new Colle information Jack and I had been discussing—there was just so much stuff in this office that we wouldn't want her to see. I caught my fingers in my blonde curls and pulled a second to send blood to my brain and gain focus. Was running the answer? Or should I shelter in place?

"It was a nice try office," I muttered. "But she's much stronger than I am. I can't risk her getting the door moving again."

Everything that could fit into the Prada went inside, and I filled every vest pocket as well, beginning by putting Jack's phone and the charger in the pocket with my key ring. I shrugged into the bomber jacket and slung the purse strap cross-body to be hands free. I teed the tables perpendicular, using the legs of the moved table to serve as an anchor to attach the heavy curtains. I pulled down a third drapery and added its length to the end of my makeshift escape route. Still not long enough, but it would get me past the middle of the ground floor. It would have to do.

My gaze quickly inventoried the space. I scooped up anything left that we didn't want the enemy to see, packing it in one of the filing boxes. Then I grabbed the gloves from the floor and put them on for the third time. I slid open a window. Scooping up handfuls of the hefty make-do curtain rope, I dumped it out to hang down the side of the building. The file box went under my left arm. I anchored it against my body, using the Prada to hold a short side close to my hip, with the bottom angle supported by the leather purse. With my left arm across the top, my hand grabbed the carry handle on the opposite short side. The box was going to have to precede me out the window, the only way to go.

The lock disengaged once more, but I didn't try to fly over and relock it this time. The last struggle took too much energy. I needed all remaining reserves.

As she clunked the heavy door against the heavier tables, I sat on the sill and steadied myself to begin the descent. I prayed I wouldn't spill the contents of the box at the same time, but it wasn't far, and this grip was steady in the short term. I double checked the sharp narrow edge of the box bottom to be sure it was effectively anchored against the leather Prada for no-slip balance. Time to rock and roll.

With only one hand, I couldn't do a normal rappel. Instead, I wrapped my freehand in the curtain, holding tight as I moved off the sill and did a modified one-armed slide down the scratchy curtains. Nothing elegant like acrobatic silk dancers, but it was effective. Thankfully, the gloves helped my grip and kept me from getting substitute-rope burns. My face, however, wasn't so lucky. I made the final drop and my heels hit the sidewalk, with the curtain stopping about a foot above my head. My right cheek and the end of my nose felt like the skin had gone through a dry ice epidermis peel treatment.

I steadied myself, then looked out at the street, hefting the box one more time to keep it from slipping, then I caught the other grab handle with my right hand. I hurried down the block, my legs hitting the box as I moved as quickly as possible down the pavement. When I got to the corner, I looked back and saw the Amazon staring at me out the window. I doubled my speed and buzzed around the corner to keep her from following my progress. A number nineteen bus stood midway down the block, and I headed for it, jumping on before I had unearthed my Oyster card from the Prada.

"Hurry, people are waiting behind you," the dreadlocked driver chastised me.

"Trust me, I want you to go as much as you do," I replied, moving to the side so others could pass me while I looked.

"What's that box? You get fired today or something?" he asked.

"Or something," I said, finally locating the damned card. The driver pulled back into traffic before I even got to an empty seat. I looked back through the windows and caught a glimpse of the Amazon as she got to the corner and swiveled around trying to spot me. Another double decker bus came up behind us, and the red metal of a second one traveled two cars lengths ahead of us on the street. If she figured out I grabbed one of the buses, I prayed having three to choose from would be enough of a shell game to give me the advantage I needed.

FIFTEEN

"That's how you escaped?" Jack pointed at the curtains puddling the office floor. He was still tense when I first saw him from the landing below our floor—pacing with the door propped open so he could watch for me. By the time he met me halfway down the stairs though, I could almost see most of the stress visibly roll off him. He hadn't been six inches away from me since.

During my great escape, I'd switched buses until I reached Cassie's street, then called Jack from her flat. Luckily, I'd caught him before his head exploded. Because when he saw the SOS text I'd sent and tried to call but couldn't reach me, he'd contacted Timms and learned the police had already arrived. Timms said they'd found the office empty of people but in a state of chaos inside. Dropping the file unceremoniously on Cecil's desk, he'd shouted that he'd call later and was en route back to the office when I'd reached him via the burner phone Cassie kept in one of her kitchen drawers. I promised I'd meet him back at the office as soon as I could contact Thomas for a ride. His voice calmed down a smidgeon.

Leading ultimately to this question about my escape.

I nodded. "I was afraid she'd shoot at me up the stairwell if I ran for the fire escape, so going out the window seemed the only recourse."

"Quite brilliant. Resourceful."

"Nothing any ten-year-old who's mad at a parent hasn't employed as a method for running away from home. Though the climb down was usually only one story instead of a bit more than two."

"Speaking from experience, are we?"

"I'm an escape artist from way back. Just ask your sister," I said. "But what would have really been handy is my backpack from the other night, if I'd left it in the office instead of at Cassie's. I could have used that escape line, except it would have ended shorter than the curtains. This experience proved we do need to get the long rope or the collapsible ladder we've talked about for several weeks."

"You have an ax now," he teased. "Get handy with the other tools and make one yourself. You know where the home improvement store is located."

I punched his shoulder and he laughed.

He'd already pulled the entire length of curtains up from outside when he arrived, and I kicked the fabric into a corner and closed the shutters I'd opened earlier. First to watch the street scene. Then to escape. Thank goodness I'd decided to stand there and watch Jack walk back to the Underground, so the Amazon didn't take me by surprise.

"Do you think she watched me leave?" he asked, making me feel like he was reading my mind. Again.

"My guess would be yes. But she had a gun." I shrugged. "I can't imagine even the two of us would worry her since she had firepower."

"You saw a gun?"

I nodded. "When I checked the stairwell cams."

"She might have felt she needed the equalizer since you bested her in Barcelona."

"Only because I had surprise, a travel-sized hairspray, and rose thorns on my side. I can't count on that lethal combination every time I cross paths with her."

Jack belly laughed, and I knew he was completely back.

I walked to the door and moved the umbrella stand he used to prop open the entrance.

"Don't do that." He grabbed the door and took the umbrella

stand away from me, returning it to the previously unusual position. "We can't let that door close while we're in here."

"Why?"

"The police shut it when they left, and I had a devil of a time getting it open again when I got here. I don't see any damage to the lock or the strike plate, but I don't want us to get accidentally locked in."

"The Amazon left the door open when she left?"

"Must have, since the cops were here."

I remembered the Amazon's hardworking black box. "My guess is the keypad is toast inside. She used an electronic device to generate the pass code three or four times when I kept relocking the door. It probably didn't save the code when it discovered the correct one and overloaded the keypad software from hitting again and again with hundreds or thousands of attempts in just a few seconds."

Jack walked out the door and looked at the keypad. "It doesn't look burnt out or anything."

"No, but the software is probably compromised inside." I leaned against the doorframe. "I doubt we'll have any difficulty opening the door from this side."

"Forgive me for believing you, but remaining suspicious just the same. This is no longer my week for taking any chances." He walked back in and waved a hand toward the tables I used for a blockade and pseudo-escape route anchor. "Why move the tables?"

Both were still catty-whompus in the middle of the room. I briefed him on my barricade idea, and how the Amazon had to push the door with the additional table weight to move into the office. He was wide-eyed when I finished. "She moved both heavy tables with the door? I'm not sure I could do that."

"She seemed to have anger cheering her on from the corner," I said.

"I'm guessing a regular steroids regimen as well."

I shrugged, continuing to sweep the room with my gaze. After six months in this ongoing investigation, we'd digitized most of the data, but at least I'd carried away the most sensitive of what had been in physical form. She'd taken everything I had to leave behind. Nothing we didn't suspect they already knew that we knew, yet irritating all the same. She left the widescreen, and the ceiling cams were too high for her to reach. In seconds, Jack connected his phone with the television screen. He queued up my departure and her entrance into the office a couple of minutes behind my disappearance out the window. After she'd squeezed into the room, she slammed the tables into the center of the space, clearing the door. Then she'd made a perfunctory exploration around the nearly bare office before flying into a rage. Once her volcanic state died down, she made a phone call, spoke quietly for several minutes, then grabbed every loose paper she could find on the floor or wall and left. Jack zoomed in on her phone display.

"I can get five of the numbers she dialed, but not the entire exchange," I said.

He nodded. "That's my take too."

I pulled a small notebook from my purse and recorded the numbers. "Just in case."

"Good idea. But the beginning looks like an international exchange. One calling Paris."

"We need to tell Nico."

"Agreed."

"It also makes the requested trip to Paris sound like something we need to do soon." I sighed. "Guess we also need to get a better lock or find new offices."

"I'll look into retinal scanners," Jack said. "But moving might be the best option."

"Maybe we could buy a food truck, work from inside while we stay mobile around the city."

"And you could pick up extra money working the lunch hour," Jack said. "Max would love the idea. You'd be a new revenue stream for the organization."

"Nah, he wouldn't want to split the profit with your boss," I returned, grinning. "Because I'd make sure you worked right beside me anytime our canopy was out, and we were open for business."

The rest of the video shots showed the police storming in minutes after she left, two police cars with lights, sirens, and four uniformed PCs. One of the constables looked out the window at the curtains and said they probably needed to get a picture from outside. I was surprised they didn't pull up the fabric. The cops called in to their superior, dusted the keypad and the door for prints, took a few pictures with their phones, and left. I knew they wouldn't find her prints. She always wore gloves. As the screen showed them leaving, Jack shut down the video.

Jack disconnected his phone from the widescreen. "I'll call Williams—"

"Hello."

We turned and found Timms standing in the open doorway.

"Looks like someone has been doing a little redecorating," he said. I was beginning to wonder how far down Timms was going to land on my list of not-so-favorite people.

"We're going for that minimalist look," Jack said. "As of this moment, we're definitely a paperless operation."

"Anything of value stolen?" Timms asked. "Anything which could compromise your foundation's work, Miss Beacham?"

I shook my head. "I spotted her through the security cams and was able to load up the more important and confidential items and take them when I left."

"Out the window, I understand."

"Yes, Inspector."

"You're quite resourceful, Miss Beacham. Do you often leave buildings in such...an unusual manner?"

Uh-oh. Don't panic, Beacham, I thought. Aloud, I said, "Nothing like sheer panic to get the creative juices going, Inspector." I pretended to laugh. Jack didn't buy it, but Timms seemed to and chuckled. "But it isn't anything I ever want to have to do again," I added, crossing my fingers behind my back for the second time in two days after responding to something Timms said.

Luckily, I'd left the work vest and gloves at Cassie's before I returned, so while I still looked dressed down in my jeans, I didn't have the kind of clothes on that would raise Timms's suspicion meter to high alert. Given my current fear of saying too much, I offered to make tea and let the boys talk amongst themselves. It was a good plan. By the time I was playing mother with the teapot, Jack had Timms agreeing there was no reason for me to remain tied to London.

Personally, I think with the Amazon situation happening, Timms feared I would be involved in something else soon that would add to his workload if I hung around town. Which meant he might have been saying okay so I could find safety in another location. Or he hoped I would be killed or abducted elsewhere, leaving him with just Melanie's death to solve.

"And you think this woman in the video feed is the one whose hair the crime scene people found in Miss Beacham's hotel suite?" he asked.

"We believe there's a very high probability," Jack replied.

SIXTEEN

Timms left after finishing his tea and securing a promise from Jack that copies of our security cam files which included the Amazon would get forwarded to his Met police inbox. We replaced the tables in their original positions, checked to make sure there wasn't anything left in the office we could take with us—there wasn't, the Amazon was thorough—and made sure the door locked fully when we left. Since the same security firm installed our cameras and the keypad for the door lock, Jack asked them to service the keypad when he called and requested today's video files be emailed to him.

"I'll forward it on to Timms," Jack said when the call ended. "But I think it would be a good idea for us to have control of the copy too."

"Whether I meet with Arlo or not, I think we need to go to Paris and back up Nico," I said, as we entered the Underground station on our way back to the flat. Then I stopped and touched his arm. "I think you were going to contact Danny about tracing the Amazon's route when Timms walked in. At least you said you were calling him."

"Yes, yes, yes. Damn." Jack pulled out his phone and dialed. "Williams, yes, hello. You may get another call from Inspector Timms, but in case the request goes to someone else in your department I'm wondering if you can do some video tag again for us."

He listened to Danny's reply, then said, "That's right. The break-in at Laurel's office. I'm getting the video from the security cams sent to me, and I'll forward you a copy when I send one to

Timms per his request. The video should be date and time stamped, so if you could back-follow anything you can about where the ginger assassin came from or what route she took when she left, we'd be most appreciative."

"How appreciative? No, I won't agree to let you go out to dinner with Laurel." He winked at me. "But I can see if Cassie isn't totally put off by you yet."

Danny talked, then Jack said, "I'm using Laurel's mobile because my battery is dead. Feel free to contact us on either line. Mine should be charged up again this evening. And we may be leaving the country in the next few hours, so if you find anything I need to see, call as soon as possible. Thanks, mate. Cheers."

He handed me the phone. "Text or call Cassie and see if she's on her way home yet. If she isn't, we can meet her on the way."

"I'll ask where she is, but I don't think I should meet her anywhere we could be followed," I said, texting *Where are you?*

She responded back immediately: *my flat.*

"She's home." I turned the screen to show him. "Why don't we make a circuitous route back?"

It took a train, two buses, another train, and an extra twenty minutes, but we finally arrived at Cassie's flat feeling confident we had no one tailing us.

"But if the Amazon knows where the office is, she might already know where Cassie lives too." I chewed my lower lip as I inserted the front door key.

"Definitely something to consider. Maybe Cass needs to come along to Paris with us," he suggested, following me up the stairs. "Be nice to have the gang all back together again in one place. Didn't you say she has a friend who lives there?"

"Monique."

"Monique, right."

As we reached the landing Cassie threw open the door. "Thank goodness. I was hoping that was you I heard talking. Where have you guys been? You should have arrived here half an hour ago."

"Actually, twenty minutes," I said.

"Huh?"

"We're twenty minutes late. We've been planning a trip to Paris."

The compiled video from the office security camera arrived in Jack's inbox a minute after he took it off the charger. He forwarded everything to the inspector and Danny, while Cassie and I checked plane schedules. When he finished, he said, "I'm going to my place to pack a bag and fetch my car. I want us taking a less direct route to the airport."

I walked him out and handed him my key to the front door. "Be careful, and don't do anything risky while you're gone."

"Like use my curtains to climb out the window?"

"You called that brilliant when you saw what I'd done."

He laughed and pulled me close. "It was inspired, without a doubt." He kissed me, and after a second I kissed him back. When we separated, he said, "Keep the alarm on, and don't open the door for anyone. I mean that."

"Will do," I said, feeling a shiver race up my spine. "We'll be busy packing anyway. Hey, can you bring me a bag of some kind to use for luggage? A duffle? Anything?"

"I'm sure I can find something." He kissed my forehead and disappeared out the door.

Cassie sat cross-legged on the sofa, balancing the laptop with her knees. "There's a flight in three hours with available seating, and another in four and a half hours. Should I book one or both of them?"

"I doubt we can make the one in three hours," I said. "Jack plans on taking the long, long way to the airport, and it may be an hour before he gets back here anyway. Why don't you book us on the later flight and see if there's anything five hours or more out that offers an option. I'll get my credit card to use for another booking."

"Don't worry about it," she said. "I can use the corporate card and one of mine for the second round of booking. But seats are filling up, so we definitely do need to double book if I can get through using two cards and different carriers."

I headed into the bedroom to pack, and Cassie brought me a carryon when she finished on the computer.

"Here you go," she said. "I heard you ask Jack to bring you a bigger bag, but I have this one to spare. And if you need clothes to fill out the gaps in your wardrobe, I'm happy to share anything you need."

"Thanks, Cass." I had my belongings folded and laid out on the bed, so I could visibly see what items I lacked. "While I appreciate you trusting me with your things, given my history the past six months of losing luggage, I'm not sure it's a good idea though."

"I'm not worried," she replied. "If getting your packed bags pinched by a murderer isn't a world class case of lost luggage, I don't know what is. I figure the trigger has already been pulled on your curse this time, and the things you borrow are effectively curse-proof."

"Shh, not so loud," I replied. "The curse might hear you."

By the time Jack returned we were packed and ready to go. Well, I was packed once I moved the rest of the clothes and shoes I had stacked on the bed into the soft-sided bag he brought for me to use.

The drive to the airport was long but uneventful, and no one complained. We were all living on the "better safe than sorry" principle, I believed. Like we'd assumed, the first flight out wasn't an option, but we made the second one with time to spare. Cassie had already phoned Monique but texted her the plane's carrier, flight number, and ETA when we knew for sure which bird was taking us to Paris. I texted the same information to Nico.

"Now, you know if you need me in Paris, just call," Cassie reminded us. "I feel kind of guilty going along with your plans to just hang out with my friend."

"In the short term, this is much safer, and we're nearly to the weekend already, so don't feel the least guilty," I said. "We have no idea how the Amazon is getting in and out of the country. Network while you're there if it helps you feel like you're working instead of vacationing. We want you close, but not too close to me until we have a better idea what's happening."

A young woman walked to join her boyfriend ahead of us in line, and Cassie gasped.

"What's wrong?"

"I just realized what I noticed about the party cam views," she said. "In the later views of the party, after you returned, there was a young woman who looked a lot like that girl there, and who stayed glued to the Russian's wife. I watched that group a lot when I was there in the interim, and she was never with the wife's entourage then. But she was easily the same size as the woman we watched the police chasing away from the house."

"You think one of her friends was the thief?" Jack asked.

The PA came on and announced our plane was ready for boarding.

"I'm not positive, but I think I'm pretty sure," Cassie said, grabbing her carryon and her purse. "I know that sounds weird but—"

"No, it sounds exactly right," I said, following her lead. "High probability, but more evidence must be considered. What was she wearing?"

"I'm not sure. An emerald green dress, I think? She was a brunette. Danny should be able to tell because all the rest of the girlfriends stayed ringed around the wife the whole time. Well, a couple of them spiraled off short term. I'm assuming to use the ladies. But the posse stayed mostly in attendance the entire night."

Jack had his phone out. "I'll text Danny to follow up on this tomorrow. If the woman was the thief, do you think the wife was in on it?"

"I'd bet on it," I said. "She was probably planning a little insurance fraud to build a personal slush fund. And I'll bet only jewelry was supposed to be stolen."

"Do you believe that's why the wife disappeared when the cops showed up?" Jack asked, looking at his phone and texting as he talked.

"No, I think that was mostly due to her hitting cocaine in the bathroom. But she couldn't have been happy to hear the bust was stolen too." Then I reminded, "Don't forget Danny doesn't know about the bust, so don't add that info to your text."

"Absolutely. Thanks," he said. "Williams is already suspicious because the thief's bag looked like it held more than the reported missing jewelry. He'd be royally pissed off if he found out I wasn't telling him everything."

"Especially difficult when you can't tell him how you know," I replied.

Nico met us close to baggage claim, and Cassie spotted Monique nearby. Nico texted Cassie what hotel he had the three of us booked into for our stay, and she texted back Monique's address. On the plane, the three of us had decided on regular check-in times we would all keep, no matter where we were each day. Just quick texts were enough. Once all the locations were exchanged, we promised to keep in touch and went our separate ways.

"From what I've been able to determine, Arlo is in the Montmartre area," Nico explained. "But I have us booked in a luxury hotel more centrally located to everything. While a room in Montmartre might be more convenient for connecting with Arlo, until I know what he looks like I didn't want to run the risk of him knowing who I am before I know how to spot him."

"Right," I agreed. We were in a rented Peugeot, and I scrambled for the grab handle above the car window. Nico drove as crazily as any native Parisian driver, which was probably tamer than the way he'd learned to drive in Italy when I thought about it. Regardless, I was glad I had a back seat and thought I might need to crawl into the floorboard. "Montmartre is almost like a village inside the Paris city limits. If he's lived there a while, he could have all kinds of people spying for him and reporting back."

"Did you tell Arlo we were coming?" Jack asked, putting his hand out to brace against the dashboard as Nico stomped hard on the brakes to keep from hitting the car in front of him after that driver halted unexpectedly.

But honestly, crazy driving aside, I could almost forget my anxiety by focusing on the view out of the windows. I didn't think any city in the world was more beautiful at night than Paris. From the twinkling lights on the Eiffel Tower to radiant light touching all the streets and buildings across the rest of the city, Paris was as beautiful as any woman could ever be. Oh, sure, the streets were made for military processions, and the monuments championed victories, but this city always made me think of a lovely, strong, feminine spirit.

"No," Nico answered Jack. "As far as he knows Laurel is still waiting for permission from the London police."

When we got checked into our hotel and the bellman took us up to our room, I saw Nico had really outdone himself on the booking. Paris was literally outside our balcony, with a distant view of the Eiffel Tower, the lit-up pyramid of the Louvre, and the Tuileries Garden sat across the street. The night air was cool, but not so cold I wanted to step back inside. Jack joined me, wrapped his arms around me from behind and rested his chin on my head. Things felt pretty perfect.

"We're having breakfast right here in the morning," I said. "Feeding our souls with positive vibes while we eat to feed our bodies."

"I've already placed the order."

I squeezed his hands. "Gotta tell you, Hawkes, you scare me sometimes with how well you know me." Not that I had a clue even half the time about what he was thinking.

"We just like the same things," he said.

Good enough, I thought. I twisted in his arms to face him, and our lips met. As I fell into the kiss I could feel Paris' approval.

SEVENTEEN

As planned the night before, Nico left early in the car to Montmartre, intending to network until he heard from Arlo. Jack and I finished breakfast and dressed in clothes we could comfortably walk in all day. I wore my hair up, hoping it made me look less like my internet image. But if that and a change in locale didn't do the trick I'd be buying a dark wig like Jack suggested. The nearest Metro stop sat at the end of the block.

"I love Paris for so many reasons," I said, as we held the handrail and made our way down to the train tunnels. "I think public transportation is one of my top three. So many gorgeous entrances." I pointed to the unique decorations. "Look at this one with its gold and silver balls floating above us. You're never more than five hundred meters from a Metro stop or another form of public transport. Though it almost seems a shame to ride the subway because it means you miss seeing the city when you do."

"You realize you're arguing both sides of your own issue."

"Yes, I'm versatile that way."

In minutes we had tickets, found our platform, and could see the light on the train hurtling toward us from its tunnel. I took a firmer hold of my Prada. Pickpockets seemed at their worst at points like this, often boarding with passengers, then grabbing bags and jumping off to escape just as the doors closed.

"Enjoy your Metro beauty moment," Jack said. "But don't complain when you have to climb all the stairs out at the Abbesses."

"The bakery down the street won the best baguette in Paris award," I said. "Knowing world-class bread is so close makes the stair climb worthwhile. President Macron even initiated a measure asking that the baguette receive a World Heritage cultural designation for France, like Italy accomplished for pizza from Naples."

"Bet food is your number one reason for loving Paris." He grinned.

"Of course. That's a given."

Because of the hilly region that comprised Montmartre, the Abbesses station was the deepest in the Paris Metro system. But oh, the views from Montmartre—spectacular. The only point higher than Montmartre was the Eiffel Tower. And because so much of Paris was flat, the view always seemed to go on forever.

When we came out at Montmartre, I acted like any tourist and turned in a circle to take it all in. What was once a small bohemian village on the hill had become one of the most famous areas of Paris, yet still retained its boho charm. In the past, the rolling hills were covered with vineyards, and more than two dozen windmills to ground grain for the residents' bread. This was where the working classes and artists came to live, an attractive area to these groups because rents were low and wine priced cheaply. All the great artists called the hilly region home at some point: Lautrec, Renoir, Picasso, Van Gogh. Plaques around Montmartre pointed out the houses where famous artists lived, and at places like the Lapin Agile Cabaret, tourists learned how the smaller clubs catered to artists and gave them a place to hang out, while the better known Moulin Rouge Cabaret was more for the wealthy and the tourists. Sometimes, in small clubs, artists exchanged paintings for food or a pitcher of wine. Even Picasso bartered his art in this fashion when he went through his own starving artist phase while living and working in Paris.

I pulled a pair of sunglasses out of the Prada, and hoped they helped in my disguise, wondering if we'd have time for me to do some shopping to replace my missing clothes and see what new up-and-coming designers were making their name onto the scene. My fingers itched to pull out my overused credit card.

"Shall we head for Place du Tertre and see if we spot any artists we know?" Jack asked, lacing his fingers with mine as we strolled.

"Okay, but I don't want to sit for any portraits—and especially no caricatures—no matter how much they try to twist our arms," I said. The Place du Tertre was about a block from the Sacre-Coeur church and teemed with artists who created street art for tourists and offered their own studio works for sale each day. "If Arlo doesn't make contact with Nico, we can hang out on the church steps later. Someone there likely knows him. I think half the population of Montmartre is on those steps most days."

We took a few side trips a block or two off the main tourist routes and let the neighborhoods show us their charms. The houses weren't the kind of stately Haussmann architecture that helped define the Latin Quarter. Here the designs were more wonderfully artistic, and each seemed to possess its own unique spirit.

"I adore how quiet it is in Montmartre," I said.

"Yes, the twisty cobblestone streets discourage anyone from wanting to drive anywhere," Jack said.

"I wonder why Nico decided we need a car. Parking here has to be difficult."

"I'm glad he did. With all the unknowns in this case, it's good to be certain we can make a fast getaway if necessary."

Jack's phone rang, and the screen showed it was a call from Danny. We moved into a little alleyway before he hit the speaker. "What did you find, Williams?"

"It was exactly like you thought. I pulled the films all the way back to the start of the party, and she was in the thick of things for the first hour or so. Then she disappeared, and I couldn't find her anywhere until after you and Laurel took your walk and came back through the front door. Finally, just before the police arrived, she reappeared and rejoined the party, with all the girlfriends pulling her back into the group and keeping her close."

"Have you called DI Markham yet?" Jack asked.

"No, I just finished confirming the hypothesis and thought you should know first."

"To be honest, it was Cassie who spotted it. Remember the other night when she said she noticed something in the videos, but couldn't put her finger on what bothered her?"

"Tell her I owe her dinner," Danny said.

"Will do." Jack scratched his chin. "Not to pressure, but did you get the security cam footage from Laurel's office?"

"Yes, and I started on it a little yesterday but moved on to this today after your call last night. This afternoon, I'll get back on tracking the woman who broke in, but I have to tell you, she is cagey. I about lost her a couple of times yesterday and had to backtrack."

"Cagey is one adjective that would fit her," Jack said. "Okay, thanks, Williams. And make sure Markham takes you out for beers. You saved him a ton of legwork."

"Couldn't have done it without Cassie. Talk to you later."

"The interview with the Russian's wife regarding the appearance and disappearance of a certain entourage member should be interesting for DI Markham," I said. "Wish I could be a fly on the wall.

Jack pocketed his phone. "Probably even more enlightening to her husband. Hope the Russian had her sign a prenup, because he should definitely entertain divorce options."

We linked arms and continued our stroll. I was back to wearing low-heeled boots to accommodate the hilly cobblestone streets. I'd left my steel-toed beauties in London. Still, it didn't take long for me to start feeling the effects of the terrain in my calves, and as we neared the Place du Tertre I was ready to find a sidewalk café and people watch. Tourists with maps were likely looking for Picasso's apartment or the house where Van Gogh lived with his brother Theo. I had other goals.

"Do you want to get some coffee?" Jack asked.

"Yes, bless you."

He laughed and steered us toward a small shop with a bright awning and several sets of tables and chairs outside. We were settled in nicely when a third chair was pushed up to our table and Nico dropped into the seat.

"I thought you'd call," I said, taking a sip of my heavenly coffee flavored with a cinnamon stick.

He shook his head. "I've been following your progress on GPS. I've already touched base with Cassie, and Arlo is set to phone in a few minutes."

Jack squinted in the sun. "Can you put the call on speaker, or will that spook him?"

"Everything spooks this guy." Nico frowned. "I just hope he has something worthwhile to tell us."

Nico ordered a cup of coffee for himself, and Jack gave an update on what Danny had found after Cassie's *aha!* moment regarding the CCTV video. He laughed. "That does not surprise me at all. She's smart."

His phone rang then. Nico looked at the screen, nodded, then spoke in French. I didn't even try to follow the conversation. I knew Jack was, and he would interject if necessary. A few seconds later he did shake his head fiercely in obvious disagreement with what was being said. Nico made a calming motion with his hand and spoke for several seconds. I heard silence on the other end, as if Arlo was thinking about how to answer, then an onslaught of French followed.

The phone call lasted several minutes, with most of the talking done on the other end. Nico said a final "*Oui,*" and hung up, then turned to Jack. "Did you catch most of that?"

"Yes. So, Laurel will get the meeting place and time from a street artist."

"*Sì.* I know which artist he means," Nico said and sipped his coffee.

"If the artist only speaks French, one of you will have to come with me," I warned. "Will Arlo and the artist go for that?"

"No need to worry," Nico said.

"He'll write the instructions at the bottom of the art he draws for you," Jack said, grinning.

Their devilish expressions set off warning bells for me. "Exactly what kind of artist is this?"

"A caricaturist," Nico replied. Jack started laughing.

"Dammit, I already said—" I stopped and stared at the two gleeful males. Time to resign to fate. "Damn."

EIGHTEEN

The street art portrait wasn't half bad. I had the oversized head, of course, but the artist took pains to give the composition a nice balance. He drew me at a table in a garden behind a mint-colored house, whose corner appeared on the left side of the page. Which I presumed pointed to where I would meet with Arlo. When he finished, he signed his name with a flourish and added an address. I gave him fifty euros—the agreed upon price—and handed the picture to Jack as I walked away. Luckily, Arlo was waiting for us. Whatever way this ended it would at least be soon.

When the mint green house was in sight, Jack stopped us and said, "Wait here. Let me do a quick recon to see if I spot anything that shouldn't be there."

"Sì," Nico said. "Arlo told me he has no trouble with English, and Laurel can do the interview herself. You can keep an eye on the perimeter until their meeting is over."

"Where will you be?" Jack asked.

"I'm going to get the car," Nico said. "If we need to go fast, I don't want it to be on foot."

"Fine, both of you, leave and do your thing," I said, making a shooing motion toward each of them. I was ready for something good to happen, and I was counting on this being where we'd receive marketable information. My hopes were high.

Nico disappeared down a side street, and Jack headed toward the house. I stood under a tree with tiny spring buds bursting and waited until I received the high sign from Jack. Then I made my way around the side of the house, looking for a table by a garden. It was exactly like the picture, except that instead of me being at the black wrought iron table, the occupied chair held a wizened little gray-haired elf of a man whittling on a stick.

"*Monsieur* Arlo?" I held out a hand.

He set his knife and stick on the table and rose slowly. "*Oui, Mademoiselle* Laurel." He motioned for me to take a seat.

Nothing was blooming yet, but the green shoots and leaves showed great promise for gorgeous flowers to carpet the garden by April. Letting my gaze sweep the surroundings, I said, "You have a lovely home."

"*Non*, the house is borrowed for this purpose. I let no one know where I live. Life has become *très dangereux*."

"Believe me, I understand. When did you begin worrying about your life?" I asked.

He twirled the open knife on the tabletop. It was a well-used Swiss Army knife, but from the ease with which he'd whittled the stick, I assumed the blade must be extra sharp. Finally, he said, "About a year ago. But the last six months...*Merde!*"

"First, I want to assure you that I'm only here to try to gather information," I ventured, moving carefully. "We will not be telling authorities anything about this conversation, and we have no desire to see you prosecuted. I simply wanted to meet with you to ask about your work."

"I know your reputation. You are spoken of highly in our community, and if I can help..." He waved a hand over the tabletop. "Ask. Please."

"We've discovered several remarkable pieces of art done in different metals and wondered if they were completed by your hand, or by someone you know. One was a seventh-century broadsword, another was a seventeenth-century silver snuffbox, and the last a bronze bust duplicating a work by Rodin," I said, then held my breath as I waited for his reply.

"Did they have a mark?"

"Yes, on the snuffbox and the bronze bust." I reached into the Prada and pulled out a card with the drawing of the forger's mark.

"Each carried this symbol on the bottom of the work."

He held the card for a moment before dropping it to the tabletop and saying, "*Oui*, I did two of the items. Not the sword."

"Wonderful, thank you." I slipped the card back into my purse. "Can I ask who hired you to make those copies?" I figured it was best not to use the terms forgery or fake.

He responded by shrugging.

"Are you saying you cannot tell me, or that you won't?" I reined in my impatience at his response. As much as I would have liked to remind him that he was the one who demanded to talk to me when Nico contacted him, I knew it was crucial I curbed my sarcastic tongue.

He shrugged again and picked up his tools and resumed whittling.

"Did you make several copies of the pieces? Or only one of each?"

"Only one," he replied, scowling. His gaze remained on the knife as it easily sliced the stick. "I only make one copy, always. No matter how a man pushes me for more."

Deep breath, Beacham, time for another approach, I thought. I asked, "Do you mark all of your work with those marks, or just the two pieces?"

"I do whatever the client wants." He waved the knife in the air. "This one wanted the marks added. I added the marks. Simple. But I will no longer work for that client."

His jaw tightened, and I realized I'd probably gained all I could from Arlo on this subject. At least for now. Time to switch topics and maybe back into this later from a different direction.

"Nico said you wanted to talk to me about Melanie Weems's murder," I prompted.

"She wanted you killed," he said, punching the table with his stick as he spoke. "She came to Paris, looking for an assassin."

"To kill me?" Sure, we never got along. But, an assassination? Kind of drastic. "I knew she hated me, but I never imagined her hatred ran so deeply."

"She was not doing it for herself," the elf explained, shaking his silver head. "She came looking for another person. Someone who could not do the hiring."

"Was it someone she was involved with?" I asked. "A man with money?"

"*Oui.*"

"Was the man someone you'd ever worked for?"

He shrugged a third time. Damn. There had to be a better way to do this. I reviewed my mental list of questions.

"What kind of things are you doing to help keep yourself safe? Maybe I can do something similar."

He smiled then, and I congratulated myself for making inroads. Dropping the stick, he touched under his eye with his forefinger. "You must watch. Watch everyone. Watch everything. When something isn't as expected, leave quickly. And this..." He closed the knife blade and handed the weapon to me, closing my fingers around the handle. "Keep a knife you can always hide in your hand. Or a gun. Something small. Never be without means to fight an enemy."

I opened and closed the blade, thinking about how easily the knife held its position as I asked, "Do you have any idea who killed Melanie Weems?"

"Someone protecting y—"

A shot rang out and Arlo made a strangled noise. His head hit the tabletop with a thud.

"Get down!" Jack yelled, running toward us.

I started to reach for Arlo, to try to help him in some way, though I knew he was already gone. A head wound like that was always fatal. Instead, Jack grabbed my hand and pulled me to a sidewall built up with stones to hold an elevated garden plot. He pushed me down, then crouched beside me, a gun in his hand.

"Where did you get the gun?" How did he do that?

"Nico gave it to me last night in the car."

I heard sirens in the distance, grateful someone had called the police. Nico pulled up on the street in the Peugeot and waved us to come and get inside.

Jack and I hurried to the car, running a zigzag pattern to shelter behind trees and shrubs. Nico pushed open the passenger door as we neared, and Jack shoved me inside. He handed Nico the gun and said, "Get her someplace safe. I'll stay and talk to the police."

"Jack, you need this for protection. The shooter may still be out there," Nico said.

"You and Laurel need protection. I got this. Now, get out of here and meet me back at the hotel." Then he ran back toward Arlo.

"No, we can't—" I argued and started to climb from the car.

"Yes, we can," Nico pulled me back and accelerated, my door swinging shut with the velocity. "Buckle up."

When I grabbed the seatbelt, I realized I still had Arlo's knife in my hand.

It was over three hours before Jack showed up again at the hotel. I'd given up on waiting in the room and haunted the lobby for at least half that time. He looked absolutely done in when he pushed through the revolving door.

"Come on," I said. "Let's go get you a drink in the bar."

"Brilliant. I'm feeling a bit knackered."

As he drank a scotch, he gave me the CliffsNotes version of what happened after we drove away. Then he immediately wanted a detailed account of what Arlo told me.

"First tell me about the shooter. Was Arlo the target, or was it another close call for me?"

"I'm thinking Arlo since there weren't any follow-up shots," Jack said. "The *Sûreté* seem to agree with that theory too. Arlo was known for being a forger, and the police are chalking this up to jealousy, turf wars, dangerous occupation, you name it."

"I almost told him that he didn't have to worry anymore because the person who caused all the forgers to be killed off was dead," I said. "Boy, was I wrong."

"Maybe, maybe not. Tell me precisely what Arlo told you in the garden and we'll try to determine whether there's a new trail to pursue."

Since I'd already covered this with Nico, I breezed through my delivery, hit all the fine points and gave the conclusions I'd drawn. He remained quiet throughout, finished his scotch and ordered another.

"You'd better eat a sandwich before drinking much more."

"Too true. We never had lunch."

The second scotch arrived first, but he was smart enough to wait for the food.

"So now what's the plan?" I asked.

A rough London-accented voice, one that hinted at years of cigarettes and liquor, called out my name. "Laurel Beacham, is that you?"

Clive, roadie extraordinaire for the heavy metal band Whyte Noyse, lumbered in toting an oversized carryon. Jack and I had each shared planes with the band during different legs of our investigative journeys, and Nico was an even more frequent traveler due to his connection with the band's lovely publicist, Patricia.

"Hey, Clive, good to see you." I stood and hugged him. "Are you checking in?"

"Nah, I'm leaving. Like I told Nico yesterday, I have to get back to the tour."

"You talked to Nico? I wish he'd told us you were around."

"Ran into him at the airport. Told him where I was staying, and he said he'd have to try out the place. Looks like he got you in here too, right?"

"We arrived last night." I turned to point at Jack.

As Jack stood and held out a hand, Clive did a double take. "You get beat up again, mate?"

"No, it's just been one of those weeks."

Clive turned back to me and grinned. "Yeah, I saw Laurel had her turn in the spotlight. Bit of a surprise that was. Never expected it of you."

I covered my face with my hands. "Don't remind me. I'm trying to hide while I'm here. I kept getting recognized in London."

"Now you know how the band feels," he said, chuckling. "Though their exploit videos were never put to any music other than the songs they played."

"You saw that one too, huh?"

"Kind of hard to miss it." He slapped me on the back. "Don't worry. Fame is fleeting."

"I can only hope," I said, then asked, "What are you doing in Paris?"

"The guys needed me to take care of some paperwork for the European end of the tour. I've been with them longer than any of their managers, so I get courier duty to iron out details they feel requires close attention and confirmed receipts."

"The U.S. tour is going well?"

"Brilliantly. I'm heading back to New York tonight or I'd see if you wanted to go to dinner."

I shrugged. "We were supposed to be in New York today too, but the trip got scrapped."

"Well, hey, ride back with me. I have the whole plane to myself." He waved a hand toward the elevators. "Go on up and pack to check out. I'll wait for you."

"Thanks," Jack said, smiling for the first time since he returned.

However, I threw a wet blanket on his happiness. "Call and see if you can catch the detective first, check if he'll be available tomorrow. No point in us going otherwise."

Nodding, he pulled out his phone and connected right away with the retired detective, Douglas Harmon. "Okay, thank you. We'll meet up with you tomorrow morning in Scarsdale by ten," Jack said, wrapping up the conversation.

He ended the call and pocketed the phone. "Perfect timing. He's between test dates and looks forward to meeting us." Then grabbing my hand, he said, "Come on, Laurel. Let's go pack."

I called back to Clive, "He has a sandwich order coming. Ask them to wrap it to go."

"Great. What about this scotch?"

"Are you driving?"

"No. Got a limo."

"Then drink up. Free booze."

He lifted the glass. "Cheers."

When we got to the room, Jack finally slowed down enough to catch on that I wasn't thrilled about the prospect of spontaneously going to New York. I made an effort, but Jack finished packing long before me and got a little ticked when I dissuaded him from helping. That's when he realized my slowness was procrastination. My arguments were just another form of the same.

"Besides, you need to let Nico and Cassie know where we're going. This trans-Atlantic trip wasn't on anyone's agenda." I was carefully setting a sweater into the carryon. He pulled the bag from the bed and made me sit there instead.

"Tell me, how much of not wanting to go to New York is avoiding the risk of dredging up old memories, and how much is just avoiding Max?"

Wow! He really was perceptive. Or I was more transparent than I'd thought. "Honestly? Probably sixty-forty avoiding Max. No, seventy-thirty. I know it sounds ungrateful of me, but I feel so much more under Max's thumb than I ever felt when I was just troubleshooting art recovery. Being in the same time zone with him makes it all worse because he thinks I should sit and stay whenever he gives a command. And now I have to cyber-meet with him regularly on budgets and projected expenses and all the other administrative stuff I've never had to do before. So, I'm kind of Max-ed out on my best days."

He sat beside me and took my hand, rubbing my fingers when he said, "Part of the problem might be that you still have to expend tremendous energies on art recovery. You and the foundation must face facts—you might be stretched too thin. You have a good team to rely on with Cassie and Nico, but you're still in the trenches every minute. Having to stop and take a conference call would be justifiably irritating. You can only palm so many off on Cassie, and she's expanding her role every day besides. Taking extra calls may soon be too much for her as well."

"You're right, I know, but Max will never understand that dilemma. Part of the reason, of course, is I can't tell him everything we do because of the risk of information falling into the wrong hands. If I felt like Max could be counted on to keep a lid on intel, I could speak more freely and not shoulder everything so much of the time. But he gets excited and has to tell what he knows when trying to impress people. We've already had problems on this front with the little he's learned, or when people in our investigation run into him. I can't risk it."

"I get it, I do. I also remember a discussion we had in the Peter Paul Reubens Room at the National Gallery a few days after your promotion. You had reservations then, and they don't seem to be lessening."

"I was afraid of being hobbled by the new job, I remember. While I've forced my way through some restrictions, others remain, and I can't see how to avoid them."

"Like being tied to the U.K. and the European continent."

"I miss being able to travel the whole world for art."

Jack shrugged. "You can still travel anywhere you like. You just have more status and recovery latitude in Europe."

"Are you kidding me?" I laughed, but my tone was sad. "When have I traveled anywhere since we've met that wasn't foundation related, or to give me a modicum of safety from threats resulting from my work?"

"Touché."

I gathered steam and my hands started moving with my words. "Even this discussion we're having right now stems from the fact I can't even buy my own trip to New York and try to set aside the ghosts of my own mother's death without Max adamantly decreeing I come into headquarters for a command performance. Despite the fact anything I do for him in person while being physically in the New York office is equally deliverable via phone or internet. It's the way he has his thumb pressing more solidly against the top of my head that makes me fight against the New York trip."

Jack shook his head. "I've heard you go after him. You have no trouble standing up to Max. Why don't you just lay it on the line?"

"Probably because he might see that kind of response as the final straw and fire me. Yes, fear is a real thing in this case. Remember, the board put me in this higher position, not Max. He doesn't know what I know, and he has no idea what you, and I, and Nico and Cassie have been working on. Which brings us back to that same Catch-22 because I can't trust him enough to tell him."

"What about stepping away from running the London office? Go back to the way things were before?"

"That would put Cassie in limbo unless the new office head took her on."

"What makes you think he wouldn't keep her on the payroll?"

I snapped my fingers and jumped to my feet. "See, that right there, Jack, is a huge consideration for me. The talk will be the woman couldn't cut it as an office head and a man had to come in and take over."

"Wait a minute, I—"

"No, you said it yourself. 'What makes me think HE wouldn't keep her on the payroll.' I'm the only female office head in the foundation, and despite how far-reaching the story is about my father losing everything to gambling, booze and floozies, no matter how I've overcome that stigma, I'd wager a majority of the people both inside the foundation and out still think I wouldn't have the position at all if my last name wasn't Beacham. Which, of course, may not be the case anyway, but we haven't had the luxury of time or opportunity to either prove or disprove that conundrum either. But it is one more reason we should go to New York. Especially since Clive is giving me a way to sneak in without Max knowing."

He grinned.

"What?" I frowned.

"I just like being included in that final decision after you mention your personal issues. Oh, and it's fun to see you fight yourself in an argument. That's the second one in twenty-four hours."

I felt a lump in my throat and stepped next to him, putting a hand on his shoulder. "You know I wouldn't try to face half of the mystery about my parents without you, Jack. I may not trust my boss one iota, but I've come to trust you implicitly." My words came out thick, holding back tears.

He pulled me into his lap and kissed me, soft at first, then the kiss deepened. I was ready for more, but the room phone rang, and we got up so he could answer it. I went back to packing.

"Yes, great. We'll be down in a minute. Thanks, mate." Jack said. After he cradled the phone he said, "Clive is getting antsy and already paid for our room while he waited. Hurry. We have a luxury plane to catch."

NINETEEN

Cassie bubbled with excitement when I called her from the limo and explained where we were going and how. Conversely, when Jack told Nico the same thing, Hawkes's body language implied the excited feeling wasn't a universal experience—at least not in Nico's case. I mentally kicked myself for not doing the Nico call instead of connecting with Cassie. Despite the fact he'd volunteered for the current gig because it started in Rome, my techno-geek always got his nose bent out of shape when he had to do fieldwork. Especially when gunplay erupted. Not to mention he still blew hot and cold about Jack. All I needed now was for my favorite hacker to stomp off the job in a huff.

I started to ask for the phone, to shift Nico's attention by suggesting he get current again on the *Portrait of Three*, and we would focus on the auction card when we returned. Until I remembered one of the Whyte Noyse band members, Gordon Silver, had already said he hoped someday to purchase the centerpiece of the grouping, the painting known as *Juliana*. Clive might know nothing about the works, or possibly had heard Gordon's wish list countless times. Except Gordon was obsessed about his art collection and what he liked, so my money was on the latter. I didn't want to run the risk of Clive mentioning it to Gordon after hearing me talk about the trio of masterpieces. We had a big enough risk for leaked information as it was, without contributing to it myself. More secrets to keep.

A surprise call from Danny immediately after, however, put Jack back into a good mood. At first, anyway. "The wife broke down? That fast?" he said, then added, "Danny, I'm going to put you on speaker so Laurel can hear this. We're heading to New York on the Whyte Noyse plane with their roadie, Clive. He's in the car here with us."

I knew that last bit of information was to warn Danny not to spill confidential information. It didn't seem to bother Clive, though. If anything, his smile went broader.

"Okay, I don't have a full report yet," Danny said. "But I do have one friend who's in the same district as DI Markham, and he's giving me updates. I figure Markham will give me more once all the holes are filled. He was fairly chuffed when I took the video information to him that I'd sorted about the appearing and disappearing friend."

"As well he should be," I said, smiling inside because Cassie had been the linchpin for breaking that portion of the case.

"The friend is a new one for the wife," Danny explained. "They were introduced by a friend of a friend at some posh end-of-the-year event held a few months ago. Suddenly, they began bumping into each other on a daily basis, and it was this friend who helped the young wife plan her husband's birthday party, and who suggested she needed to build a rainy day fund in case her husband ever cut her off financially."

Interesting. A con for sure, but a targeted one. The thief was patient, making the contact, then already knowing the mark's pattern enough to happen to run into her often afterward. Probably a six- to eight-month con in the making. The couple had just married last summer, according to Jack's notes. The thief obviously took her time, leaving me to think her setting off the alarm that night might have been more calculated than I'd thought.

"Was she also the one who suggested using insurance fraud to do so?" Jack asked.

"The very one, according to the wife."

"And they planned to let the party create a loose alibi for everyone?"

"Yes, they were all going to say they were together nearly all night, and two of the women separately left the group for a short time whilst the thief was away, so they could say later they were each with her during the time she wasn't in the group."

My gaze met Jack's, and I maintained eye contact to get him to understand what I couldn't say out loud when I mused, "So she's been planning a heist like this for three or four months? Or more. Building the friendship day by day. Is she a London native?"

"No, she's French, twenty to twenty-three, no more than twenty-five, and obviously operating under an alias since her background only begins November of last year. Also, the Russian's wife said she wore gloves constantly. Said she had a medical condition and needed to protect her hands."

More likely, she had a need to protect herself from leaving behind fingerprint evidence. "I'd forgotten about the gloves she wore at the party. They were frilly and glitzy and made from green fabric to match her dress. I just assumed it was part of her look for the night."

"Does the wife know where she lives?" Jack asked.

"No, just a general area and her name. Jacqueline Aubertine."

"What the hell," I cried.

Jack cursed, "Bollocks."

Recovering a second later, I asked, "Are you sure about that last name, Danny?"

"As sure as I can be at this point. But like I said, it has to be an alias."

"Or it's her grandfather's real last name," I said. To Jack, I added, "Remember I told you Rollie mentioned a sister."

"You think this is her?" he asked.

"It's the best theory I can come up with spur of the moment." I looked at the phone again and said, "Have Markham look for a Jacqueline Baroux. If she's Rollie's sister, that would be the name on her original birth certificate. She may have others she uses too."

"Certainly, but who's this Aubertine grandfather?" Danny asked.

"Moran," I said. "Devin Moran."

Danny whistled into the phone.

"I'll fill you in by text later," Jack said. "But for now just know I've determined Moran's real name is most likely Phillipe Aubertine."

"I'll make note of that. And she definitely disappeared into thin air," Danny said. "But she left the jewels behind. So even if we do find her we can't charge her. When a search of the home was conducted, the pieces were found in the wife's jewelry case on her dresser. No way to prove the thief ever had them. Her black bag was loaded with some kind of swag when she ran that night, but the Russian and his wife wouldn't budge about the theft being anything but the stuff found in the jewelry case."

"Did the wife hide them there? Or were they left by the thief?" I wondered if that was the real reason the thief doubled back the night of the heist.

"The wife said she had no idea the jewelry was inside, but hers were the only fingerprints found on the outside of the case. No one believes her."

Which may have been part of the appeal of the game all along for Jacqueline.

"Do you know what the husband said when the jewels were found?" Jack asked.

"Not exactly. But from what I understand he's still ballistic about the robbery. Guess that's a logical reaction when you learn it was planned by your gold digging young wife."

Or when the fake Rodin you believed was real, and which you had locked in your safe, actually disappeared with the thief. I looked at Jack and he nodded.

"I also have news about the interviews with the three idiots who attacked us in the National Gallery," Danny said. "I thought I was saving the best information 'til last, but your bombshell about who the missing woman is overshadows it completely."

"Sorry, Danny," I said. "We didn't mean to quash your surprise. What have you learned?"

"Motive. They were avenging some kind of battery you did on

their boss."

Jack and I looked at each other and smiled. We'd been right. Repercussions of our escape from Colle in Baden-Baden.

"It wasn't well planned, of course," Danny continued. "But the stories of the two guys who jumped Jack and I corroborate one another. Apparently, the big guy had a few pints and ran into his mates, then they wandered by the National Gallery and the big bruiser saw you go inside. He wanted to barrel in right away and attack you, but the two smaller guys convinced him the Beacham Foundation would pay a ransom for you."

I snorted. Max pay a ransom for me. This I had to see to believe.

"The two guys admitted they were afraid when Jack and I fought back and the big guy walked away with Laurel. They'd wanted to stay with him, so he wouldn't hurt her. Their fighting with us was as much to get away and guard Laurel, as it was to take us out. Jack and I just hit harder."

"I think I prefer when my inconvenient heroes aren't part of a plot to kidnap me," I said.

"You mean you won't be a character witness at their trials?" Danny teased.

"Have them put me on the docket right behind yours and Jack's testimony."

The guys talked shop for a bit, and Clive followed every syllable. But the roadie did give me a soft elbow jab to get my attention and whispered, "You attacked their boss?"

I put my head next to his and said, "The guy abducted me. I tend to fight back when I'm taken against my will."

"Your life is never boring, is it?" he whispered, grinning.

Smiling back, I thought, you have no idea.

Clive returned to eavesdropping, and I leaned back in the seat and contemplated a little more about what Arlo said. How Melanie tried to hire an assassin to kill me at the request of someone else. It had to be Colle, even if Arlo hadn't named his client. Nico and I had already discussed the conversation and the implications when he drove me from Montmartre to the hotel earlier, and I knew he would start hacking on the Swiss clinic info as soon as possible—if he wasn't already. But was locating Colle's new profile enough? Could we even do it in time? How risky could it be for him if I testified that Ermo Colle and any new persona he used was actually the man I grew up thinking was my father? There was plenty of truly damning evidence if police could just lay hands on the man. My knowledge was probably more embarrassing than anything else. Except the Beacham family fortune vanished quicker than anyone imagined—he had markers to dozens of loan sharks and gambling dens when he supposedly skied off the mountainside and was presumably buried in the avalanche. Could he be afraid more that the police would come after him if I testified about what I knew? And how information about his past life could more greatly impact his future persona? How badly did he not want to be connected to his Beacham profile—not simply for the debts incurred, but because of the potential wrath of the crime bosses he swindled?

When we reached the airport, Clive took charge, easily cutting through any and all red tape and got us boarded hassle free. I'd watched him in action before and marveled at his talents. This time was no exception. We mostly slept on the return flight, which was kind of dumb on our parts since we gained five hours in the crossover. But as Jack said earlier, we all felt knackered. Emotional exhaustion if not the physical type.

Once we landed at JFK, Clive again got us through customs quickly and efficiently. He already had a hotel reservation and a limo waiting for him. Just before he left, he reached into the side pocket of his carryon and said, "The band will be back here for their New Jersey concert date in about a week. Take these passes in case you want to attend."

I took hold of the lanyards and added the passes to my Prada's treasure trove. "Thanks so much, Clive. We'll see what our schedules allow and let you know."

"And thanks again for inviting us to stowaway," Jack said.

Clive gave us an abbreviated salute, hefted his carryon, and headed for the limo line to find his newest driver.

Jack turned to me and said, "Airport Hilton?"

"Sounds perfect."

The next morning, we were up early and renting a car before dawn. I again cursed my idea for toting two bags. "I should have left the big one in Paris and told Nico to ship it back to London," I groused.

"You can freight it from here. All the big shipping companies have outposts at JFK."

"No, I've carried it this far, and it can stay in the trunk until we leave and have to turn in the car," I said, knowing I sounded contrary. "Just as sure as I get rid of it, I'll find an hour later there's something I need inside."

Thinking of using Nico to ship my bag reminded me I wanted to talk to him about the *Portrait of Three*, so I used the car as my mobile office. I looked at my watch and determined he was probably near a lunch break. My stomach rumbled at the thought. We hadn't stayed in Paris long enough to scratch my itch for French cuisine or all of the wonderful ethnic options in Montmartre and the Latin Quarter.

Nico answered on the third ring.

"Hey, is this a good time? Or should I call back later?" I asked.

"We can talk. I'm walking to meet Cassie for lunch."

"That's one of the reasons I'm calling. Can you please convince her to stay in Paris through the weekend? Or at least until Jack and I return to London?"

"Why?"

"Given what Arlo said, and the way we suddenly disappeared last night from the hotel and the city, I don't want Cassie in London by herself. It's too risky in case someone decides to try to get information from her."

"You think they believe the two of you returned to London?"

"Well, our names don't appear on any commercial passenger

manifest. Likely the moles that we know they have in law enforcement and intelligence circles could dig up how we left Paris, but it wouldn't be a quick and easy task."

"*Sì*, makes sense. I'll talk to her about this at lunch. If she stays on with her friend I'll change hotels, so I can be nearby."

"Thanks, Nico. One other thing. The night of the heist there was a large postcard in the safe advertising an art auction. There wasn't a name, date, or anything to help us know when or if the auction had already happened or if it was scheduled for a future time."

"Secret membership?"

"Maybe. Well...likely. But what I'm really interested in was the fact three paintings were featured exclusively on the postcard. It was the *Portrait of Three*."

Nico gave a low whistle. "Didn't you think Tony B had copies made?"

"Yes, but he was known for playing mind games. He said he'd brought them to Florence because the gallery owner wanted them for his personal collection, but he never clarified if what he brought were copies or the originals. We just know the originals were gone from his Miami office the next day. We also knew at the time the Florence gallery was funded by Ermo Colle, but we didn't know my connection to him then, just the name."

"Do you think the originals are for sale? Or a copy of each?"

"Again, I'm not sure. The photos were high def, and I looked for a visible forger's mark like Cassie found in the published book of art masterpieces. I couldn't see anything that sent up red flags."

"Why would he sell them?" Nico mused.

"Money? His competition with Moran must take huge regular outlays, and we've been getting more and more of his copies confiscated, so ready cash could be the best incentive. Plus, with Simon and Rollie having decimated the forger population, Colle has needed to constantly find and sign on new talent."

"That reminds me," he said. "The police acted on an anonymous tip and believe they have the person who shot Arlo."

"Do you think it's the real shooter?"

"Truthfully, no. I think he's taking the fall for someone else. His crimes before this consisted of petty thefts, and rumor has it the man has advanced cancer."

"He pleads guilty to get money for his family, and the real murderer is free to kill another day."

"My thoughts *essato*."

A car horn blasted through the phone, and when Nico came back on the line I said, "Tell me you didn't walk in front of a truck."

He laughed. "*Non*, just a crazy Parisian driver. These people make drivers in my home country look sane."

"Sane drivers in Italy? I don't think so."

"Point taken." He was still chuckling, but asked, "What do you want me to do about the paintings and the auction? Use the card to trace the printer? See if I can find who ordered them?"

"That's an idea. And if we can find the printer we may be able to learn if they used any kind of bulk mailing service and see who the cards were shipped to." This was opening up all kinds of new ideas, and I made a mental note to see if I could find a list of service businesses who did confidential mailings for clients like Colle. "I realize you can't do any of those things until we get the physical card to you, Nico. I was thinking that in the interim it might be worth it to see if there is any new chatter from our sources about a secret auction or the three paintings in the grouping."

"*Sì*, I can do that."

"But finding Colle's new look takes priority," I reminded.

TWENTY

The Friday morning rush was heavy, but since traffic isn't ever light in New York we moved about as fast as one could travel to exit the metro area. The ugly gray leftover snow from a couple of days before lined the roadway. It was cold, but at least we didn't have to deal with any precipitation. Another benefit: we drove the opposite direction from most of the workday vehicles. Bumper to bumper went out of the city, too, but our car did move markedly faster than those in the oncoming lanes. Our destination lay only about thirty miles north, but it still took us over an hour of drive time.

To me, Westchester County was beautiful year-round, but the hints of spring were everywhere, and Scarsdale was no different. Jack had agreed to meet the detective downtown, at the Village Center. The scenic town might have been well-funded and boasted all the amenities, but its downtown sector still resembled a kind of upscale Tudor village surrounded by parks and green spaces.

"Does it look any different since you left?" Jack asked, gliding into a parking space near a main street restaurant that was open and advertising breakfast.

"Scarsdale is like most towns. It updates, but never really changes," I said. "I have many good childhood memories of living here. Not so good after grandfather died and his son started his wastrel campaign to reduce the family holdings to penury status."

Jack raised an eyebrow, and I added, "I know, that sounded over the top. But it feels better when the fall of the Beacham fortune sounds like something you'd read in a reference book, rather than the hard-luck tale of my personal history. You can't really be poor and live in Scarsdale. At least, I couldn't. Give me my scholastic illusions."

"Paint your story any way you prefer," he said, chuckling.

We went inside, and Jack texted the detective that we'd arrived. We each ordered all-American breakfasts of eggs, toast, hash browns, and bacon. He added a short stack of pancakes too, but I'd never been a pancake-eating girl. The best part was the way the waitress never let my coffee cup get empty.

Our plates were taken away just as a white-haired, smiling man arrived at the door with a younger brunette woman, obviously his daughter, pushing his wheelchair. One of the waitresses opened the door and welcomed them. When the man asked something, the waitress bent down to listen, then pointed toward our table. Jack jumped up to move away one of the chairs and make room for the wheelchair.

I stood and held out a hand, "Detective Harmon, thank you so much for meeting with us. I'm Laurel Beacham."

He grabbed my hand in both of his. "It's nice to meet you. I'd know you anywhere. You look just like your mother."

"This means a lot, Detective Harmon."

"You can call me Doug. It's been ten years since I was Detective Harmon."

"But he's still everyone's first call when they have a problem to solve," his daughter said, smiling and resting a hand on her father's shoulder.

When he let go of my hand to shake Jack's, she stepped up and introduced herself, "Hello, I'm Joanne Kocourek. I'm Doug's daughter, but I wanted to meet you because I was a nurse in the hospital when they brought in your mother."

"Wow! Really? Thank you for being part of the team who worked so hard for her." I felt tears in my eyes.

She leaned over and grabbed a couple of napkins from the silver holder in the middle of the table and pressed them into my hands. "She fought hard. I remember your grandmother sneaking you into the ICU, so you could sing to try to make her better. I can still close my eyes and see you singing."

"I'd forgotten all about that. I remember being so worried because there was a big plastic tube thing in her mouth, and I thought that was why she couldn't open her eyes and smile at me." I wiped away a tear. "That was the last time I saw her until the funeral."

Joanne pulled out a chair and motioned for me to sit down, then took the remaining chair adjacent to mine. Jack and Detective Harmon were already going over data in the files. The pages were photocopies, and I could tell some of the originals had been carbonless multipage documents and were a little harder to read in the black and white form, but the detective seemed to know all of it by heart.

"I never believed that one-car-accident verdict, but we couldn't get enough evidence for anyone to press charges."

The waitress brought two fresh cups of coffee and refilled Jack's and mine. A minute later she brought over a basket of mini muffins. Doug gave a shout of thanks.

"We appreciate this, Vicki," Joanne said.

Walking around Doug to give him a one-armed hug, Vicki said, "Have to keep my favorite customers happy."

Doug's files were thorough. When it looked like crime scene pictures were coming, I excused myself, "Have to go powder my nose." I waited about ten minutes before returning. There were close up photos of car parts, witness statements, and even interview transcripts lying around the table, but it looked like I missed what would have been upsetting to hear and see. I let the sound of the talk wash over me and contemplated what I'd said last night to Jack. Now that I was here and faced with the facts, the ratio was more fifty-fifty, though my not wanting to meet with Max when I came to New York still took a slight lead.

I thought back a couple of decades to that day in the ICU. Grandmamma wasn't fooling anyone, obviously, but at the time I thought we were accomplishing the best kind of stealth. I saw my mother and put my hand on her arm, planning to shake it to try and wake her, except the many I.V. lines frightened me, and I was afraid my doing so would hurt her. That's when Grandmamma suggested I sing a song. I sang "Twinkle, Twinkle Little Star" because it was one my mother and I often sang together. I sang it over and over until I started to cry. That was the last time I sang those words. I couldn't even sing the alphabet song in kindergarten because it used the same tune.

The next piece of evidence Doug pulled out and unfolded was a large-scale map. It showed the area's topography and natural structures around Scarsdale. He'd made endless notes and small sketched drawings on the page. He showed us where my mother's car apparently began having difficulty in slowing down or stopping and the route she traveled, her speed more than twice what the safety limit was on the curvy road. Finally, the spot where her car sped so fast it hurdled the tall rocky outcropping, went over the top, and hit a huge pine tree on the down side of the hill.

Because the rocks didn't show her tire marks, no one realized her car was wrecked on the other side. It was hours before a couple of hikers found her and called for emergency crews. The medical team fought to save her, and Joanne patted my arm as her father and Jack talked, telling me how people still remembered my mother. But she never woke up. She'd lost too much blood. It had taken too long to get her to the hospital.

The detective's words caught my attention again when he spoke about the scene. "Your grandfather hired demolition guys to come in and blow up that rocky hill," he said. "Made it a straight view from the road to the green fields beyond. Now, of course, some developer went in and filled up the field below with houses." He shook his head and drank from his cup.

Doug had copies of everything in his files so Jack and I could take the evidence back with us.

This has definitely been a week for files from the past, I thought.

We stayed through the lunch hour, and I ate the best meatloaf I'd had in years, along with loaded mashed potatoes and brown gravy. I wanted to pack a suitcase full of nothing but the yeast rolls. I loved traveling around the world with my job, but at that exact moment I realized I really wanted roots. No, I didn't want to come back to Scarsdale permanently, but I was ready to get a place of my own. With my own furniture and my own alarm system. Maybe learn to cook more than scrambled eggs. I couldn't play tagalong with Cassie forever. She'd already set the pace and I needed to learn to keep up.

When we left, we carried go-bowls of cherry pie, because even I couldn't find room to eat it. I hugged Doug Harmon goodbye and thanked him again for his help. While he and Jack traded last stories, I walked over to Joanne.

"He's a very special man, your dad," I said.

"I know," she said. "He's never let this one go. No matter how much evidence he brought in, the case was turned away."

"You think the DA or someone higher up was bought off?"

She shrugged. "I know it kept Dad up nights, trying to figure out another strategy. Another way to deliver a fact no one could misconstrue or deny. I was surprised when he said Jack contacted him about the case. Dad was surprised, too, but happy the case was getting reexamined. We all figured once your father died in that skiing accident everything was over."

"Yes," I said, trying to smile effortlessly, but knowing I wasn't succeeding. "Life is funny. Sometimes the things you think are over are only on hiatus."

She stared at me for several seconds, then said, "I think you want to tell me something, but you can't. You know, if you ever need to talk, there are counselors who want to listen, and are ethically bound not to let the words go past the office door." She pointed at Jack. "And see those files under his arm? I put my address and phone number inside the green one. I'm never more than a phone call away. You're never alone."

I chewed my lower lip for a second, then got my mouth working in a real smile. "Thank you, Joanne. I was honestly afraid about what this day would bring up and what cracks it would make in the armor I'd built around myself. But I'm leaving here feeling stronger than I felt even an hour ago. Thank you, and please thank your father for me."

She pulled me into a goodbye hug and I think we both shed a few tears.

"Are you going to drive by your family's old home?" she asked.

"I don't think I want to," I said. "I'd rather keep it in my mind the way I remember the place."

"I can understand that," she said.

Jack was pushing the wheelchair out to the sidewalk while Joanne followed him and I brought up the rear. He turned his head and gave me a raised eyebrow. I smiled, and he turned back around, heading for the SUV that Doug pointed to down the block.

"I do wish I could talk to my old nanny," I said. "She got married and moved away about fifteen years ago."

Joanne stopped. "Do you mean Kelly Hobbs?"

"Yes. Did you know her?"

"Of course. We're friends. She moved back three years ago."

I set the pie containers on the hood of our rental car and asked, "Can I find her today?"

"In about thirty seconds," Joanne said. "She works a couple of doors down. Follow me."

I forgot about Jack and Doug, and the fact they probably didn't know why we were heading the opposite way. All I could focus on was seeing Kelly again.

The business was a delivery dinner service, with food prep employees working at stainless counters and appliances while they chopped, cooked, and packaged up food specialties. Joanne led me to the office and knocked on the doorframe. "Hey, Kelly, I have someone here who would like to say hello to you."

"Who?"

I heard the voice and knew immediately. Joanne stepped aside and waved me in. When Kelly saw me, she covered her mouth with her hands, burst into tears and pulled me into a hug. "Oh, Laurel, honey, I've thought of you so often."

Joanne spoke up then, "Well, I'll leave you two. I need to get back to Dad."

I pulled out of my hug with Kelly and gave Joanne another quick one. "Thank you so much, Joanne, for everything you've done. You made a special day even more special."

Kelly and I sat on the sofa in her office and fired questions and answers at one another. She'd moved back after her husband passed away because she still had so many friends in the area. She'd trained police recruits in hand-to-hand combat for a while, and admitted she had the martial arts training I'd had my suspicions about. But when she got tired of not knowing how to cook the food she really wanted to eat or was too exhausted to try, and saw so many people like herself eating unhealthy meals they took from the grocery freezer, she opened this storefront business. She now had two dozen employees.

"I just take the money and keep the books, and I leave with delicious meals that are foolproof every time," she said.

"What a great story."

"And the best part is I can employ moms who just need part-time positions too," she explained, brushing her bangs aside with one hand. "We have three full-time positions shared by six part-time employees. As one leaves, the other takes the station and finishes the day. I love giving women flexibility."

"So, no more training police for martial arts?"

"I lead tai chi every morning in the park for a crowd of about thirty. But no more aggressive training. I work out to keep my skills, but that's all." She raised her hands to encompass her business. "This place keeps me busy enough."

She asked about my career. She'd followed my name when she caught it in the papers but wasn't sure exactly what I did. I honestly would have loved to tell her everything—I doubted she'd be frightened to hear it, but I imagined it would worry her—so I gave her the *Readers' Digest* condensed version I relied on when I was afraid I might say too much.

When I finished, I said, "I don't want to put you on the spot, but I'd really like to know exactly why my grandparents hired you, given the training you had. I've been putting some memories together lately. Having known your skill in martial arts, and the fact I received Bruno our German shepherd about the same time...well...Were you really hired as my nanny?" Then I stated what I really felt, "Or my bodyguard."

"I always knew you were sharp," she said. She looked away for a moment as if deciding what to say. When she turned back, there was something in her eyes that told me she'd made peace with whatever it was. "I've never tried to get between someone and their family. But I always wondered why your grandmother hired me too. I had no nanny training, just experience being an older sister with younger siblings. But she got my contact information from a friend and came to see me. Gave me this song and dance about how she was frightened you might get kidnapped. Asked me to come and just see if I liked the job. No pressure."

She got up and walked over to a bookcase and removed a framed picture to hand to me. I was small, looking even smaller from the weighty expression on my face as I held a wildflower in my hands. Kelly was kneeled down beside me in the shot, looking at me but pointing to the camera. I could still hear the words she'd said that day, trying to coax a smile from me.

"That was you and me the first month I began working for your family," she said, pointing to our images in the picture. "Your mother had just died, your father was barely around, and when he was, your grandmother watched his every move. And you were the sweetest, saddest little thing I'd ever seen. You missed your mother so much. I remember lying on the bed and holding you as you said prayers and asked for the angels to let your mother come back. I was hooked. I had to stay and help you smile again. Then I had to stay to help you laugh again. Then I had to stay because I didn't want to leave."

"Thank you." I stood and walked over to return the frame to its shelf. "I can honestly say that most of the best memories of my childhood included you. I'm so glad you decided to stay, Kelly."

"Me, too, honey."

We talked a bit more, then I looked at my watch and realized I'd left Jack to fend for himself for nearly an hour without even letting him know where I was going.

"Don't worry, I'm sure Joanne told him," Kelly said, placing a comforting hand on my arm. She rose and moved to her desk, plucking a business card from a standing holder. "Here's my address, phone, email, Skype, Facebook, Twitter, Instagram, you name it," she said, smiling. "Let's keep in touch, okay?"

I pulled one of my own cards from the Prada and swapped it for hers. "Definitely. It's been so good to catch up with you. I guess the only person I haven't talked to is Dexter, our chauffeur. I still smile when I think about him saving *Mad Magazine* for me each month, so I could fold up the back cover and see the secret picture."

Kelly shook her head and crossed her arms. "I don't know what happened to Dex. Even after I moved we kept in touch. For a while, he worried he'd lose his job after your grandfather died, but the last time we talked he was so excited. Said your father suddenly offered him free dental insurance. Dex had a toothache, and your dad said that was the worst kind of pain, and he should have offered dental coverage years ago. Your dad made an appointment for Dex right then with his own dentist and told whoever he was talking to on the phone to get Dex fixed up with all the crowns he needed to keep him from having to get dentures. I still remember the excitement in Dexter's voice when he told me. Repeated the conversations word for word. Made me glad your dad was so unexpectedly thoughtful because Dex would have just lived with the pain otherwise."

"Do you know when this was?" I asked, getting a funny feeling in my stomach.

"Maybe a month before your father was reported missing in the avalanche," Kelly said. "I remember thinking how lucky it was that Dexter received his dental work when he did. Your father said he was keeping Dex on for some kind of special project that was going to turn around the family's bottom line. This was at a time money was already getting tight after your grandfather's death, so the news sounded especially hopeful."

"That's very interesting," I said, smiling despite my desire to scream. "Do you remember Dexter saying anything about the special project?"

"Just that he had to go to Europe a couple of times a year with your father. I figure he got a job over there after your father was killed."

"I'll have to see if Jack and I can find him," I said, though I knew how unlikely it was.

We said our goodbyes and promised to keep in touch, and I returned to find the car empty. I looked around and saw Jack sitting on a bench in the park across the street. I walked over and asked, "Hey, is this seat available to rude girlfriends who run off and leave you in a strange town?"

"Absolutely." He grinned up at me. "I've already had to run off three other rude girlfriends to make sure it was available for you."

His arm was stretched across the back of the bench, so I sat close and rested my head on his shoulder.

"Did you enjoy your reunion with Kelly?" he asked.

"Yes." I sighed and watched a chipmunk scamper across the lawn. When the critter disappeared in taller grass, I said, "I'm pretty sure I know who was actually killed in the mountain avalanche too."

He turned so he could look at me. "Who?"

I relayed the story Kelly told me about Dexter. The surprise dental gift. The special project requiring he travel to Europe.

"I don't know if my father bought off the dentist or the receptionist, but I figure one of them switched the chauffeur's dental records for those of my father."

"That would work."

"Dexter told Kelly my father said to get any amount of crown work needed to keep from him having to get dentures."

"Because dentures would render the chauffeur an unsuitable candidate," Jack mused.

"Yep."

"I'm sorry. I know you wanted to know who it was, but I never imagined it would be someone close to you."

"Amazing how whatever I learn, Daddy Dearest continues to disappoint."

TWENTY-ONE

The only other person I'd wanted to try to see was Mrs. Conner, a woman who had two original paintings of which forged copies of the works ended up in a coffee table art book Cassie discovered last Christmas when visiting her aunt. My desire to see her was actually a fishing expedition to test a theory. I hadn't really needed to meet with Mrs. Conner about her art, Cassie and Nico had already done so in January, but I wanted to see if there was a reaction when she saw me in person. So many people had told me recently how much I looked like my late mother, and what I wanted to know from Mrs. Conner was if she knew my family. In particular, whether my father could have gained access to her Central Park apartment and art collection.

However, as we motored back into the city, I phoned and was told by the maid that Mrs. Conner was at her home in Bermuda. Nope, I wasn't planning on heading south. Besides, with all the mounting evidence we'd been gathering for months, plus the answers I'd learned from Arlo based on the questions he wouldn't answer, the evidence was stacking up solidly to back up my team's hypotheses regarding the number of crimes to be laid at the Moran organization's feet or which were high treason art crimes by Ermo Colle. Meeting with Mrs. Conner would simply offer additional confirmation to give me peace of mind. It wasn't crucial and wouldn't change the plan. We needed to get Colle's new identity, turn everything over to law enforcement so he could be arrested, and let the legal system dismantle all facets of his operation.

I thanked the maid and said I'd try to see Mrs. Conner in the future, when she and I were both in New York at the same time.

"So back to London?" Jack asked. "Or do you want to spend a couple of days enjoying a little R&R touring New York before Max learns you're here in the States?"

"I think you know the answer to that."

"You want to get home because you're worried about Cassie and Nico."

I smiled and didn't answer for a second. "Yes, I want to go home. And yes, I want to know Cassie and Nico are safe."

"What was the hesitation?"

The sky had been clouding up ever since we'd left Scarsdale, and I hoped we could get out of town before any bad weather struck. My brain was feeling equally cloudy. I removed my shades and dropped them into my purse. "No hesitation. Just a little tired."

We hit a light, and he put his hand on my thigh. I looked over at him.

"You don't have to tell me now if you don't want to," he said. "Wait until you're ready."

"It's not anything really." I shrugged. The light turned green and we continued moving. "I just kind of decided during this trip I want to find some place to live that truly is mine. No more hotel rooms. It's time to set down some roots."

"That's a big step."

"I think I'm ready," I said, then grinned. "Besides, it gives me lots of new shopping options since I'll have to furnish the place."

"I have little doubt," Jack said. He had his phone mounted to the dash and the GPS guided us along the way.

"Which airport are we flying out of?" I asked.

"While I waited for you and Kelly to get reacquainted, I checked airline availability on my mobile and found LaGuardia gave us better options tonight."

"So that whole line earlier about a weekend of R&R..."

"I knew you wouldn't go for it," he said. "Besides, Danny's getting bogged down in work requests, and it might be a good idea for me to go in and try to do some video back-checking on the

Amazon's route myself. If we wait much longer it may not even be worth the trouble."

"You're right. You talked to Danny?"

"Nothing as good as what he told us last night, but he's keeping me updated. They still haven't found Jacqueline Baroux, but having her real name is giving Inspector Markham a little more direction. I gave them Moran's former address in Mayfair, but I figure she's already out of Great Britain. Took too long for us to know about her."

An airport sign flashed up ahead. I pointed. "Thank goodness, we'll be out of this car soon."

"Getting tired of car travel?" he asked.

"To be honest, after this week I'm getting tired of travel period—Paris yesterday, New York today, London by morning because of the time change—I may sleep for a week."

He raised an eyebrow. "Not a bad idea."

Two seats were available in business class on a flight leaving in an hour and a half. We checked our bags, so only the Prada had to get past security. After we made it through the line and gained directions to our gate from one of the TSA agents, we arrived at check-in with just minutes to spare.

I was about to put my phone in airplane mode when it rang. "It's Nico." I answered. "Hi, we're just about to take off for London."

"Okay, great." He sounded absentminded. "I've gained some information on Colle's new look."

No wonder he sounded like he wasn't listening to me. "Do you have it in email form yet?"

"I will soon. I may have more by the time you land."

"I'll look for it then. But remember that it's middle of the night in Paris now. Don't work twenty-four seven. Max won't pay overtime."

He blew out a long breath. "Don't I know it. I already have

Cassie acting like she's my mother. I don't need it from you too."

"She's also telling you to get some sleep?"

"Women," he said, and hung up.

"What was that?" Jack asked.

"Nico's tired of people telling him to take care of himself." I turned on airplane mode and stuffed the phone into its pocket in my Prada. "But the reason he called is that he's broken the code on the new identity for you know who and will have material emailed to us by the time we land."

I pulled my coat over my arms like a blanket. "It's okay to wake me for dinner, but otherwise I need to sleep."

Plane noise and food woke me up a couple of times, but otherwise the flight was uneventful. We landed at Heathrow at half-past it's-too-damn-early, and I woke up enough to negotiate my way out of the plane and into the airport. By the time we'd found our bags and cleared customs, I was exhausted again.

"I think I need a roadie slash travel-sherpa like Clive full-time," I said. "Travel was so much easier when he took care of everything."

Jack laughed. "Sure. Take that up with Max during your next conference call regarding budget issues."

"Spoil sport."

We almost got on the train before Jack remembered he'd driven there, which meant we had to schlep our bags to long-term parking. The dark morning was cold, and mist was falling. I missed the spring preview I'd had in Paris...was it really only a day ago?

"Are you going home with me? Or am I dropping you at Cassie's?" he asked.

"When I drop these bags, I may never pick them up again, so take me to Cassie's, please."

When we arrived at her flat, he came in with my luggage and we discussed what we were going to do with the information we'd gained in the New York fly-by. I found most of a bottle of good wine in the refrigerator and carried it and two glasses into the lounge. Jack already had the files out on the table, including the copy of the file we'd found in Simon's desk, and he was rereading the email attachments Nico sent while we flew home. He tossed my phone onto the table and held the glasses while I poured the chardonnay.

"There's plenty of material in Doug's files to make a case for your mother's murder," Jack said, nodding toward the small stack of files on the coffee table. "We can get Colle held on the murder charge while a multi-country task force has the time needed to pull down his organization—both art forgery and import/export business.

"What would I need to do to get things started? Or does that have to come out of law enforcement, too?"

Jack picked up my phone from the table and reread the email Nico sent with Beacham/Colle's new identity. "Even without knowing his new name, we can turn this and Simon's original information over to the New York State Police and ask the Westchester prosecutor to file charges for your mother's death."

"Can I do that by phone or email?"

"I'll talk to my solicitor in the morning...well, later," Jack said, looking at his watch. "See what the procedure is exactly. Unless, of course, you want to go through the foundation's lawyer."

I shook my head. "Not while there's a high risk that Daddy Dearest has a mole in the foundation. I don't want him learning what we're doing and disappearing again. Just go ahead and have your lawyer start doing whatever needs to be done."

"Probably a letter to start." He took another sip of wine.

"Okay. Tell him to bill me. I guess give him the office address."

Jack snapped his fingers. "That reminds me. I need to call the security company and see whether they sorted the problem about the keypad or the lock. Find out what alternatives they have for us too."

We added another couple of tasks for our individual to-do lists, then finished off the wine. But as we headed to bed I came to a decision I'd been weighing ever since Jack mentioned going to his lawyer.

"When you get the job started with your solicitor regarding the letter asking for prosecution, could he also get a DNA test run on me to compare with the hair in the file?"

Jack stopped and leaned on the doorframe. I turned and met his gaze. "You're sure?" he asked.

"I think so." I sighed. "I may not open the envelope with the results right away, but I need them available when I'm ready."

He pulled me into a hug and spoke into my hair. "We can do this ourselves. I'll grab a swab kit and get your sample, then we'll send it and the hair off to see if they match."

A lump in my throat kept me from saying thank you, so I nodded into his chest instead.

When we woke a few hours later, we found Nico had apparently worked all night, because he now had a fresh alias to go with Beacham/Colle's new look. Albert Bentley. Daddy Dearest was trying to do the full Brit this time around.

Jack called his solicitor. The lawyer said to meet him at the office and bring the files he needed.

I forwarded Jack all my emails from Nico about the new persona, so he'd have them handy on his phone, and he headed out the door. I watched from the window as he drove away and had a sudden feeling of calm. I knew what I had to do.

Despite my resolve, I spent almost a minute staring at my phone. This request was one I never dreamed I'd make, and I wondered what kind of reaction I'd receive. A swipe at the top of the contacts screen took me to the right number. Well, the number necessary to start this quest. He picked up after two rings.

"Nico, I need you to find a way for me to contact Moran."

His reply was a choking sound, followed by, "What? Am I dreaming?"

"I don't know," I said. "You just emailed me ten minutes ago, so I assumed you were still awake. But if you heard me say I need to contact Moran, you heard correctly. I need to talk to him and there isn't time to do it via any roundabout ways on my own. I need you to hack, bribe or plead the information out of someone. I'll be doing the same with my own resources."

"Why?"

"Do you really need to know?"

"Does Jack?"

"Not yet."

"Are you going to tell him?"

"I'm not sure."

"Then, *sì*, I need to know. I'm not doing this if you're the only person holding all the cards and Moran is involved."

I stared unseeing out the front curtains. This wasn't something I actually wanted anyone privy to, but I could trust Nico. He might still try to talk me out of it, but I could trust him not to judge me or try to thwart my plan.

"We found out my mother was murdered. The evidence in the files prove everyone knew it at the time, but...someone...someone probably in my family...likely bribed someone high enough to not get the case tried."

"Ermo Colle? Or, I guess now I should say Albert Bentley?"

"Yes. Except to be more precise, he still used the Beacham name then." At least I hoped he was the one doing the bribing. I didn't want to think anyone further up the family tree was responsible for the cover-up that made sure a murderer went unpunished. "And since the M.O. matches the way Moran's brother died—"

"Paul-Henrì."

"Again, yes. It's not a stretch to assume Beacham/Colle was responsible for both 'accidents.' Especially since everyone I talked to in Scarsdale has always thought he had my mother killed. The assumption wasn't that he did it himself. He hired someone. But he murdered her, Nico."

"*Sì*. Are you contacting Moran to inform him, or—"

"It's a...courtesy call. That's probably the best name for what I'm doing at this point. I want him to know what information is getting turned over to international authorities. Jack is with his solicitor now, who will notify the New York State Police, and we'll make sure they have everything we have that they need. I also have a probable name for the body used to help Colle disappear ten years ago."

"When he faked his death with an avalanche?"

"Exactly," I said. "If Swiss authorities exhume that body, there's a high possibility they'll be able to identify the victim as our family chauffeur Dexter. I can also prove how the body was erroneously identified without anyone the wiser. And Jack's lawyer will write a letter on my behalf saying in no uncertain terms that I want Daddy Dearest prosecuted for my mother's death, and for the death of Dexter as well. I'll look to see if I can find family for Dexter, but I don't remember any in all the years I knew him. In the meantime, I'll ask that Dexter's death be charged as a homicide. I think I can do so through New York, so it can tie to my mother's case since that was his state of legal residency. But even if it must start by going through Swiss courts, the prosecution should be able to cite Dexter's death when prosecuting for my mother's murder—and show the duplicity of the accused. The prosecution can charge him under Beacham, Colle, the new name you found—Bentley—or any other aliases he's used in the present or past. I don't know how quickly anyone will respond, but in case Moran wants to...mete out his own justice a little sooner...I want to let him know."

"You want Moran to have him killed."

"I want a fair and just outcome for the murders. I know if the authorities catch him and arrest him and try him, I will get that. But history makes me worry. Unless Moran steps in too, a murder charge will only be for my mother and possibly Dexter. Not Paul-Henri. Giving a heads up before Colle is tracked down and arrested gives Moran a bit of latitude. Besides, as long as Colle is free, I'll have a target on my back. I want him caught quickly, as much to save myself as to make sure justice is done for all the deaths. If Moran finds him first, I'm certain he will bring in a lawyer to furnish the necessary evidence to charge Colle in this third murder, or...he can handle things in a less conventional way."

"You know what Rollie would choose."

"Yes, the Amazon. That's why I want to talk to Moran instead. I prefer the kind of outcome where Colle has years in prison to think about his crimes."

"Are you saying you don't want Colle killed?"

"As I said, I want justice. If he's tried and convicted for my mother's murder, he should receive the punishment he deserves. But even in a perfect world...Sometimes we need to make sure there's backup. I want all parties to have enough information to not only catch him, but hold him, and put him away for the rest of his life."

"Which means a race to see who collars Colle first, the cops or the criminals."

"Or Jack and me. Just because we've found the answer, it doesn't mean the problem is resolved."

"You really need to stay out of this, Laurel. This could bring long-term problems if you do anything...off the books."

"I won't kill him, Nico. At least, not on purpose. I save and recover art. I catch crooks and turn them over to the authorities. That's all I intend to do here, find the truly crooked art criminal and turn him in. The path toward the murder convictions will already be in play by the end of the day. I won't be involved other than passing along information."

Nico gave a long sigh over the phone line. "Okay. This shouldn't take long. I still have a couple of options from when I hacked Rollie's guys' phones in Barcelona. It may not be a direct number, but I can find a connection and get back to you soon. Don't make any other phone calls until I see what I can find. The less anyone else knows about you talking to Moran, the better it sounds."

I walked into the kitchen and grabbed the burner phone I'd used a couple of days before to connect with Jack. "If you can't get a direct number for Moran, leave this number and ask him to call me." I rattled off the digits.

"Is this a burner?"

"Yes. I wasn't planning on calling Moran on my line anyway. I think it's safer if I don't leave a digital trail."

"Ahh, you've learned well, Grasshopper."

I couldn't help it, I laughed. *The Karate Kid* reference, coupled with seeing Kelly again yesterday, was too much.

Nico broke my good mood, asking, "What if he calls when Jack is around?"

"If you're as fast as you claim to be, Moran should get the message before Jack returns from seeing the solicitor. I have Cassie's flat to myself until then."

"Guess I'd better get to work," Nico replied and hung up.

TWENTY-TWO

After talking with Nico, I decided to vary my plan a bit. Because of Melanie having tried to hire a hitman to kill me, and the three goons at the National Gallery whose plan had been to use attempted ransom to avenge their boss, Colle was still a menace to me. However, I needed to make sure I didn't look like the person turning him over to anyone. I didn't want any other henchmen to concoct future revenge plots against me.

Plus, it didn't feel right making it super easy for Moran.

I still felt I needed to give Moran the information, as much for self-defense for myself as justice for his brother—and my possible father. Only DNA testing with Paul-Henrì's relatives would let me know that for sure. And I wasn't about to ask.

When Jack sent the electronic copies of Simon's file to Nico a couple of days ago, he'd cc'd me as well. I pulled up the email on Cassie's laptop and downloaded the image files to a flash drive, then I slipped the drive back into its tiny hinged case.

The phone call came twenty minutes later. Nico was even better than I'd thought.

A voice with a Continental accent I recognized said, "I was given this number, am I speaking to—?"

"Yes, Moran, it's me."

I spent a good five minutes telling him a lot of what we'd learned lately, and the risk I saw for Beacham/Colle not being prosecuted for the murder of Moran's brother unless steps were taken soon. I didn't give Moran the new identity Nico found this morning. That was part of my plan to at least try to play fair with law enforcement. Jack was offering everything. I was simply offering what was in Simon's file. Minus the DNA evidence, of course.

"So, that's the deal. I give you the flash drive with information to use in locating Colle's new name and face, while law enforcement is looking for him as well. If you decide you want to prosecute, I'll make sure you have evidence from my mother's case that could be useful in tying her murder to your brother's."

"And if I decide not to prosecute?"

I knew he was baiting me. He wanted to see how far I would go.

"We're not playing this game, Moran. If you choose not to prosecute, you don't need the Scarsdale material. And if you aren't interested in finding Colle—"

"*Non. Attendez.* I'm sorry, wait...wait a moment."

I got a mental picture of him using his hands to make a calming motion as he spoke. The line was quiet for a short time.

"I would like the material you have to help find Colle's new persona," he said, finally. "I believe it would be in all our best interests for him to be arrested on a number of charges. Not the least of which is attempted murder of you."

"Yes, I'm aware of that recent risk, and it's part of the reason we're working so hard to get enough material for law enforcement to make a case. We're also working with other countries' art task forces for the same reason because you're correct, there are many ways he can be charged. However, his risk to me is no different from that of the redhead who works for your grandson, and who stole everything she could out of my office a couple of days ago. And my packed luggage from my hotel suite when she left behind a dead body."

"She'd come to protect you. She killed the woman who went to your room to kill you. She knew the woman was a threat."

"But the redhead had the telescoping baton handy to kill Melanie in my room. That was the only weapon on the scene."

"The baton arrived with the victim. The redhead, as you call her, entered your room after the drunken woman went inside. This, Melanie, tried to attack, and our woman took away her baton and hit her instead."

"Multiple times in the head," I said.

"Her anger was unleashed," Moran replied.

I thought back to his previous statement. Our woman, he'd said. This was the first absolute confirmation the Amazon was part of Moran's organization.

But he had more to explain. I said, "The redhead had a gun when she came to my office. Why was she armed if she was there to protect me?"

"She always has at least one weapon, usually more. She heard about the attempted abduction in the museum and realized your young man wasn't enough protection. She went to your office intending to move you to a safer environment. Per our instructions."

"Then why didn't she knock?"

"She didn't believe you'd open the door for her. There's evidence, she knows, about some of her previous...work...and she wanted to get close enough to communicate more personally."

I wasn't gullible enough to completely believe him, but it all made a weird sense when coupled with everything that happened whenever I was near a Moran associate in the past. I shook my head in frustration, disbelief—who knew. "Tell her thanks, but I'm picky about wanting to only use my own bodyguards. Please tell her I prefer to see her as my enemy for the time being. Or at least a disinterested party. Too many people have switched sides on me lately and I'm getting a little dizzy trying to keep up. Besides, she may be quite busy soon defending herself for the murder of Melanie Weems."

"I doubt very much that she's concerned."

"They've found evidence an auburn-haired assassin was in the room with the murder victim."

"Maybe they have, maybe they haven't. But she was only there because Melanie came to kill you when you returned that night.

She'd taken a job as a maid in your hotel a few days before, to keep an eye on you."

"There were no redheads—"

"She wore a wig while she worked. Very easy to change one's looks that way. I understand even you have done that on occasion."

Huh. He was trying to sidetrack me. Stay focused, Beacham, I thought. Now I had a hit woman turning maid-bodyguard, and a former art museum director murdered because she couldn't find a hitman and decided to kill me herself. But it was his casual tone about the evidence that I addressed.

"Are you telling me the crime scene evidence has been taken by one of your moles in London law enforcement?" I asked.

"I believe small items like that strand of hair get misfiled quite easily. Of course, I have no idea if it has happened this time. I simply wanted to bring up the possibility, you understand."

I rolled my eyes. "The fact you already know about the hair evidence, and informants have come into the conversation—"

"I believe you brought that topic to the floor, *mademoiselle*."

"Be that as it may, I'm going to be giving you exclusive intel on a flash drive, and I want to make sure the information isn't accidentally leaked to someone affiliated with Colle. Please choose carefully who you assign for this sensitive hacking job."

"I understand your concerns."

Then, while I seemed to have the upper hand, I delivered the pièce de résistance. "You might also want to start double checking the information of whichever mole told you about the recent hopes for recovering the Rodin bust for the British government from the Russian official living temporarily in Knightsbridge. If someone had spent a little time double-checking that intel, your granddaughter wouldn't have had to lug around a forgery by a metal expert from Paris as she ran from the police."

Moran sucked in a breath.

Bingo, I thought. I knew I wasn't being completely fair denigrating his informant that way, since we hadn't known it was a fake either until I cracked the safe. But I'd wanted a reaction, and I scored this time. I started to mention that she didn't look anything like Rollie, but I hesitated pushing my luck.

"Also, that particular forger was killed in Montmartre a couple of days ago. I'd thought the forger wars were over when Simon...stopped."

"I get your point, and I will see what I can do."

"Thank you. There have been far too many deaths." I pulled a pad of paper and a pen from my Prada. "Back to the business of getting this flash drive to you. Where can I mail it?"

"I think a dead drop would be a preferable method in this case. Perhaps attached to the bottom of a bench?"

"Sounds doable." I pulled the package of super strong adhesive pads from my purse that I used to leave listening transmitters when I needed to unobtrusively keep tabs on people.

He gave me a location in St. James Park near the playground and asked if I could manage the drop within the hour.

"I can probably make it in half an hour. Tell your pickup person I'll try to leave it under the seat on the north side of the bench. It will just be the little plastic case, not an envelope or anything large that could be spotted by a passerby."

We rang off, and I changed into jeans and a sweater, then shrugged into Cassie's purple hoodie. It was raining again, but with the hood up and an umbrella, I figured on staying fairly dry. Into various pockets, I distributed my phone, key ring, wallet, the flash drive and the pads I'd use to attach it to the bench. The burner phone went into a back pocket, so I could grab it quickly and toss it away when I noticed a handy trash bin. I left the Prada behind. I'd have to hurry and get back since Jack didn't have a key to the door and I didn't need anything slowing me down.

I bought a paper from the news agent on the corner and tucked it under my arm. The Tube was packed with people set to enjoy their weekend, rain or no rain. I got off at the stop for St. James Park and strode Birdcage Walk to get to the rendezvous point. Buckingham Palace stood in the distance, majestic even in the drizzly gray day.

The bench I needed was in sight while I was still under my half-hour goal. No children were in the playground at the moment, so I had no competition for the spot. I sat on the folded newspaper and clamped my umbrella between my torso and left elbow, so I could leave both hands free to work inside the big front pocket of the hoodie. It may have looked like I was watching people walk their dogs, and kids jump in puddles—in fact, I hoped it looked exactly like that was all I was doing. My hands were busy, however, removing a couple of the super sticky pads and affixing them to the small plastic square case. Getting the thin plastic off the adhesive sides was always tricky without looking, but I'd had plenty of practice, and today's task wasn't under a time limit like I usually had when I did this kind of thing blind.

All set, I held the readied case in my pocket with my right hand, careful of the adhesive, and withdrew my left hand again to hold the umbrella. I looked around at the people in the park, trying to determine who would be coming by for the flash drive. There were more people than I'd expected for a rainy day, but it was a Saturday after all. Dogs still needed to be walked, and the Brits truly enjoyed their park strolls. I looked at my watch and prepared to go, letting my right hand grab the front slat of the bench as I rose, firmly attaching the flash drive underneath. I picked up my paper, folded it again, wet side together, tucked it under my arm and walked away.

I felt like a spy, making deals with the enemy for the greater good. At the next bin I spotted, I tossed the burner phone.

TWENTY-THREE

Jack had his phone out when Cassie's building came into view, and he sheltered under the porch overhang. My phone rang a second later.

"Hello?" I said, grinning as I walked down the sidewalk. His attention remained fixed on the front door.

"Can you come and let me in?"

"It'll be a minute."

"All right?"

"Everything's fine." Except you may want to kill me when I've admitted what I just did, I thought.

"Come on down when you're free," he said and hung up.

Then he turned around and saw me. He was frowning when I joined him on the stoop, but he stayed quiet when I handed over the key. My phone rang again as we climbed the stairs. This time it was Cassie.

"Nico said you're back in London."

"Early this morning." I followed him inside and punched the disarm code. He walked to the lounge and pulled the files out from under his coat and dropped them on the table.

"Are you at my place?"

"Yes. Is that okay?"

"Sure. But could you drop that brown reference book on my nightstand by the British Library for me? My friend, Ian, the guy who's so helpful to me there, called and said they could really use the book for another patron. I was finished with what I needed it for anyway. Just using it for bedtime reading."

I walked into her room and picked up the book in question. A tome on historical furniture and fabrics. A little light reading.

"I can leave immediately."

Jack started shaking his head. I nodded twice, then added, "Text your friend and see if he can meet me at the door or the reference desk, so I can make sure it gets turned over to the right person."

"Great. I'll text you back after I hear from him."

I cradled the huge book in my arms and started to leave the room. Until Jack's arm shot out to block my exit.

"Why do I get the feeling you don't want to tell me where you've been?"

"Because you're paranoid, Hawkes." I ducked under his arm and took a seat on the sofa. Then I hid my crossed fingers and pretended I hadn't told Nico earlier what I knew I'd said. I made my gaze stay locked on Jack's when I replied, "I have every intention of telling you where I was, but I didn't want to do so on the street or while we climbed the stairs in the public area. Want to come get comfortable?"

He took the space beside me, and I kept the book in my lap in case I needed to throw something. I turned slightly, so we were practically facing each other.

"First, can your lawyer help us?"

"Yes, it went pretty much as I expected. He looked at the file information but will begin with a letter. I told him we are very concerned about leaks, and we're keeping a tight lid on the evidence in all the files for the present. But we will share it with law enforcement for them to use to locate the suspect and build their case." He raised an eyebrow. "Now, your turn."

"I left a flash drive in St. James Park for Moran."

I let him bluster a minute, knowing he'd eventually calm down and listen. One of the things I appreciated most was Jack's ability to understand my squashy ethics. He never liked me stealing back art work, but it was more because he didn't want me to get hurt or caught than it was because I was stealing. I always gave the pieces back to the rightful owner, after all. This transgression regarding Moran, however, was different, and I'd known it from the start. I was giving information to the enemy that law enforcement would rightly assume was on offer for just their benefit.

Before our decision to go to the solicitor, Jack had only given the hair and a few pictures to Cecil. I gave Moran the clues to find the man growing the hair.

Once I explained I wasn't giving away everything, just the raw data Nico started with, his face relaxed a bit. Then when I said I did it as much for self-preservation as justice, since the more people looking to punish Colle for all his crimes the faster he would lose the ability to send people after me, Jack nodded, and I knew I was in the clear.

"Still, Interpol will get him behind bars, Laurel. Especially since Nico has found the new identity."

I demurred, "As long as one of the Colle moles doesn't find out as well and tip off the boss."

"We'll be very careful in how we release the information."

"Moran's granddaughter pulled the heist because they thought the Rodin was the real thing. They could have only known about it because of a mole in the British government, and I can't help thinking that secret was one carefully kept to a tight circle as well."

Jack's face paled. "You learned that from Moran? It was definitely his granddaughter like we guessed?"

I nodded. "Absolutely."

I knew I was probably overstating, but something inside me had to get out all my reasoning for doing what I'd done. Looking down, I realized I'd braided my fingers. Nerves. I took a deep breath. "Even if Colle doesn't learn from leaked information, just think about how many people like him purchase high-priced attorneys who work their legal shenanigans until the felons die a natural death, never spending a day in prison. That alone bothers me on so many levels."

"And in prison, he could..."

"Continue to order hits on me," I finished the sentence he let hang.

He grasped my shoulders and said, "Please don't tell me Moran promised out loud to kill Colle."

"First, no, I would never ask him to do that, and I would have shut him down if he'd started to say so. But he wouldn't. We both used burner phones. I put the information on a flash drive to avoid having an internet connection with him. He was the one who suggested a dead drop so there wouldn't be any mail or video trace between us."

I recalled a phone conversation from years ago I had with one of the crime bosses who made me pay off part of the debt accrued by Daddy Dearest. "If I really wanted to be sure Colle was killed fast, Moran would not have been the person I'd have called."

"You have a direct link to a hitman?" Jack asked, a dark eyebrow shooting toward his hairline.

"Next best thing if I intended to use that option. One of the loan sharks my father was in debt to when he died used to call me every week. He'd ask me in his gravelly voice how I was doing in school and how I was holding up. And finally, like any regular debt collector, he'd ask how much I could pay down on the debt. Then he would send a man by to pick up whatever money we agreed to. After a couple of months, I walked into the university bursar's office to explain why I couldn't pay my tuition and learned the semester was already paid in full. When I'd paid twenty percent of the original debt, he said I could stop paying him, but I'd better stay in school. He may have shown kindness to me, but I'd wager if I contacted him and asked if he or any of his working associates might want to 'talk' to Colle before he was arrested by Interpol, the conversation would be between Colle and an assassin's bullet." This knowledge was what I'd come to realize was likely the real reason he wanted me dead. "If I'd wanted to put out a contract on Beacham/Colle, I wouldn't have risked just calling Moran."

"Wow." Jack shook his head. "That was one of the most frightening and sexiest things I've ever heard you say."

I gave his shoulder a shove. He laughed and reached out,

grabbing the back of my head to pull me close for a kiss. The big brown book played chaperone.

As we broke from the kiss, I said, "And face it. With the kind of money and connections Moran has, he may want Colle to serve time in a French prison for his brother's murder. A French prison where Moran likely has his own paid guards, maybe even the warden. Where he can get the prisoner moved to a miserable cell in solitary confinement, so Colle can't even order his own dinner, let alone order a hit on me or anyone else. In that scenario, if he tried to get anyone assassinated, it would likely be himself to end the misery. I'd be completely good with that too, by the way."

"Brilliant summation. I know you trust Moran." Jack chuckled. "Though I honestly don't understand why. But after charming loan sharks, I guess talking to crime bosses is kind of your superpower. If you call each of the guys you paid off back then and tell them how to find the very much not-dead Beacham/Colle, and who the guy really is, think they'd give you all your money back from the estate?"

"I'm not proud to admit the thought has crossed my mind," I said.

He kissed my forehead. "Be proud. Your admission of thinking about it but not following through proves you're not his daughter. No DNA test necessary."

"I forgot, you were going to bring a swab thingy," I said.

Jack pulled a long silver cylinder from his pocket. "Open your mouth."

He pulled out a swab and ran it all around my mouth, then slipped it into the container. "You're done," he said and returned the cylinder to his pocket.

"Easy," I said. "I've seen them do it on television, but always imagined there would be blood involved."

"Old school. We only use the new and improved methods. Less icky," he replied. "But speaking of blood, what was Moran's explanation for the Amazon continually coming after you?"

"Believe it or not, she was protecting me. Just seems to be

lacking in interpersonal people skills. You can give Timms another heads up as well about how she got inside the hotel. She'd been on the housekeeping staff a couple of days already."

"Seriously?"

I nodded. "Go over the hotel videos again paying attention to brown-haired maids, or have Danny do so." I gave him the rest of the synopsis about that part of the conversation with Moran, finishing up just as my phone buzzed with a text from Cassie. I picked it up and saw I'd be met at the front door of the British Library by her friend Ian. I removed the hoodie by pulling it over my head and refluffed my blonde curls with one hand while shoving my phone into my pocket.

"You coming with me?" I asked Jack.

"I will since you've changed out of that hoodie."

"Good, you can carry the book." I stood to get my coat and dropped the heavy tome onto the sofa beside him.

TWENTY-FOUR

The rain had stopped, but I got a plastic bag to protect the book just in case the weather changed again. Before we left the flat, Jack said, "The British Library isn't far from the office. Let's stop in and see if the keypad has been improved while we were gone."

"Will they use the old code? Or change it?" I asked.

"I just want to see if the unit's been pulled or changed out," he said. "There's nothing inside to protect anyway."

"I should have asked Moran to get the Amazon to return the papers she took from the office and my suitcases, but I was too busy trying to outwit him on evidence." I snapped my fingers. "That reminds me."

I ran back to the bedroom and grabbed the backpack I'd used for the heist, pulling out the auction card to leave on the bed.

"Why are you taking the bag?" Jack asked when I reappeared.

"I want to leave the escape line. I figure if it's in the office we'll never need it, but if it's not there I run the risk again of having to use the curtains. My face still burns from my cheek rubbing against the rough fabric on the way down." I also pulled Arlo's Swiss Army knife from my Prada and added it to the front pocket of the backpack. For the last day and a half, I'd felt guilty every time I'd accidentally touched the knife while it was in my purse. Maybe having it in our escape bag would take away some of the taint.

Two bags. Did I really want to carry two bags?

"Do you have the keys?" I asked Jack.

He dangled the key ring.

I hung my purse on one of the coat hooks. "Come on, let's go."

Cassie's friend was waiting exactly where he said he would.

"Hello, Ian." As he walked toward us, I said, "I'm sorry. Thank you for waiting for us." I hurried to shake the man's hand. "I'm Laurel, and this is Jack."

"No, no need to apologize. I'm sorry for the misunderstanding." He shook Jack's hand and accepted the book, taking a peek inside the white plastic bag.

It took several minutes of small talk, then Ian went back into the Library, and we headed for the office.

"Well, that was a nice yet awkward encounter," I said, as I slipped my hand into the crook of Jack's elbow, the backpack-Prada-replacement-bag dangling from my other shoulder.

"We Brits tend to apologize more than other people." Jack covered my fingers with his free hand. "You started the whole thing by apologizing first. Then old Ian felt compelled to apologize for making you apologize, and you can see by that exchange how a situation of the kind can snowball."

"I promise never to say I'm sorry again."

"Then I think you have to become a lawyer."

"I don't like the white wigs."

"Those are barristers."

"So, do I need to stick with being a solicitor?" I asked.

"How about if you stay an art recovery expert and I clap a hand over your mouth anytime I hear you start apologizing?" he responded.

"Deal."

The office building was in sight, the front door of the ground floor restaurant busy with Saturday lunch customers. We picked up our pace and angled for the side entrance.

"Where do you want to eat lunch?" Jack asked as we reached the first landing.

"I don't know...Paris?" I twisted on the stairs to face him and grinned.

"Are you serious? I mean..." He shrugged. "Lunch would be late and all, but I guess we could."

I turned back around and resumed climbing. "No, I'm kidding. I just think we got a little shortchanged from our Paris trip this week."

"Definitely." A couple of steps later, he added, "Not feeling a little jealous Nico and Cassie are still there, are you?"

"No." I looked over my shoulder and frowned. "Maybe. I mean, I know I told them to stay the weekend to be safe while we were traveling with Clive, but now we're back and they're still there, eating the great food and seeing the great sights, and...Yeah, I'm probably jealous."

Jack rubbed his free hand up and down my back. "Remember neither of them knows a crime boss who'll take out a hit anytime they ask."

"You are never going to let that alone, are you, Hawkes?"

"I'm telling you, ask any guy and he'll admit that story is a turn on. Ask Williams, he'll back me up on this. No, don't, Williams already fancies you. We don't need to make it worse."

I laughed. "Danny just wants to get your goat."

"No, he wants to get my girl."

I knew I was blushing, and Jack immediately went silent. I had the feeling we both knew we were suddenly on a slippery verbal slope. We hadn't talked about where we were in our relationship, but we'd been together enough that I knew we were pretty much exclusive. Even if we hadn't verbalized any promises. Still, I thought it best to let the comment slide, particularly since I wasn't ready to address it. When we got to the top floor I said, "I need to use the restroom. Check out the keypad and I'll be back in a minute."

Two steps into the hallway, however, and a huge blur suddenly emerged from behind the blind corner and slammed me into the wall. It took a second to get my senses back, and I saw the damned giant from the National Gallery charging Jack. He jumped out of the way a second before King Kong could knock him down the stairs.

I pulled out my phone and dialed, choosing Timms over 999.

"The giant is trying to kill Jack," I screamed when Timms answered. "We're in the hallway of our office, top floor." The giant grabbed my phone—"Send help!" I screamed—and he backhanded me with the meaty paw he was using to crush my phone. I remembered hitting the floor and having the impression of something being thrown down the stairwell. I hoped it was my phone instead of Jack.

A second later, Jack landed beside my head, and I worked my way back to a sitting position. I saw the giant coming at us slowly, wearing a wicked smile with bad teeth. His huge hand clutched a lethal-looking knife.

Scrabbling into the front pocket of the backpack, I pulled out Arlo's Swiss Army knife, opened the longest blade, and pressed it on Jack. He looked at the knife as if in disbelief, before giving me an apologetic look like all was lost. I realized what he was thinking: the giant was seven feet tall with a longer knife blade, and Jack's reach was at least six inches too short. The ogre could swing his knife, cut Jack, and only risk losing a finger.

"Fire escape. Go!" Jack whispered, pulling me to my feet as he stood up. Double vision hit when I tried to turn my head, and I was incredibly dizzy. When Jack let go of me, I grabbed the door frame to keep on my feet. No way I'd make it down the outside fire escape without falling over the edge.

Jack launched himself at the giant's leg, aiming Arlo's knife toward the femoral artery. While the giant's thinking was slower, he still recognized a threat.

"No!" I screamed, grabbing the ogre's attention.

But getting stabbed got his attention right back on Jack and made him mad. The giant roared and swung back his leg. I looked for some way to equalize things. Jack rolled, and the kick missed his head by mere inches.

The fire extinguisher.

I unclamped it from the wall, nearly falling over.

"Hey, loser!" I yelled at the giant, pulling the pin on the fire extinguisher. He looked at me, while holding Jack's arm and plunging the knife into Jack.

I blasted his face with the white foam.

He let go of Jack to claw at his face. I kept the foam pumping right into his eyes and nose. But the weight of the extinguisher was getting heavier instead of lighter. I saw spots before my eyes and knew I was about to black out.

Jack wasn't moving. Under his coat, a red stain expanded across his shirt.

"No, no, no, no, no," I cried.

Aiming at the floor, I hit the whole area around where the giant stood with foam. My legs were giving out. While the big man roared and tried to clear his eyes, I dove for his legs, pushing King Kong toward the stairs.

The foam made the concrete floors slippery enough that my nudge sent the ogre scrambling, trying to keep his balance in the slickness. Just when I was afraid the effort wouldn't be enough, his boot caught the edge of the top step. He slid off and began tumbling down the flight. He didn't move once he hit the landing.

I crawled over to Jack, praying, reaching to touch his neck, and begging the heavens for a pulse. It was slow, but it was there.

Suddenly, I heard sirens. That was when I finally passed out.

I woke strapped to a gurney outside the building. Emergency personnel and vehicles were all around.

"Jack," I screamed, trying to grab someone dressed in white. "Did you get Jack? He's been stabbed."

The EMT spoke softly, "Yes, miss, don't worry. He's been transported to hospital, but he should be fine. He's lost some blood, but the punctures didn't look like any major organs were hit. We're getting ready to transport you there too."

TWENTY-FIVE

We didn't get a trip to Paris. We did spend the weekend in bed, but it was at Cassie's instead of a room overlooking a fabulous, world-class view.

The hospital didn't want to let us go, but Nico showed up a couple of hours after we arrived. He got concerned when he couldn't reach either of us by phone, and my GPS charm said I was in the middle of a London street and not moving. Well, concerned is probably an understatement, because he was worried enough to call a friend of his who got him on a fast chopper for the hop over the Channel. That was telling information, because while Nico isn't a fan of flying, he particularly dislikes helicopters.

It was still several more hours before Jack's x-rays and my CAT scan said we were able to sign ourselves out of care. Though we were highly discouraged to follow that route. By then, Cassie had received Nico's panicked text and grabbed a seat on the first available flight home. So, she was on hand in all her mother hen efficiency to make sure she understood every necessary instruction for our care and feeding during the convalescence period. She had a few things to say to Nico too. As if she could get him to change his night owl ways.

When we were in the cab on the way back to the flat, her phone rang.

"It's Danny Williams," she said, then hit the speaker button. "Hi, Danny, what's up?"

"Cassie, I know you're in Paris, but—"

"No, I'm home. Jack and Laurel were hurt."

"That's what I was going to tell you."

"Hey, Williams," Jack said, his voice quiet and raspy enough that I took the phone from Cassie and held it closer to him. "Why didn't you let me know Colle's big hood from the National Gallery was turned loose?"

"Someone came in and got all three out on bail," Danny said. "I didn't hear in time to warn you."

"Given that one of them tried to beat the hell out of you too, you might ask your superior why you weren't one of the first people notified about the release."

"Already said almost that exact same thing," Danny replied. "My supervisor promises to get an accounting of the situation and suggest new protocols."

"We're on our way to Cassie's place," I said. "And I don't know about Jack, but I'm only going to tell this story one more time. If you'd rather hear what happened from us, you're welcome to come by the flat tonight. Otherwise, you can read the police reports."

"I'll get there as quickly as I can."

When we got to the flat, Cassie immediately ordered us to bed.

"Nico and I can bring chairs into the bedroom, so we can all talk and listen. You two need to be resting."

I found the auction card where I'd left it, scooped it up and pointed to the bed as I told Jack, "Sit here and wait until I get this to Nico. I'll be right back. You're going to have trouble getting that shirt off again without help."

"No argument from me."

I found Nico in the lounge and handed him the card. "This is the one I was telling you about. Whatever you can find out is more than we currently know."

He checked out both sides, then used his phone to do a scan of the images. "It doesn't look like much, but I'm often amazed at what I find once I start digging."

"I'm always amazed at what you find." I looked to the kitchen but didn't see Cassie anywhere. "Where did she go?"

"The Tesco on the next block. The nurse suggested soup for

you and Jack. Cassie didn't have any and was determined to follow orders."

Smiling, I shook my head. I grabbed a pair of scissors from the desk and went back into the bedroom to help Jack.

"I don't know if we're going to survive our period of recuperation," I told Jack.

"What do you mean?"

"Cassie is following hospital orders to the letter."

The trauma team had sutured his wounds and braced his arm to help the muscles recover. "I'm going to cut off your shirt. It's a goner anyway, and even if it isn't I never want to see the thing again. Hold still."

"Don't like the shirt, or don't like the memories it brings back?" he asked, barely moving his lips as he spoke. I wanted to laugh, but I was afraid he'd join in and it would have been painful for him.

"I don't like remembering how dead you looked in the hallway with this shirt getting redder and redder by the second. Plus, it has holes from the damned knife. There." I pulled out the last strip of fabric and nearly cried when I saw the bandages on his side and back. "I am so grateful the stupid ogre didn't know anatomy."

He chuckled. "Ow!"

"They told you not to laugh."

"I wasn't laughing."

"Your muscles won't find anything even slightly humorous at the current time." I kissed his forehead. "Try to remain stoic."

He grabbed my waist and pulled me down to sit on the bed beside him. With a finger, he lifted my chin. "Just before we were attacked, I think I said something that made you...uncomfortable," he said. "I didn't mean to—"

"No, no." I jumped to my feet, but he grabbed my arm and pulled me back down again. I waved a hand. "It's okay. We were just teasing about Danny, I know."

He used his free hand to trace down my cheek and under my lower lip. I started chewing the corner of my lip, and he leaned in and kissed me, starting softly with that corner, then covering my mouth with his.

When we broke from the kiss, his mesmerizing teal eyes held my gaze, and he said, "What I said wasn't to pressure you. It was simply a quick quip to reply to what you said. But I do want you to know I'm committed to us. I know we said we were going to try this, see how it went, but you can trust me. Even if I did try to con you a lot at first. I'm not asking for promises, just letting you know I'm willing to put just as much into this relationship as you are."

I felt tears welling. I looked down and cleared my throat, willing my voice to stay steady, as I said, "That means a lot." I took a deep breath, then forced a light laugh and patted his thigh. "But no worries. I knew the 'my girl' thing was in response to what I said about Danny trying to get your goat. It was the perfect retort." I stood and waved my arms a bit as I looked down at him and added, "I knew...all this...don't worry. I understand the Jack you were last fall was the Jack you had to be at that moment in time...and place...all."

He grabbed one of my flying hands. "But you do understand the Jack I really am, right?"

There had been so many men I couldn't trust through the years, so many who helped me create the armor I wore against getting too close. He knew that—well, he knew enough to understand it, even if he didn't know all the particulars. Hell, for a while he was the male I was least convinced about in my life. Until I learned more. In that moment though, I couldn't speak. I used the hand he wasn't holding to cover my mouth for a second, then I reached down to grip his hand with both of mine. "I know...it takes me some time...and I don't forget things easily, I have to be convinced. But I have us in perspective—you in perspective—the real you. I know. It wasn't anything today...I just hadn't stopped and thought in that direction yet."

Which was a load of bull. Anytime Jack talked about us in any kind of steady or future tense I had to stop and recalibrate things in my mind. But those experiences had always been my internal thinking, and I'd believed I was getting better with each evolution. This was the first time we'd actually discussed anything like this, and it wasn't hard to see I wasn't as prepared as I might have thought.

He stood and hugged me, and I thanked the heavens again that we'd come out of another deadly situation alive. Once I knew I wasn't going to start crying, I pulled away and touched his cheek, saying, "This heart-to-heart conversation is over, lover boy. Let's take off your pants so you can get into bed."

The smile and soft chuckle my words produced made it all worth it.

"I'll go get a wet cloth and try to wash off some of that iodine stain." I moved my hand near the yellowed area I was talking about, and Jack caught my wrist and held it.

"Get pajamas on so you're presentable for company and get in bed," he said. "I can wash myself one-handed, or I'll get Nico to help. You're three shades paler than you were when we arrived. You have a concussion, remember? Get in bed and rest so Cassie can wake you up every couple of hours."

"I forgot I have that to look forward to."

Besides, I couldn't argue. Once he took my focus off him and his care, my energy level hit the basement. I pulled on pink silk pajamas and nearly crawled to the bed.

I woke when I smelled soup and realized I was starving.

"What are you doing out of bed?" Cassie cried when I wandered into the lounge, tying the belt of my robe around me. Jack was stretched out on most of the sofa wearing just pajama bottoms. I pointed at him and raised an eyebrow.

"I know," she said. "I've been trying to get him to go to bed too, but he said he didn't want to wake you." She clapped her hands. "You're both awake now. Go to bed. I'll bring you soup in a few minutes."

"She's not going to feed us if we don't follow orders," I said. "And I'm hungry."

"Fine. Lead the way."

She swooped in minutes later, with a tray for each of us. Nico brought in a chair and sat working his phone. A second later the doorbell rang, and Cassie left to let Danny in.

"Get well soon," Danny called out, as he entered the room with a huge bouquet of Mylar balloons.

"Danny, this is so sweet, but you shouldn't have," I said, stopping my spoonful in mid-taste. I shook my head. "You *really* shouldn't have."

"I can't stay long, so this is kind of a get well and peace offering," he said. "I have to do a double shift to try and catch up on requests. But I have some time slotted to find your redhead, don't worry."

Jack waved his good hand. "You can forget that. Laurel learned it was a misunderstanding. We don't have to worry about her anymore."

"I know I didn't alert you about the Colle muscle getting out of the nick, but—"

"Danny, this is no reflection on you," I said. "It really was a big misunderstanding. She learned about what happened at the National Gallery and wanted to protect me."

"But the redhead broke in." His light brown brows furrowed together.

"She does that," I said. "Bad people skills."

"You know I'm not completely buying this," he said. He took the chair Cassie handed him and placed it near the foot of the bed, letting go of the balloons so they wafted along the ceiling.

"Can you accept at least half of it?" Jack asked. "With a promise you'll hear the rest as soon as we're able to tell you?"

He rubbed his chin. "Okay, yeah, I can agree to a partial explanation on those conditions. Especially, since it cuts down on my workload tonight. However, I'm assuming Inspector Timms isn't going to get this same deal."

Jack grinned and shook his head. "This is one of those 'by invitation only' explanations. Consider yourself part of our inner circle."

"At least halfway," Danny clarified.

"At least that," I seconded. I pointed to my Italian geek. "Have you met Nico? He's the only one of us not based in London, but we try to keep him here as much as possible."

Nico set his phone aside for a moment and shook hands with Danny. Cassie came back then with a tray of cheese and crackers, beers, wine and water, and set it on the blanket chest at the end of the bed.

"Snacks," she said. "We're set to hear the whole story."

"I'll take a beer," Jack said.

"You'll take water," she said.

"I don't have the concussion." He jerked his thumb at me. "Laurel does."

"But you're on pain meds, so no alcohol."

"Remember what I said when I first walked in," I reminded him.

"I'm starting to understand," he replied, taking another spoonful of soup.

"Hey, Laurel, Jack." Nico hurried over and held up his phone screen.

"Jack, you look," I said. "My eyes still hurt when I try to read anything."

He looked up at Nico. "This is great. I can't believe you already found something."

"What is it?" I asked, getting seriously peeved.

"Looks like we're heading for Italy by the end of summer," Jack said.

"Do you mean—?"

"Auction on the Amalfi Coast," he said. "No date yet or location...?" He raised eyebrows at Nico, who nodded in return, then added, "Yet we know we're a bit ahead of the game for once, and that's something."

I'd never seen his smile so wide, but I understood completely. This was worth any amount of recuperation tedium. A chance to recover *Juliana*.

Seeing Nico's phone reminded me mine was still DOA at the bottom of the stairwell. "Cassie, when you get a chance, I need another phone..."

"Nico's already working on that," she said.

"I have some programming to do on it to shield your location," he replied. "I'll bring it by tomorrow. Along with another bracelet with a GPS charm."

"You guys are the best. Thank you." I rubbed my eyes. "Not that I'll be doing any texting for the night anyway."

"The doctor suggested you avoid reading and doing close work for several days," Cassie added.

"No argument," I said. At least not until morning.

Jack's phone erupted then with a cacophonous ring. "It's your pet reporter." He handed the phone to me. "No doubt he's found your number is out of order."

I sighed. "Hello, Linc."

"Hallo, Laurel. You sound awful. How are you?"

"I'm sure you already got a detailed report from your hospital Deep Throat."

He chuckled. "I heard a little about yours and Hawkes's condition. But you're okay? Just a concussion."

"Yeah, just a concussion." I started to roll my eyes, but it hurt, and I quit. "And a headache as a bonus, so please don't make it worse."

"I would never—"

"Can the puffery, Linc. What do you need?"

"Are you pursuing inquiries into the Met police about their release of the man who attacked you again after first trying to kidnap you in the National Gallery?"

Great, I thought, he put that together already. Not that it really surprised me. Lincoln Ferguson never came off as a slacker. "No, I'm not pushing for any inquiries."

"It was obviously an egregious slip on their part," he argued. "Are they pursuing inquiries internally? This is the second time someone who attacked you was released by the police."

Another landmine to tiptoe through. Rollie was spirited away after getting arrested in February and, unfortunately, Linc was on hand during the capture, filming the entire event. Now the giant was added to Linc's repertoire of questionable evidence that I didn't want to explain. "I can only assume all protocols were followed, and if there is a need for internal questioning, I'm sure the Met police is completely capable of making departmental changes. I don't feel I need to be involved in anything of the sort."

He was silent for a moment. I didn't know if he was making notes or figuring out a new tactic to get on my good side. Fat chance of that. "I would like to add, Linc, if you're taking notes of this conversation, please be sure to quote me accurately, as I've appreciated all protection I've received from all avenues of London law enforcement, and I don't have a desire to criticize anyone or any department at this time. We're clear on this, correct?"

"Crystal. And I'd like to offer you a means of saying exactly that on air. Tell the public what happened and—"

I started shaking my head, but it made me dizzy again. "No. Stop."

"Laurel, you've been quite the sensation lately, all over social media. Our audience is clamoring for more information about the gorgeous blonde art recovery expert. To know you've come through things in one piece."

"Going overboard on the flattery, Linc."

"Is it working?"

"Not even a little."

Jack chuckled beside me.

"Just one on-air interview," Linc almost pleaded. "I have no problem if you want to make it a one-off exclusive interview. No qualms—"

I laughed. "Like an exclusive is a bad thing for you?"

"What I mean is, I won't come back for a follow-up."

"But others will, Linc. If I give you an exclusive, it would fuel other reporters to see me as fair game. I prefer ultra-exclusive."

"As in no interview?"

"Exactly."

He tried again. "Your pictures have been ahead of breaking news for days on all social media, and yours and Hawkes's attack today is—"

"No, Linc. No. The fact I'm still trending on social media is exactly why I don't want any new exposure."

"The public wants to hear your story."

"The public will just have to get over it."

"You're currently a media sensation—"

"Linc, you aren't listening." I blew out a long breath. Getting mad wasn't going to help, but the guy simply wasn't backing down. "The last thing common sense says for me to do is agree to give interviews and see my face plastered all over television and print media, when what I really want is for the social media furor to die down. You have to see that."

He began saying something more, but I felt a sudden wave of utter fatigue and interrupted him. "Thanks so much for the offer, and for calling to check on Jack and me. But this isn't a good time to talk to either of us. If you need any more information, please coordinate with DI Timms or his DS at the Met police. Goodbye."

I could hear him still talking as I ended the call.

TWENTY-SIX

Two days later a flurry of messages began a back and forth journey across the Channel. Despite still being out on doctor's orders, Jack was called in for a few hours, and when he returned, he said, "I think the French have Colle, but no one is naming names yet. Just a person the French government is holding in connection with long ago murders."

"They didn't mention art crimes?"

"They wouldn't if the perpetrator came to them via Moran."

"Did they mention anything about Swiss authorities?" I asked.

"Only that another country's law enforcement arm is also an interested party."

"They're sending out feelers to see who'll bite?"

"Possibly. Or they're trying to determine exactly what kind of fish they've landed. I'm thinking Moran is pulling strings on this thing, given the way they seem to be working in the dark."

"If you and your Home Office buddies can follow any of this communication trail, it could help you ferret out who is a Moran mole in your organization. As little as it seems like they know, it's surprising they would reach out otherwise."

Jack nodded. "Cecil is already on it. He agrees it's important to see who is particularly interested on the British law enforcement side—and who might be trying to act uninterested. He also understood when I suggested this apprehension is quite possibly based on the quiet feelers he's put out about Colle. He asked the French to get a DNA sample and will have the tests expedited."

Which reminded me about my own DNA comparison. I steeled myself to the fact I would have to decide whether or not to open the results when they arrived.

Jack did that mind-reading thing he was so good at and said, "You'll get an initial summary of your results via email. A lengthier analysis will arrive by post."

"I know, I'm fine."

"I know." He hugged me. Then his phone dinged another text. "Need to run. Have to make a report."

"They do know you're supposed to be resting. Doctor's orders."

He grinned and waggled his eyebrows. "Be here when I get back and we'll play a round of doctor and patient."

"Sorry." I grabbed the Prada from the table and slipped the strap up my shoulder. "I'm leaving with you. Cassie and I are meeting an estate agent to tour some open listings."

Jack slipped on his leather coat. "She's probably rather sick of roommates."

"Speak for yourself, buster. She loves having me here." I laughed at his expression. "I'm just kidding. But one bathroom for three adults is getting a bit much."

"I guess I could go back to my own flat," he said.

"She'll never go for that until the doctor says so. She'd be running to your flat every hour to make sure you weren't passed out and unresponsive."

"But she's okay with helping you find a flat of your own?"

"We'll see. She hasn't let me sign a lease yet."

Not that it mattered. We didn't find anything that made me want to sign on any lines. We lunched later at an Indian place down the block from Cassie's flat, and I was surprised at how little energy I had just from walking around and asking questions. I was ready for a nap.

"The nurse told me that's the nature of a head injury," Cassie replied, scooping her naan across the plate as she spoke and popping it into her mouth.

"I'll be glad when it stops. Flagging energy isn't a favorite of mine."

"Don't worry. You're welcome to stay as long as you like."

"Your landlord might have other ideas about that. I'll bet your lease doesn't tolerate extended house guests without official roommate status."

She waved a hand. "He's a pussycat, and he's not going to say anything." She finished off the last bite and used a napkin to wipe her mouth. "Not to change the subject, but since you and Jack are presently off-duty, do you want me to use the airline credit balances you have to get you back to America for the Whyte Noyse concert? It's just a few days away."

"Let me talk to Jack first. But thanks for mentioning it," I said. I finished off my chai and set the cup by my plate. "Until we know what's going on with the French authorities, I doubt he'll want to be far away for any reason. And if Nico discovers anything new about the auction, we may need to cross the Mediterranean instead of the Atlantic."

"Okay. Just let me know and I'll work anything out for you."

"Thanks, Cass."

When I spoke to Jack later about Cassie's suggestion, I was surprised to hear, "I think that would be a very good idea. We should both be approved to travel in a couple of days, and with the backstage passes we shouldn't be jostled too much by the crowds."

He'd already told me they were nearly positive of Colle's identity, though he looked different from an obvious facelift, and was still adamantly professing to be Albert Bentley. I asked, "Don't you want to be close by for the interrogations?"

Jack shook his head. "I won't be invited in. MI-5 and MI-6 are coordinating with all of it since they have a shot at connecting him through DNA evidence. You might be called in to tell how you found the file. So far, there hasn't been a connection made between Colle and his original Beacham identity. I'll make sure that comes out soon. Simply the fact that Colle didn't even exist a dozen years ago makes that connection mandatory."

"I'm surprised Moran didn't already do so if he's trying to get a tie to his brother's death."

"We know Moran is crafty—and patient. It wouldn't surprise me if he already has his own evidence about the Beacham/Colle connection squirreled away somewhere, and he's letting the law enforcement noose tighten first to see which way to use his material to the best advantage."

"All well and good," I said. "But I still question your agreeing to cross the Atlantic for a rock concert."

"You don't want to go?"

"That's not my point."

He took my face in his hands, and I stared into those teal eyes, thankful I didn't see pain there for a change as he said, "Colle's men have already attacked you twice to avenge a perceived grievance against their boss. And Colle tasked Melanie with the job of finding an assassin. We know this. For now, your name is completely out of the current investigation, but they can only hold the suspect another day or so without charging him. He already has a lawyer. And while Colle may be hanging on with white knuckles to the Bentley surname, by the time he or his lawyer gets out of the interrogation room today others will know about his apprehension."

"So, we hide in New Jersey?"

"Can you think of a better place?"

"St. Tropez comes to mind." I grinned. "I get what you're saying, though. Being backstage with rock star security will put me off-limits for that evening at least."

"And give Cass a break from having houseguests who overstay their welcome. Unless you want to invite her too. Do you think Clive would offer another pass?"

"I'm sure he would," I said. "Except Cass hates Whyte Noyse and all groups like them. She suffered in silence in college, but I doubt she'd jump at the chance to join us."

"It's settled then. I'll run it by my doctor and you notify yours."

"Just that I'm flying?" I asked. "No destination."

"Correct."

Cassie kept Max from bothering me during my "convalescence." She and I went out one more day on our flat-looking quest. Colle was charged on the unrelated burglary to keep from having to set him free while more evidence was established for the prosecution's case. Cecil kept Jack abreast of everything going on during the interrogations and even got the videos sent to Jack, so he could view the questioning phase and offer any additional insights.

Yes, he let me watch too.

While Cassie was spending the afternoon at the British Library, and we had the flat to ourselves, it seemed a good time to binge watch French interrogation videos.

"I have to say, it's really weird seeing a voice a lot like one I've known since birth—just slightly changed—coming out of the mouth of someone who looks completely different," I said. The plastic surgeon had done a real number. All traces of Beacham and Colle were gone. He had dark hair this time and much fuller eyebrows. It was obvious he was going for a real desire to hide too, as instead of a fine jawline like before, his new look sported the beginning of saggy jowls. I would have felt sorry for him if I hadn't hated him so much.

Despite listening to hours of interrogation, we had nothing to add that the French police couldn't discern from the facts they'd gathered. Albert Bentley, as he now called himself, pretended he didn't speak French, so most of the interrogation was carried out in English. Cecil had already told Jack about this, and since MI-6 knew Colle spoke French and Italian fluently, they'd already alerted French law enforcement, so anytime the officers needed to speak amongst themselves they left the interrogation room.

"The only way they're able to hold him at this point is due to three fingerprints that suddenly appeared in Interpol files," Jack explained. "So far, the interrogations haven't worn down Colle, but the fingerprints put him solidly at an art heist in a Paris museum five years ago. For some reason, the fingerprints were forgotten, and the case went cold."

"Or the heist was done by Moran's men, and the fingerprints were added to the file by a mole he has placed in Interpol," I said.

Jack grinned. "At least he's doing our work for us. Regardless of how unethical it is."

I paced Cassie's lounge. "You know my ethics always lean toward doing the greater good. I'm Machiavellian that way and won't apologize for it. But it concerns me the French may decide to focus on pinning the museum break-in on him and not prosecute him for any of the murders that can be laid at his feet."

"I felt the same way when Cecil first briefed me," Jack explained, hitting the pause button on the video. "I wasn't sure how to proceed yet in that regard, since the idea was to get him apprehended as quickly as possible, then let New York take the lead on the murder connection."

There was the conflict. Did I speak up right now? Tell who Colle was originally? Or did I wait? "When they brought him in, you said part of the reason the French police were holding him was in regard to a long-ago murder."

Jack nodded. "Again, fingerprint evidence that came from a document ordering the death of one Paul-Henrì Aubertine. But they can't corroborate enough yet to charge him for the murder."

My legs gave way, and I sat on the coffee table. "When did you learn this?"

"About an hour ago." Jack scratched one eyebrow with his thumbnail. "To be honest, I'm not sure it will stand up as evidence, and even if it does, it's dated before Colle existed. So, to use it to tie to—"

"Do it." I wasn't sure I spoke out loud at first, so I said it again. "Do it. Tell who he really is."

"Once this gets released, you can't stop it," Jack said. "And frankly, for your safety, I'd prefer we let the international police close up the Colle syndicate ahead of letting everyone know about your personal connection to Colle."

"I just want...I want the murders known and prosecuted," I said. At first, the words were difficult to form, but soon they rushed out faster than I thought I could speak, "I didn't know Paul-Henrì, but nothing anyone has said would give a valid reason for his murder. And I know my mother and Dexter didn't deserve death. I know it will give Colle great pain to see his crime empire fall and his new address be some prison cell. But I don't want anyone to forget his crimes when he went by the Beacham name. Those crimes were personal, and he believes he's gotten away with them."

Jack walked over and took my hand, pulling me to my feet and into his arms.

"I promise, I'll make sure the right people know all the evidence against him," he said, stroking my hair. "But we need to do this in steps. To keep you safe. You didn't take the risk of contacting Moran and getting this thing accelerated just to bugger it by bringing the earlier murders up too quickly."

Passion is a difficult emotion to contain, especially when it's tainted by revenge. However, I knew when to step away from the edge. "You're right. The idea was to not only get him prosecuted for his crimes, but to try to get my life back to some semblance of safety and sameness. I'll be ready to step forward when anyone needs me, but I'll keep quiet while the cases are being built."

"I can only imagine how hard it is for you."

"Don't even try," I said. I pulled free and headed for the bathroom, so Jack wouldn't see my tears of both relief and fury.

Cassie got us terrific seats on a trans-Atlantic flight a couple of days later, after we both had doctor's approval that cleared us for flying. She also promised she would keep Max from learning I was in his time zone and just a bridge ride away. Actually, we were even closer than that, as we spent over twenty-four hours seeing a couple of Broadway shows, devouring the best New York prime I'd ever eaten, and even doing a late-night carriage ride around the Park.

The trip was a far cry from the flight in and out we experienced just a week before, and though the pace wasn't as frenetic, we still fell into bed exhausted.

The night of the concert, Clive sent one of the group's limos to pick us up, and a tall attractive brunette met us at the back door.

"Hi, I'm Shannon Binegar-Foster," she said, shaking each of our hands. "I help Gordon Silver with his art, and Clive thought it would be a good thing if we met so I could be a kind of point person for you tonight. These concerts get really crazy as everyone in the group and crew is doing their job, and Clive didn't want you feeling like you were on your own." She grinned then and added, "Plus, Gordon thought it was an excellent idea if you and I met, Laurel. Sorry, Jack, but my boss is a little focused."

"Yes, we know," Jack and I said together. We all laughed and climbed into the rear door. The chauffeur soon had us motoring across the bridge and out of New York.

"Have you worked for Gordon long?" I asked.

"About five years," she said. "I'm an artist and was also a small business owner. Both of those combined have kept me versatile and still help me on all ends of being Gordon's art-girl-Friday."

"So, you assist him in acquiring art?"

"I tend to intercede when it's necessary," she said, waving a hand as she talked. "Gordon doesn't have time for detail work, of course, so I do that. And I look at all the upcoming catalogs to see what sales are coming at Christie's and Sotheby's, both in public and private sales. I also talk to art sale agents. Sometimes Gordon will go after a piece that sold with a collection, for instance, because he's only interested in the one work. Other times he wants to know all the works an artist or seller has for sale."

"He told me that he tries to stick with British artists."

"Exactly."

But she wasn't British. Her accent was definitely American. "Did you answer an ad when he was looking for an assistant? Or did someone introduce you?"

She laughed. "Believe it or not, I was visiting London and

wandering through the National Gallery and found myself in the same room as Gordon. In fact, he stumbled into me while he was too busy looking at the paintings to realize anyone else was around. We started talking—well, mostly he did. I honestly didn't know who he was, and just thought he was an art lover like myself. He told me about his collection, why he liked what he did. I lost track of time and suddenly realized I had to leave. He asked how he could get ahold of me, as he wanted one of his representatives to call me. I was hoping I could get something going for my artwork, so I gave him my card and pointed out I lived over here, not the U.K. A week later, I had a job offer, and I've never looked back."

She then switched the conversation to us, and admitted she recognized us from the media coverage. Especially me.

"Don't worry," she said. "Security around the group is tight, and you'll be close enough to be part of the invisible cordon. I'll get you a couple of Whyte Noyse caps if you want. That can help hide your eyes from gawkers."

"Yes, thank you."

The ride in was smooth and excitement free. Our reception at the venue was hurried but warm. Shannon was exactly right, everyone moved with purpose and had something to do all the time. We talked a few minutes in the group's dressing room. The guys were the complete opposite from their crew, relaxing and picking chords on guitars. A makeup artist was working on Gordon, brushing his dark hair back from his face, and when we drew near he motioned her aside and waved us closer.

"I thought you and Shannon should meet," he told me, pretty much ignoring Jack after a quick handshake.

"I absolutely agree, Gordon," I said, finally pulling my hand out of his grip. "The next time you're buying something at Sotheby's or Christie's let me know. If I'm free, I'll meet her there."

"Fab, fab, yes." He nodded and clapped Shannon on the shoulder. "I don't buy in person. Tend to drive the price up that way, so I use phone bids. But I like having Shannon at the auctions, so she can give me the read of the rooms."

She'd told us all of that in the car on the way over, so Jack and I just nodded and let Gordon talk. We'd found that was the best approach. Eventually, someone reminded Gordon he needed to finish getting ready, which was Shannon's cue to usher us out again. We ran into Clive, who looked like he'd pulled an all-nighter. This was the first time I'd ever seen him in concert mode, and the only time he'd ever appeared harried about anything since I'd met him.

Our seats were perfect, the hats Shannon gave us helped disguise me from any social media lurkers, and soon the houselights came down, the show lights came on, and the music swelled as the group hit the stage. I'd never been that close before at a concert, and while I knew it was a perk, I never wanted to sit that close again. But it really was a new experience. I wondered if the doctor would have been as accommodating with his medical release if I'd told him I'd be hit with that many decibels on the trip. Jack had thought ahead, of course, and pulled earplugs out of his pocket and slipped two into my hand.

The music was still overwhelming, but manageable.

Much like the party we'd used for cover about a week ago, the music kept a driving beat I could feel throughout my veins. Not having a theft to orchestrate, however, made the evening much more enjoyable. Plus, the company was better. Even the fifty thousand or so in the surrounding seats and standing in the aisles.

It seemed too soon when the rock ball was over, and this Cinderella had to return to her mundane life. Okay, I was hoping it would become more mundane.

Shannon took us backstage again to say goodbye to everyone and then led us to where the limo waited.

"I'm heading on home from here," she said. "But the driver will take you back to your hotel. And if you need anything before you leave, please give me or Clive a call. Here's my card."

She passed her business card and I traded it for one of mine.

"Be sure and call me when you're in London," I said. "Well, anywhere you're going to an auction. I'm on the run a lot, so even if you're in a different country I might be nearby."

"Sounds like a plan," she said, grinning. "I'll email you when I head out of town, just in case we can meet."

"Definitely."

On the ride back, all of the energy that pulsed through us from the music and the crowd suddenly vanished.

"I feel zapped," I said.

Jack pulled out his phone. "You and me both. I'm going to check my messages, then knock on the window and tell the driver to wake us when we get there."

"Oh, I hadn't even thought about messages," I said. I'd turned off my phone at the concert. When I pulled up emails, I felt like I got socked in the stomach. Before I could speak, Jack said, "The DNA match came back on the hair we gave to Cecil. It matches the sample the French got from Bentley. They can prove now that Bentley is Colle."

I stayed silent, staring at the subject line of my email.

"What is it?" Jack took my phone and turned it so he could read. One of the entries earlier that evening was from the private lab where Jack sent my DNA swab and the hairs we found in the plastic bag in the file.

"You don't have to open it," he said, putting the phone back in my hands.

"I know." Then I touched the screen. Putting off the information made no sense. I may not have known which result I wanted—or which was the most tolerable—but putting off knowing wasn't going to change anything. I touched the screen and opened the message.

"My DNA doesn't match the hair sample in the comparison." I scratched my forehead. My emotions were so torn in that moment.

Jack stayed quiet for several minutes, then said, "You have options now."

"Yes. I've been thinking that I may take my mother's maiden name, regardless of the outcome. I was thinking it could distance me from more Beacham scandal when he's prosecuted for her murder. Now, I can do so since I don't have Beacham blood."

"Will any of that matter for the foundation?"

I took a deep breath and considered the same question I'd asked myself time and again. I knew I'd earned my position. I knew I did it better than anyone else was capable of accomplishing—especially given all the daily challenges my team and I handled that Max and the board knew nothing about. But if I changed my name, what would that do to my standing with the board? Or my standing in the art community?

"I don't know. But if they find out Colle murdered my mother, my keeping his name would look like I identified with a murderer. I can't imagine they would be happy with that either. For that matter, I have no idea how angry they'll be when they find I initiated things to get him arrested on every level I could find. No way they'll be happy with me about that either."

"So, we'll just take things as they come," Jack suggested, wrapping an arm around my shoulders.

"After the foundation's board recovers from learning he's actually been alive all this time."

"It will be interesting to see if any of them appears less shocked than the rest," he mused.

At that moment, my phone rang. It was Cassie. "Can you take it please?" I asked him.

"Sure." He answered the phone. "Hi, Cassie, what's up?" When she responded, he said, "She's right here, but she's not—okay, I see. Yes, I'll get her."

He covered the phone and said, "She said she must talk to you."

Since it was about six in the morning Greenwich time, I wasn't concerned at first at getting the middle of the night call in New York when I saw Caller ID, but Jack's reaction alarmed me. "I'm here, Cass. What is it?"

"Laurel, you need to get back here as soon as you can."

"What's wrong?"

"There's someone here you need to meet."

"Cassie, have you been taken hostage?"

Jack grabbed my phone and put it on speaker.

"No, nothing security wise." Her voice echoed in the small space. "It's just... Laurel, there's a boy here. About ten years old. He says he's your brother, and he has a birth certificate to prove it."

RITTER AMES

Ritter Ames is a *USA Today* bestselling author who lives atop a high green hill in the country with her husband and Labrador retriever, and spends each day globe-trotting the art world from her laptop with Pandora blasting into her earbuds. Often with the dog snoring at her feet. Much like her Bodies of Art Mysteries, Ritter's favorite vacations start in London, then spiral out in every direction. She's been known to plan trips after researching new books and keeps a list of "can't miss" foods to taste along the way. Visit her at www.ritterames.com where she blogs about all the crazy things that interest her.

**The Bodies of Art Mystery Series
by Ritter Ames**

Henery Press Mystery Books

And finally, before you go...
Here are a few other mysteries
you might enjoy:

ARTIFACT

Gigi Pandian

A Jaya Jones Treasure Hunt Mystery (#1)

Historian Jaya Jones discovers the secrets of a lost Indian treasure may be hidden in a Scottish legend from the days of the British Raj. But she's not the only one on the trail...

From San Francisco to London to the Highlands of Scotland, Jaya must evade a shadowy stalker as she follows hints from the hastily scrawled note of her dead lover to a remote archaeological dig. Helping her decipher the cryptic clues are her magician best friend, a devastatingly handsome art historian with something to hide, and a charming archaeologist running for his life.

Available at booksellers nationwide and online

Visit www.henerypress.com for details

FIXIN' TO DIE

Tonya Kappes

A Kenni Lowry Mystery (#1)

Kenni Lowry likes to think the zero crime rate in Cottonwood, Kentucky is due to her being sheriff, but she quickly discovers the ghost of her grandfather, the town's previous sheriff, has been scaring off any would-be criminals since she was elected. When the town's most beloved doctor is found murdered on the very same day as a jewelry store robbery, and a mysterious symbol ties the crime scenes together, Kenni must satisfy her hankerin' for justice by nabbing the culprits.

With the help of her Poppa, a lone deputy, and an annoyingly cute, too-big-for-his-britches State Reserve officer, Kenni must solve both cases and prove to the whole town, and herself, that she's worth her salt before time runs out.

Available at booksellers nationwide and online

Visit www.henerypress.com for details

I SCREAM, YOU SCREAM

Wendy Lyn Watson

A Mystery A-la-mode (#1)

Tallulah Jones's whole world is melting. Her ice cream parlor, Remember the A-la-mode, is struggling, and she's stooped to catering a party for her sleezeball ex-husband Wayne and his arm candy girlfriend Brittany. Worst of all? Her dreamy high school sweetheart shows up on her front porch, swirling up feelings Tally doesn't have time to deal with.

Things go from ugly to plain old awful when Brittany turns up dead and all eyes turn to Tally as the murderer. With the help of her hell-raising cousin Bree, her precocious niece Alice, and her long-lost-super-confusing love Finn, Tally has to dip into the heart of Dalliance, Texas's most scandalous secrets to catch a murderer...before someone puts Tally and her dreams on ice for good.

Available at booksellers nationwide and online

Visit www.henerypress.com for details

THE AMBITIOUS CARD

John Gaspard

An Eli Marks Mystery (#1)

The life of a magician isn't all kiddie shows and card tricks. Sometimes it's murder. When magician Eli Marks very publicly debunks a famed psychic, said psychic ends up dead. The evidence, including a bloody King of Diamonds playing card (one from Eli's own Ambitious Card routine), directs the police right to Eli.

As more psychics are slain, and more King cards rise to the top, Eli can't escape suspicion. Things get really complicated when romance blooms with a beautiful psychic, and Eli discovers she's the next target for murder, and he's scheduled to die with her. Now Eli must use every trick he knows to keep them both alive and reveal the true killer.

Available at booksellers nationwide and online

Visit www.henerypress.com for details

www.ingramcontent.com/pod-product-compliance
Lightning Source LLC
Chambersburg PA
CBHW060543260626
47161CB00003B/1038